What Critics Have Said

Nora Eckdorf (Eyre & Spottiswoode, 1967)

"Leon Whiteson's first novel strives for greatness, and achieves it."
New Statesman, London, August 20, 1967

"Leon Whiteson's remarkable talent is already fully mature."
Doris Lessing, London, 1967

White Snake (General Publishing, 1982)

"Leon Whiteson's novel about the conflict in Southern Africa reminds me of Nadine Gordimer… This is a very good book, and Whiteson has written it well…"
Globe & Mail, April 5, 1982

"*White Snake* is a wonderful surprise: a taut and intelligent thriller about the morality of terrorism… a haunting book."
Ottawa Citizen, April 10, 1982

Fool (Mosaic Press, 1984)

"In this bizarre trip through London's underbelly… Whiteson is a master punster, scatological wordsmith, scholarly etymologist and superb phrase-turner whose profane sense of humor tickles the brain and excites the tongue."
Los Angeles Herald-Examiner, December 23, 1984

"*Fool* rummages through a whole inventory of traditions associated with literary fools… *Fool*'s fleshly passion is promiscuous, but so is his compassion for flesh and spirit alike…"
Canadian Literature 110, Fall, 1986.

A Garden Story (Faber & Faber, 1995)

"This memoir is fabulously self-absorbed but exhilaratingly inclusive in the manner of Bruce Chatwin and Andrew Marvell."
New York Times, January 1996.

"*A Garden Story* is rewarding and inspiring reading,"
Christian Science Monitor, February, 1996.

"Leon Whiteson's book is emotional, immediate and rich… a realm of primal delight."
Los Angeles Times, December 1995.

A Place Called Waco (Public Affairs, 1999)

"In its firsthand account of the 1993 Waco tragedy, this book is brilliantly incisive and level headed."
Los Angeles Times, August, 1999.

"*A Place Called Waco* tells a highly believable story… leaving you with the sickening conclusion that the Branch Davidians' fiery end was a highly forseeable train wreck."
Washington Post, October, 1999.

Killing Lanna (Mosaic Press, 2002)

"A hypnotically erotic passion play that traverses the line between madness and love… a fascinating poetic novel."
Fearless Reviews, April 2002.

Dreams of a Weeping Woman

other books by Leon Whiteson

Fiction

Killing Lanna (Mosaic Press, 2001)
In the Garden of Desire:
Erotic Meditations (Mosaic Press, 2000)
White Snake (Mosaic Press, 1988)
Fool (Mosaic Press, 1984)
Nora Eckdorf (1967)

Non-Fiction

A Terrible Beauty (Mosaic Press, 2000)
A Place Called Waco (1999)
A Garden Story (1995)
The Watts Towers of Los Angeles (Mosaic Press, 1989)
Modern Canadian Architecture (1983)
The Liveable City: The Architecture and
Neighbourhoods of Toronto (Mosaic Press, 1982)

DREAMS OF A WEEPING WOMAN

for Katrine & Daniel,
with love,
Leon

Leon Whiteson

mosaic press

Library and Archives Canada Cataloguing in Publication

Whiteson, Leon, 1930-
Dreams of a weeping woman / Leon Whiteson.

ISBN 0-88962-825-4

I. Title.

PS8595.H492D73 2004 C813'.54 C2004-905647-6

Published by Mosaic Press, offices and warehouse at 1252 Speers Road, Units 1 and 2, Oakville, Ontario, L6L 5N9, Canada and Mosaic Press, PMB 145, 4500 Witmer Industrial Estates, Niagara Falls, NY, 14305-1386, U.S.A.

Mosaic Press acknowledges the assistance of the Canada Council and the Department of Canadian Heritage, Government of Canada through the Book Publishing Industry Development Program (BPIDP) for their support of our publishing activities.

Designed by Keith Daniel
Printed and Bound in Canada.
ISBN 0-88962-825-4

Canada Council for the Arts | Conseil des Arts du Canada

Mosaic Press in Canada:
1252 Speers Road, Units 1 & 2,
Oakville, Ontario
L6L 5N9
Phone/Fax: 905-825-2130
info@mosaic-press.com

Mosaic Press in U.S.A.:
4500 Witmer Industrial Estates
PMB 145, Niagara Falls, NY
14305-1386
Phone/Fax: 1-800-387-8992
info@mosaic-press.com

www.mosaic-press.com

Mother and Son

one

THE DAY I TURNED THIRTEEN, Leila, my mother, told me she had a lover. The stiff, adult word coming out of her sensitive, pale face and delicate mouth hit me like a slap across the cheek. More than the word itself, her expression really shook me. Her green eyes were wild with shadows and excitements I couldn't begin to fathom, and the abrupt breach of her graceful pride plunged me into a panic. I finally managed a hoarse sound approximating the syllable, "mom", and she squeezed my fingers with gratitude. "I had to confide in someone," she whispered, "and today, Joelly, you are a man in the eyes of God. Besides, you're the only one I can trust."

The question, *And dad—?* stuck in my throat.

"Oh, he knows," she said, divining my thoughts. "He told me to."

I blushed. The thought of my father, paralyzed from the waist down as the consequence of a car crash three years earlier, telling my mother to "get a lover" knocked me for a loop. As my mother hurried on, the hot phrases tumbling and stumbling one over another, my head was in a whirl.

I was an only child, and my mother and I had a sensual and emotional intimacy dating back into the mists of my infancy. She was constantly touching me, stroking me, regarding me with her smoky emerald eyes, wrapping me around with her slender chalk-white arms and her soft murmurs of affection. Whenever she hugged me her thin body quivered, transmitting thrilling pulses through my skin. Throughout my childhood she was a magical force, the atmosphere in which I lived, the very air I breathed. Her electric presence and erotic energy were intrinsic to my early experience of the world, and back then that I could never really think of her as a separate person. Even now, decades later, I still can't define the original boundary between Leila's soul and mine, and perhaps it never existed.

My father, Max, on the other hand, always kept me at a distance.

He was a very private man, his head busy with secret thoughts and complicated grievances, even more so after his accident . The click and whirr of The Bounder, his motorized wheelchair, the slither of its fat rubber tires on the tiles as he roamed the house – these were the anthems of his privacy. Despite his disability, however, he continued to be a mildly successful architect, and to an outside view my family must have seemed quite conventional in the free and easy coastal city of Santa Monica, California, in the mid-1970s.

Back then it was clear to me that Max and Leila did not really trust each other. As I grew older I began to see that their reciprocal mistrust, their mutual acceptance that they could never truly be known to each other, was the real bond between them. Their shared mistrust offered a kind of certainty, a tense but somehow secure truce, and the atmosphere in our house resembled a deliberately stilled pool. All the same, I loved coming home from the racket of school to its deliberate quietude. But the fateful word, "lover," shattered that peace. Abruptly, an alien presence intruded, heralded by that loaded, oddly formal, yet unclear term, and I sensed that my deep childhood was over, breached by a foreign force shoving me over the threshold of adulthood. I was shaken and jealous, and essentially at a loss.

"*Can* I trust you?" Leila asked anxiously, on that fateful day when I became a "man." We were so attuned to each other that she was quickly aware of my confusion. "I love you, Joelly," she said solemnly. "This doesn't change anything."

That statement was patently a lie, and that truly frightened me; it cut the ground from under my feet, adding to my rushing sense of uncertainty. Suddenly I was on my own, a neophyte grown-up, confronting a vast, unknown country filled with all kinds of dangers, with no experience to guide me.

"Say something," she urged. "Please?"

"That's nice," I mumbled foolishly.

Her head jerked back. She regarded me askance. For a moment we looked at each other as if we were strangers, and the hurt in her eyes tore at my heart.

"I love you, too, mom," I murmured reassuringly.

"Really?" she asked eagerly.

"Like bubbles," I said, using the old childhood term we'd concocted as part of our personal language.

"Like bubbles," she echoed, smiling, and hugged me hard.

I struggled free of her grasp, irritated by her pretence that everything was the same despite her confession of unfaithfulness – to me, as well as to my dad. Staring at her face, I was struck by its unbearable radiance. This lover had lit her up, set her on fire, carried her off in a blaze of female glory that left me panting with jealous resentment.

"Who?" I exclaimed, and heard my voice come out raw and hard.

Moved by my anguished interest, her face flooded with tenderness. "His name is Jordan. Jordan Williams." In a rush she told me how they had met at a UCLA Extension course in French Literature – "`Madame Bovary brought us together, we were both in tears!" – and how Jordan had praised her "pretty eyes." Her cheeks were blazing as she repeated this trite compliment. "As soon as he touched me I knew, I knew!" she cried ecstatically.

"Knew?" I mumbled.

"*Knew!*" she said, with a look of fierce triumph.

As she ran on, describing her first night in Jordan's arms, offering details that made me want to shut my ears in shame, I sensed from her tone that the urgency of her feelings obliterated every other loyalty, to my father, to me. I felt numb. Leila was no longer my mother. She was someone else, a fascinating, frightening *other,* and I was threatened by a surge of panic.

Leila sensed my distress at once. She smiled, and the old Leila, warm and vulnerable, was back. Drawing a deep breath, she said: "You know, dad and I, since the accident, there's been nothing…he can't. We tried things..." She shuddered involuntarily. "Not good. I don't think he really wanted...*Get yourself a lover, woman, for godsakes,*" she declared, miming my father's impatient contempt. "Anyway..." She let the word float in the warm summer air: *anyway...*

We were silent for a long moment, surrounded by a stillness that was simultaneously fragile and inviolate. When my mother spoke again her voice was a whisper. "Trouble is, he hates me for it, all the same. `Leila, don't come to me with that glowing look. Have some *vergüenza*!' Shame for what?" she asked me. "For doing what he said I should? For being *happy*?"

At that moment the desperation of her desires was beyond the reach of my adolescent head. She seemed like a songbird that had flown out of its cage and no longer knew the way back.

"Mom," I murmured, and took her in my arms. We rocked together quietly, both of us seeking comfort in the familiar embrace. She was a woman in distress, a weeping woman, and I was soothing her unhappiness, and it felt right, and good.

two

ALL MY LIFE I've been haunted by the image of a weeping woman. I've seen her often in my dreams, and her presence is always there at the edges of my mind. Perhaps "presence" isn't quite the right description. In my childhood the woman in tears was more an atmosphere than a clear form; more a mood than any focused impression. She was my mother, yet more than my mother – a wrenching, purely female quality of sadness, an ancient, archetypal sense of sorrow.

It was obvious to me early on that Max was not aware or wasn't moved by Leila's elemental melancholy. I could never understand how he could ignore the fact that the woman he lived with, and supposedly loved, was so profoundly sad. As I grew older I began to think that maybe he just didn't want to know. Or that perhaps he had long realized that there was nothing he could do about it, personally, or as a man.

Leila's lover would never make her happy. I knew this as soon as I met him. To put it bluntly, Jordan Williams was an asshole, a man utterly in love with himself, a pompous prick who considered he was doing my mother a favor by awarding her his attentions. Sure, I was jealous of the blatant way she fawned over him, fetched and carried, gazing at the man with foolish adoration. But I understood her hunger, and hoped she wouldn't discover too soon and painfully just how shallow the man was. We all invent the people we love, and she had a powerful imagination and urgent need; but Jordan the man was so removed from Jordan the fantasy that I knew at once she would be bruised, and badly. Trouble was, I didn't know how to protect her. I could not tell her what I really thought of Jordan; that would have been too cruel. In truth, I could never bring myself to cause her pain of any kind, an inhibition that was clearly a kind of emotional cowardice.

My father, on the other hand, attacked Jordan mercilessly. "You sure know how to pick 'em, Leila," he sneered. "Of all the men you might have plucked, you selected this plum!" As her eyes grew moist, he sliced away at her lover's "fatuosity," the knuckles gripping the arms of his wheelchair white with a furious joy, his face burning with a kind of hideous delight that turned my stomach. The fact that I totally agreed with him made me complicit in his malice, and my guilt was excruciating.

"Women are strange beasts," Max told me, often. He liked to soliloquize on this topic while I walked beside his wheelchair for his evening airing, along the pathway in Santa Monica's Palisades Park. "And your mother is one of the strangest." I made a noncommittal grunt in response, and he took this for agreement, encouraging him to plunge into a monologue about the nature of the "female mystery." Wrapped in his ruminations, he seemed to forget that I was still a kid, and he revealed all kinds of intimate details about his marriage.

"I was the first man she ever slept with," he said. "She was a nineteen-year-old virgin, and frantic with it. When I touched her, in that way, she went berserk, trembling all over, twitching and howling. I was afraid she was having some kind of seizure! Her mother had episodes of petit mal, you know. But in Leila it wasn't epilepsy, just all mad virgin stuff."

He chuckled wryly at the memory. "Took me years to calm her, teach her to make love normally." He shrugged. "I guess some folk might say I deliberately dumbed her down, but they don't know how nuts she was. Besides, there's no place for such crazy sex in marriage. I had to be cruel to be kind, and it worked. Except now, I can't manage her any more. Let that moron try – he's welcome to it!"

Max often took a perverse pleasure in telling me about the effect of his spinal cord injury on his sexual life. He spoke of his "floppies" – his word for reflex erections. "It salutes and keels over, *flop!* Tried different tricks, vacuum pumps, rubber rings, and the like. Painful. Sometimes, when I beg her, Leila will use her hand. It's hard work, for both of us. She pulls this face – can't help it, I guess. Not much fun." I hated these confidences, and shut my ears trying not to listen; but the prospect of my fastidious mother on her knees between Max's shriveled legs hopelessly laboring away at his "floppy" made me sick.

Max's paraplegia was classified as a relatively moderate Level T6. He could bathe, dress and groom himself, get in and out of his bed and his wheelchair on his own, and control his bowels and bladder – though he did need to strap a plastic bladder to his left ankle for emergencies when he was out of the house. Training with chest expanders and weights had enormously developed his muscular upper body and arms, and he mockingly described his now grossly disproportioned figure as "a gorilla up top, a jellyfish down below." At night when I helped him into bed the feel of his unbalanced body, with its powerful arms and torso and dangling loins and legs reminded me rather of a hermit crab deprived of its shell.

A series of cheery nurse-aides – mostly Filipina, with sweet names like Luminosa and Caridad – visited once a week to supervise his exercise program, massage his neck and back, scold Max about the hygiene of his leg and bed bags, and check that he had taken his pain medications and stool softeners. He slept in the downstairs guest room, and the jangle of his bell at any hour of the night was a ghostly shriek in the dark. I'd rush down to find him possessed by spasms, his body twitching and shaking with agonizing pins and needles as his damaged spine played merry hell with the nerves of his dead limbs. "Don't touch me!" he'd cry. With the next gasp he begged for his pills, anticonvulsants whose medical names, *gabapentin, phenytoin, carbamazepine*, were mantras of relief. In the low glow of his night light his room had the tangy smell of deodorant undercut by a disinfectant sharp enough to mask the odor of his "purple piss," urine stained by the prune juice he was obliged to drink to move his bowels. (His morning moan: "I'd *kill* for bacon and eggs.") As his anguish eased, I'd adjust the incline of his motorized bed, my ears filled with his quiet groans, and all the other intimate complaint of his invalid existence.

Fortunately, Max could still do his job. Each weekday morning a specially equipped van picked him up and took him to an office in nearby Venice, bringing him home at five. "Without work I'd go loco," he said. "My head would stew in its own juice and my brains would leak out my ears. And Leila'd certainly strangle me. Anyway, I'm the breadwinner in this family. She couldn't earn her keep if her life depended on it." He shrugged. "That's just the way she is. You take Leila as you find her, or not at all."

On our evening walks, I always tried to distract him from his unwanted revelations, pointing out the sweep of Santa Monica Bay, the bright iron sun beating on the sea, but he would not be diverted. From time to time his attention might be drawn to a girl jogging by in Spandex tights; or he might launch into a fulmination against the ragged homeless men and women dozing under the palms. But his focus seldom strayed for long from the subject that obsessed him.

"Women have a kind of need that can kill you," he said grimly, as we paused beside the railings on the edge of the cliff. "They don't mean it to kill you, but they can't help it, no matter how much they feel for you. And if it comes to a choice between their need and your life, there's just no contest." His face softened suddenly, and a flush of tenderness suffused his lean cheeks. "I have to say, she's a generous woman," he murmured. "She gives too much...I never asked for all that, you know? Never asked for it." Abruptly, his face hardened. "She'll kill you, Joel, if you aren't careful!"

"Dad," I mumbled, shaken by his vehemence.

He struggled for control of his voice. "What I mean to say is, she doesn't know boundaries. Can't draw lines between genuine mother love and, well, the other kind. She lets it all gush out, with no regard for the consequences. God knows, I've tried to shield you. I try to keep hold of the reins, but it isn't easy, especially now that I'm a cripple, in body and spirit. That is, my soul now has a body to match." (Cripple – or the blunt Spanish *cojo* or *cojito* favored by my grandpa Enrique – was the bitter term Max preferred for his condition, rather than the more polite "disabled.") Before I could offer sympathy, he rushed on. "Now she wastes herself on pompadours like this Jordan. To mock me, maybe? Punish me for all the ways I've tried to hogtie her? No, she's just not malicious. If only she were! Then I'd know how to hate her."

This was all too much for me. I didn't want to hear any more, and for one ghastly moment I fantasized shoving my dad's wheelchair over the edge, letting it plunge down into the busy traffic along the Pacific Coast Highway a hundred feet below. The speeding cars would mangle him and his cripple carriage, and free me from the burden of his miseries. Right then I wanted to escape from both of them, to fly away across the Pacific to some distant tropical island where the world was new and free of parents. I'd be reborn there, emerging from a conch shell into the bright light of an original day. Instead, I stayed mute and dutiful, my ears ringing with my father's rancor.

"She doesn't listen to me any more. My voice sickens her. In truth, it sickens me," Max said. "No one listens to me, except you. You listen to both of us. You are our marriage!" He lifted his head and laughed, a dry cackle in the sunlight that chilled my blood.

* * *

As it was, Jordan did not last long. In a few months he drifted away like a puffball on the wind, driven off by the gusts of my mother's fierce neediness. She tried to cling to him, but the thin fibers of his being slipped through her fingers. However, she wasn't as devastated by the loss of her lover as I feared she might be. Maybe Jordan had never seemed quite real to her. Or perhaps the very notion of "lover" was unreal, more my father's bitter scheme than her own; perhaps he believed that *cojitos* deserved to be cuckolded. As he liked to say, *quien sabe lo que nos reserva el destino* – who knows what fate has in store for us.

Fate had transformed Leila Masur into Mrs. Max Bajamonde, just as it had caused her to be born in Paris on a particular day in a particular year, then abruptly transferred her to Los Angeles before she was five years old, at her mother's whim. Her intonation still retained a Frenchy lilt, especially in her rolled Rs and the trace of a Z in her "thises" and "thats," but she claimed to have forgotten most of the language, partly in reaction to searing early memories of being sneered at as *une sale Juive* – "a dirty Jewess." The gods had decreed that her true universe should be limited to herself, Max, and me, and so everything that mattered was confined to that tight triangle.

Her intense yearnings had to have a focus, however, and after Jordan's disappearance she turned back to me. In the evenings, when my father was deep into the trashy television shows he watched with avid, self-mocking contempt, she drifted into my bedroom and draped herself over my bed, watching me do my homework. I could feel her smoky stare burning the back of my head, raising the hairs on my nape. Unable to concentrate on the intricacies of integral calculus, or the subtleties of the Federalist Papers, I swiveled my seat and turned to face her, to receive the confidences she simply had to share.

"Do you know I used to cry when I was nursing you?" she'd say. "Not from the pain – though you were a greedy infant. From joy. Your smell made me drunk. Your skin was scented like a ripe peach warmed by the sun. Even the stuff you brought up when I put you over my shoulder to burp smelled sweet to me. I used to sniff your diapers before I washed them. In fact, I still bury my face in your underwear."

"You don't!" I exclaimed, simultaneously touched and repulsed.

"I do, I do," she replied solemnly. "Your body has an animal odor, for me. You're my own personal *petite bête d'amour*, Joelly."

"Mom..." I murmured, snared by her soft tone.

"When I was little I had this stuffed shaggy monkey," she said dreamily. "Harry. It slept with me, soaked up my smells. It was delicious. I thought it was as alive as I was, until I was three or so..."

"And I remind you of Harry?" I teased.

Her eyes widened in shock. "Oh no. How could that be? You are alive."

"How did you and dad meet?" I asked. I'd heard the story many times, but I knew she was compelled to retell it, perhaps in a struggle to understand fate's strange purposes.

"He claimed me," she began promptly, as she always did. "At UCLA, architecture students shared some classes with Fine Arts, and he just came up to me and took me over. I was lost. He found me. It was a huge relief."

"From what?" I asked ritually.

"From just being me."

As always, this rote reply threw me. There was an implication in it of a kind of helplessness that made my skin shiver. Was I as helpless? Would someone come and "claim" me one day? "You could've walked away," I protested.

She shook her head. "He's a man who knows his own mind. People like that have it over us every time. You can't say no if they decide they want you." The look on her face just then was the kind I imagined little Gretel had when she and her brother were lost in the forest. "You keep a diary, don't you?" she asked abruptly. "Just like me."

"What do you write in it?" I asked boldly.

"My secrets," she said, with a coy smile. "For you."

"Me?"

"One day, when I'm gone, you can read it and know everything."

"Who wants to know everything, for godsakes?"

"I do. You do. Like me, you have to know everything, or—" She broke off, leaving the dangerous consequence of not knowing hanging in the air.

I yearned to say, *I know you're unhappy, so unhappy*...But the spoken words would make it all too real, and truly unbearable. Besides, in some dim, barely realized way I sensed even then that her sorrow somehow served her. I had no idea what I meant by that, but it was an obscure truth that simultaneously clouded my mind and compounded my sympathy.

three

AROUND THE TIME my mother had her fling with Jordan I fell into my first pubescent crush.

Rory was a new student in my progressive Santa Monica junior high class. I noticed her the first day of the spring semester, struck by her brisk voice and the assured way she had of jutting her chin when she spoke. She was plump – "chubby," in my mother's vocabulary – and that unfashionable condition softened the boldness of her manner. She was from Toronto, I heard, and the flat Ontario vowels that peppered her speech made her seem all the more self-assured. Compared to me, that is; I was never much good at the desperate teenage game of "cool," of making like I knew a whole lot more about the scary business of life, sex, and love than I actually did. Rory, on the other hand, seemed to have a sure sense of herself.

Too shy to approach her, I watched Rory circumspectly for a few weeks with growing fascination. It amazed me that anyone of my age could be so self-assured. Yet I noticed that, sometimes, when she felt no one was looking, her lively round face lapsed into a sort of absence; her usually agile mouth went limp, the lips seeming to sag with the weight of their own flesh. At those moments I wanted to run up and hug her, but I didn't dare. In my family emotional attachments were never taken lightly; they were far too fraught. It was imprinted on my spirit that to love or desire someone was to plunge into complex currents that could as well drown you as exalt you, so admiring Rory from a distance seemed the safest course.

However, one lunchtime she sat down at my table and began to talk to me as if it were the most natural thing in the world. "You have a noble profile," she said. "Vaguely Mesopotamian, I think." She took my chin in her hand and turned my face to one side. "Definitely Mesopotamian."

I blushed, and damned myself for blushing. How uncool! Rory

smiled and gently squeezed my hand. "I like you, Joel," she murmured.

"Why—?" I blurted, and cursed myself yet again.

"Woman's intuition. Are you going with anyone?" I shook my head vehemently and she nodded. "Good. Let's get together after school and hang out, eh?"

I told her I had to take my dad out for his evening stroll in Palisades Park and she promptly invited herself to come along. When my father saw Rory, he scowled. But she set out to charm him, and in a few minutes he was putty in her hands. They swapped lightbulb-screwing jokes and he queried her about Toronto, displaying a level of interest I hadn't seen in years. "Your dad's a sweetheart," she said as we pedaled our bikes to her house north of Montana. The epithet "sweetheart" coupled with my father was so startling I almost fell off my saddle, but its incongruity entranced me.

Rory's encounter with my mother was less pleasant. The two women detested each other on sight. "That girl is chubby," my mother declared, loading the word with a freight of contempt.

"Nonsense," my father retorted. "It's just puppy fat. In a few years she'll be a knockout."

"She's a peasant from up north," my mother muttered. "You know those Canadians."

"You're just jealous," he said derisively. "She has your boy in thrall."

"She's chubby," my mother repeated. "I was never chubby."

"No, you were always a godamm skeleton," he snapped. "Skin and bones. Joel fancies girls with a shape to them, and good luck, son!"

"Your mom doesn't care for me," Rory said one day as we were cycling home from school. Her tone was hesitant, uncharacteristically wary.

"Well, you know moms," I mumbled.

"You two are very close."

"She's my mom!"

"Okay," she said, and changed the subject.

Compared to the charged atmosphere of my home, Rory's household was wonderfully relaxed. Her two older brothers lived at home while attending classes at UCLA, and her older sister, Juliette, was two grades ahead of us in school. At the Molloys everyone came and went as he pleased and a general easy breeziness prevailed. I tried to sniff out any murky undercurrents but found none in their blithe family cheerfulness, and that amazed me.

Rory's mother, Edina Molloy, was a big, broad-shouldered woman with a moon face and hands like baseball mitts. Like a mitt, the fingers seemed to be sewn together, separate from the huge thumbs, making her gestures blunt and bold, and somehow guileless. She exuded an air of great simplicity, as if there was nothing in life that could not be sorted out with enough goodwill and common sense. She was from a different planet than my mother, that was obvious, and I felt disloyal to Leila for liking her at once.

Rory, on the other hand, was intrigued by my mother, despite Leila's obvious disdain. "Your mom's so beautiful, so fine. How can someone like that just live from day to day?" she wondered. "She's crazy about you," she added. "I think maybe she's in love with you."

"Sure she loves me," I said defensively. "Your mom loves you."

"Love is one thing, in love's another," Rory countered. Then, seeing my discomfort, she went on to talk about other things.

Leila's antagonism toward Rory was goaded by her habit of serenading me at odd hours. Standing under my first floor bedroom window, Rory would let loose a volley of song, mostly golden oldies from the 1930s and Forties that sounded innocently silly in our rough-and-tumble times. Strains of "Chattanooga Choo Choo," "Begin the Beguine," "Jealousy," or "Shoo Fly Pie," wafted up to me, carried by her strong, husky voice. When I leaned on the sill I'd find her moon face lifted skyward, and I fancied I could almost see the musical notes issuing from her wide red mouth.

I was thrilled to be serenaded, it was so wonderfully corny. But Leila was outraged. "The girl's old enough to be your mother!" she exclaimed, grossly exaggerating the three-month difference in our ages. In furious disgust, she ran out and dragged Rory, still singing, into the house. "For godsakes, think of the neighbors," she said. "You'll set all the local dogs barking!"

My father tried to get Rory to sing indoors, but she said she could only "let rip" in the open air. "My mom says my voice is meant for big spaces," she explained. "In here, I'd rattle the china."

"F. the china," my father replied, drawing a disapproving glance from Leila.

However, Rory would sometimes sing to me sotto voce in my bedroom if my parents were out of the house. Her favorite indoor song was "Anything Goes" – "In olden days a glimpse of stocking/ Was looked on as something shocking" – which she rendered in a Doris Day-like low croon. After that we'd kiss and cuddle, and she allowed me to touch her "developers," her already bulging breasts, but only on the outside of her blouse.

"I think you'll be a terrific lover some day," she whispered. "You have such gentle hands." Hearing that, I felt terribly grown up and my blood tingled with masculine pride. After she left I masturbated like crazy.

* * *

Rory's presence in my life exasperated my mother in ways I couldn't quite fathom. When Leila spoke about her her eyes would sometimes glitter with a kind of fierceness while her whole body seemed to quiver with a barely suppressed outrage. She made wild statements, calling Rory "evil," "a demon." She warned me that Rory would "seduce" me, conjuring up images of the movie vamps I'd seen in the old films my parents rented and ran on our home projector.

"Nobody seduces anyone any more," my father cut in. "This is the Seventies, the age of the sexual revolution, honey."

My mother swung on him. "You don't mind that this – this precocious teenage hussy! – is intent on destroying your son's innocence?"

"I wish I'd been so lucky," he retorted. "Things might have turned out differently."

Leila froze, shocked by his implication. Her lower lip trembled, and at that moment I was ready to drop Rory instantly if only she wouldn't cry. I opened my mouth to make this promise but my throat was too dry. However, I silently resolved to tell Rory the very next day that I couldn't see her any more.

That night, after supper, my mother came into my room while I was hurrying to complete a class assignment I had to finish for the next morning. She draped her arms around my neck, nuzzling her cheek against mine, and her warm, deeply female smell filled my nose, making my head swim. Wordlessly, she clung to me, swaying slightly, while I sat with my fingers frozen over my typewriter.

When she began to speak her voice was a low burr in my ear. "You're my life, Joelly," she murmured, her breath brushing feathers over my skin. "No, you *are* life, to me. That may sound foolish, but I've never felt you were separated from my body, even when they cut the cord. I still know how you feel, even before you do, sometimes. I know every expression on your sweet face. You're my *petite bête,* my creature. *Mine!*"

I tried to wriggle free, gently, but her arms were locked around my neck. Part of me wanted to break her grip, even roughly; another part wanted nothing more than to sink into the sensuality of the warmth that seemed to suffuse every muscle and nerve in my body. As she went on I barely listened, consumed by the struggle inside me. Break free or surrender – which? It was as if I were trying to swim upstream and downstream at the same time, yet could not move a muscle. Panic and pleasure tugged at my heart. I wanted that moment to end instantly, and continue forever. When, finally, Leila withdrew her arms and released me I was overcome by an aching sense of loss. The joy of release was strong, but the regret was far greater. At the same time I had a feeling of arousal denied. All I knew was that the aroma of my mother's skin was the most exciting scent I had ever experienced.

After Leila left my room, I tried to describe her visit in my diary. Writing in my diary was the only way I could get some kind of purchase on things. The words I scribbled on the page helped me wrap my mind around events and feelings I could not begin to understand, charged experiences that seemed to threaten my life as a separate human being. I felt that if I could only write it all down I might make some sense out of my days, and maybe survive them.

Rory had said my mother was in love with me, and certainly her actions that evening seemed like the attentions of a lover. But through the thicket of written words I glimpsed a question that made me shiver: *Was I in love with my mother?*

In truth, I could not decipher the meaning of anything – least of all the phrase, "in love." Certainly not in regard to Leila.

I had a crush on Rory – that was clear, at least. I liked the look and feel of her body, and the touch-memory of her budding breasts fueled my masturbatory furies. Yet Leila never appeared in my deeper erotic fantasies; in fact, the very thought of such a thing shocked me deeply. Her persona was far too potent for cheap thrills.

So, were "love" and "sex" mutually exclusive? Would the feelings I had for Leila and the kind of attraction I felt for Rory ever be fused in one whole experience?

"My brain hurts," I said out loud, echoing one of my father's favorite expressions. I slammed my diary shut. As I struggled to straighten out my thoughts, floods of guilt and shame and raw desire washed through me. Most of all, I wanted to give in to my mother's call. I felt I owed her my absolute devotion, that she deserved it, in recompense for some primal, unspecified wrong she had suffered sometime, somewhere; a wrong that I had participated in, unwittingly, maybe just by being born.

In my Spanish Literature class I had recently read a phrase by the seventeenth century playwright Calderon de la Barca that sent shivers down my spine: *El delito mayor del hombre es haber nacido* – "Man's greatest crime is to have been born." My Spanish teacher, Mr. Morales, explained that Calderon was talking about the Catholic concept of original sin, but to me the words had a different slant. In being born I had somehow added to my mother's deep distress. Yet I was her life, she said. So, was life itself a kind of injury? Calderon thought so, it seemed; and so, in sense, did my mother. If both of them were right, what point was there in living?

The year before, Jack Bloy, a boy in my class, had committed suicide by jumping off the edge of Palisades Park into the traffic on the Pacific Coast Highway. Nobody told us why he had done it; some said he was depressed because he couldn't keep up in class, others that he was high on smack, though I never heard anything about Jack being a druggie. As far as I knew, his home life was okay; his parents seemed pleasant enough, and they had just bought him a new Japanese thirteen-speed racing bike for his birthday. Two days later he took a wild swan dive off the cliff, and all of us were shaken.

Maybe Jack had been grappling with the kind of mind-busting questions that were obsessing me. Questions without answers. Questions no adolescent mind could begin to deal with. Why are we asked questions we can't answer? I wondered petulantly. It was ridiculous! And cruel. It had maybe killed poor Jack.

Next day in Spanish Lit. I interrupted a discussion of Calderon's "Life Is A Dream" to ask exactly this: Why are we asked questions we can't answer? Startled by the uncharacteristically blunt tone of my query, Mr. Morales peered at me over his bifocals. "Joel?" he said gently. "I don't—"

I cut him off with a quote from the text. "`What is life? A madness. What is life? An illusion, a shadow, a story...' Is there an answer? And if there isn't, why the hell ask it?"

Morales regarded me gravely. My unusual impoliteness gave him pause; he saw at once that I wasn't being disruptive just for the hell of it. "`*Que toda la vida es sueño/ y los sueños sueños son*,'" he quoted. "`Life is a dream' – that's one answer."

"It's not good enough," I replied angrily. "It didn't help poor Jack."

There was a gasp of shock in the class. I saw Rory frowning at me across the classroom. "That's gross!" someone exclaimed, and there were many murmurs of assent.

Morales shushed them. "It's perfectly valid for Joel to relate literature to life," he said. "What value does it have, otherwise? The reasons that drove that boy to take his life aren't so far removed from the questions Calderon poses in *La Vida es Sueño*. `Why are we asked questions we can't answer?' That's the heart of the matter, my friends. It's a conundrum that can drive you to drink." He gave a complex shrug. "Part of me says it's the only question worth asking. The other part says, for godsakes don't ask it! Each one of us has to decide which line to follow through life, the asking or the not-asking. Or maybe our temperaments dictate the way. Now to proceed..."

At the end of the class Morales called to me as I was about to exit. "Something troubling you, Joel?" he asked. "Beyond the profundities, I mean."

"Well, you know," I mumbled. "Just stuff."

"Family `stuff'?"

"Yes. No. Maybe." I wriggled uncomfortably. Mr. Morales seemed far too nice and straight to bear the burden of my murky troubles.

He regarded me gravely. "You're a good student," he said. "And I appreciate your love for our literature. But sometimes we're all caught up in things we can't deal with right there and then, especially in adolescence. That's when the gap between the questions and the answers is greatest, and sometimes the people we love most cause us the worst confusion. Sometimes just to dream the dream is the wisest course, *hijo mío*."

"How do you do that?" I asked sullenly, edging toward the door. The familiar classroom, now my only safe haven, didn't deserve to be muddied by the mess in my head.

"Search me," Morales replied, dismissing me with a laconic wave.

Rory was waiting for me in the corridor outside. "What's up, J.?" she asked. Her habit of calling me "J." was yet another thing about her that annoyed my mother.

"Same shit," I shrugged, pushing past her. She hurried along after me, tugging at my loose shirttail. Abruptly, I swung around and faced her. "Let's cool it for a while, okay?" I said harshly. "You and me."

She gaped. "Cool it? Why?"

"I need, you know, space. To think."

"Seems you're thinking too much," she said dryly.

"Look, that's it, okay?" I turned and walked away, leaving her standing.

four

SOMETIMES JUST TO DREAM the dream is the wisest course, *hijo mío...*

Morales's sentence went round and round in my head, and each time it circulated I got more and more angry. I admired my teacher greatly, he was such a nice, caring man, he had taken a lot of interest in me; but it seemed to me that his response to my question was fucking fatuous! Okay, but why was I so angry? And why did the fury I felt gratify something deep inside me? Why did it give me such a feeling of satisfaction, as if I'd melted down a complex situation to its basic level, burned away all the confusing crap to enjoy a pure rage? Maybe it had something to do with my Spanish blood, I reflected wryly. Perhaps it was something I'd inherited from my beloved Grandpa Enrique: a fundamental instinct that, when it came right down to it, outrage was the only appropriate response to the human condition.

Enrique Bajamonde was without doubt the angriest man I've ever known. He was furious enough with America, which had given him refuge, but he was vitriolic about the Spain he had been forced to abandon in 1939 when Franco defeated the Republican Army in his native Andalusia, forcing him to flee over the Pyrenees to France. With the Fascist victory, Spain, he declared, had finally achieved the *desgracia* it so thoroughly deserved.

If he despised his countrymen, for the French he had nothing but hatred. He damned them for the way in which they had immediately interned thousands of fleeing Republican soldiers in freezing concentration camps in the Pyrenees. He bitterly remembered that the exhausted, miserable Spaniards were fed nothing but thin soup and bread for weeks on end. Despite the meagerness of their rations, Enrique and his fellow internees had fashioned sets of chessmen out of bread, to while away the long, cold months before the International Red Cross arranged their passage to England, six months after World War Two began. "If you won the game, you ate the pieces, and I was a champ," he said, his ink-black eyes glinting with an astringent glee.

On the boat to Britain, Enrique, then barely twenty years old, met Mercedes, a seventeen-year-old refugee girl, my grandmother. They were both descended from generations of Granadan *conversos*, fifteenth-century Jews who had been forced to convert to Christianity by the Inquisition; that, along with their common birthplace, drew them together. They married a few days after they arrived in London, just as the Luftwaffe was beginning the brutal blitz that was supposed to bring the English to their knees. The two young Spaniards were so dazed by the hardships of the previous few years that it did not occur to them to take shelter from the bombs. "We wandered around Piccadilly, blissfully holding hands among the burning buildings and the debris and the dust," Enrique recalled. "We were too distracted to be frightened. Besides, we'd already seen a war."

Enrique never forgave the English for having failed to support the Spanish Republic against the Nationalists, and only grudgingly admitted England's generosity in accepting him as a refugee. The British had not called him to serve in their army in the war against the Nazis and he resented that, even though he said he would have refused the call. "They didn't fight our war, why should I fight theirs?" When the Allies allowed Franco to survive after Italy and Germany were defeated, his resentment was intense; it meant he could not return home. In disgust, he rejected Britain and moved to the United States, to the West Coast, as far away as possible from fascist Spain.

By the time I was closest to him, between the ages of eight and eleven, before he died of lung cancer induced by chain-smoking (his explosive smoker's cough had an air-tearing sound, like the bursting of a blown-up paper bag), Enrique had long since funneled his exile's rage into angry diatribes against anything and everything. If I mentioned that the Santa Monica bus I'd taken home from school was late and crowded, Enrique would instantly launch into a fulmination in which every bus driver was *un hijo de la gran puta*. At times the torrent of words spilling from his mouth could be fiercesome, yet I sensed he was deriding himself even in the midst of his most vehement diatribes. The self-mockery might be revealed in a tangential, almost touching phrase cutting through his ferocious words. Or it might flash out in an oddly cheerful grin as he paused to draw breath before rushing on.

He particularly hated the fact that we and General Franco shared the same family name. The dictator's mother's family name, or matronymic, was Bahamonde, and he recited the dictator's full appellation, Francisco Paulino Hermenegildo Teódulo Franco Bahamonde, with bitter relish. "That bastard must've stolen Bahamonde to give himself some *categoría*," he huffed. Bahamonde, literally, "lower world," was, he claimed, a typically devilish name mandated for *marranos* – secret Jews – by the Inquisition after their forced conversion. "In the Generalisimo's case, the epithet is quite correct!" "Marrano," Enrique liked to remind me, means "swine," an unkosher beast for Jews.

Enrique's wrathful monologues were the fugues of his soul. My late grandmother, Merche, had long since dismissed these outbursts as *tonterias,* sheer silliness, but I was fascinated. The pure black-heartedness charging such furies vented a passionate energy, spiced by a sly relish for the brute facts of life.

"Lazarillo de Tormes," Europe's first picaresque novel, was Enrique's favorite book. He read me long passages from it, his crisp Castilian ringing in my ears. In "Lazarillo," the young *picaro* is initiated into the world of pain by a vicious old blind man. The sightless man dashes Lazarillo's head against a stone animal to teach him to be alert. "Silly fool," his master jeers, "learn that the blind man's boy has to know one point more than the devil," and laughs heartily at the joke. "Pain is the price of wisdom," Enrique concluded solemnly. His own painful wisdom was derived from the memory of his mother, father, and little sister Rafaela, strangled by the fascists in 1937, leaving him with an orphan's distrust of all humanity.

I knew that Enrique considered me naive, a softie from a pampered background, and was contemptuous of my childish belief in people, my "delusion that it's possible to be human," in his phrase. "We live out a life sentence, stupidly or gracefully," he said, "and our only grace is to give God the finger. All the rest is *mierda pura, mierda absolutamente pura.*" The phrase, "pure crap," was delivered with a harsh, singing rasp from deep in his throat, like a rough, deep-throated *cante jondo* phrase from the *soleares,* a kind of Andalusian blues, he listened to by the hour. "Your kind fucks about with metaphors," he said, "and in the end, you can go home to mommy anytime you wish. I'd be shot on the spot if I put my nose across the Pyrenees." Enrique was right, not about being shot, since Franco had by then declared a general amnesty for Republicans refugees, but about not being able to find the home he remembered.

When we went hiking in the Santa Monica Mountains – he loved the harsh, semi-desert chaparral – Enrique would speak about his life with a raw nostalgia that twisted my heart. "The trouble with exile, *nieto mío*, is that it stamps you forever. Exile really has no place to go, no true resolution. If I could return tomorrow, I'd still be lost. Things move on. The Spain I knew doesn't exist any more, the man I was has vaporized. I'm in exile from a past that's vanished into thin air. That's my story – so tell me, what to do?"

Troubled by his persistent question, I once suggested, with all the naiveté of a boy, "Can't you invent a new story, *abuelo*?"

His face darkened instantly. For an endless moment he glared at me with absolute contempt, reducing me from a grandchild to the status of some loathsome insect. "Spoken like a true American," he said. "Shit, this is a marvelous country! A nation in which *cojitos de seso*" – his rendering of "lame-brains" – "are free to make themselves up as they go along!"

Enrique both despised and needed my company, I realized. He required an audience, someone who would receive his diatribes, "like a kind of human toilet," he said tartly. But my compassion had to be subtle. If, in an excess of sympathy, I let him win at chess – a game he'd taught me – he kicked the board across the room, scattering the chessmen. "Smashing me is what you do!" he shouted, his face flushed, his eyes like chips of jet. "You're my master at this game, so don't pretend to be my whipping boy. It's a fucking obscenity!"

I cringed at such abuse, but I soon came back to see him again, compelled by his raw struggle with fate, a battle he stubbornly refused to concede. While I was trying to thread my way through my own childhood confusions, Enrique was fighting for his soul with his back to the wall, believing that the country he loved, the life he loved, was being strangled to death by forces he had miserably failed to defeat. In the context of a hospitable but obtuse America, he had to somehow preserve some spark of his true self; and, by extension, the flame of Spain's bitter honor.

The sheer terror in his eyes in certain moments wrenched my heart, not only with compassion, but with a scare that came from watching a man whose existence had been wrecked. Then his usually taut features seemed to sag with the gravity of his grief, until his face looked like a grotesque Halloween mask, a sack of loose old skin draped over his skull, with ragged holes cut out for his eyes. All the same, even at his most desperate, there was always a very Spanish trace of perverse satisfaction that life had proved to be the *mierda pura* he'd always known it was.

I adored Enrique, but all the same there was a laconically sardonic strain in his character that at times simply appalled me. After my father's terrible accident, for instance, Enrique cheerily dubbed his son *El Paralítico.* Max flinched at this epithet at first, then gleefully adopted it as a badge of honor. But I thought it was truly ugly. However, my grandfather was then in his last year of life, and he was even more fiercely scornful of his own body's ruin. All the same, *El Paralítico* was far too blunt for my tender ears.

Enrique's one purely tenderhearted passion centered on the hummingbirds he attracted to his backyard feeders. Ask a question about these tiny, shimmering animals, and he would respond with a rapt recitation of the hummingbird's amazing heart rate and wing-beat rhythms. Drawing me carefully close to a feeding female, he blew gently on her head to raise the glittering plumage, revealing the hungry bird's powerful tongue muscles pulsing under the paper-thin skin at the back of its skull. In a whisper he explained that the hummingbird's darting white tongue was so active, and so big in proportion to the creature's bill, it had to be anchored by sinews wrapped around its skull. But Enrique was under no illusion that hummingbirds were pure delight. "They can be ferocious," he said proudly. "I've seen them stab and strike, knock one another out of the air out of sheer viciousness. Sometimes I fear for my eyes." To Enrique, hummingbirds epitomized the dynamic tension between *ferocidad y gracia*, ferocity and grace, that, in his thoroughly Iberian view, governed all existence.

The company of Enrique's angry ghost was a true comfort to me in the miserable weeks following my messy run-in with Mr. Morales. In a world of confusion it was something real to hold onto, something essential, in the true sense of cutting right to the bone. Up against Morales's woolly suggestion of surrender to a dream state I could oppose my grandfather's crisp prescription of *mierda pura*. Life is shit, and it was right and fitting to be fucking angry about it.

In the end my "sulky mood," as Leila teasingly dubbed it, was undercut by an unexpected twist: Max more or less moved out of the house.

He won a competition to design the Engineering Sciences building on a campus in northern California. It was a project he had entered independently, not as an employee of his firm, and the commission was a huge boost to his ego and his professional prospects. However, it also meant he would have to be away from home for weeks at a time. Both these possibilities elated him, he could hardly dissemble his joy. The condition of *cojismo,* crippledom, which he had assumed with such self-derisive elan, had begun to bore his restless soul, and he clearly looked forward to escaping it, and us.

"Things have their moment," he said with a shrug when I told him I'd miss him. "Soldier on, son, soldier on. And take good care of your mom." He was so eager to escape, he refused to allow us to accompany him to the airport. One of his assistants came by, packed his stuff into a van, and drove him away, and Max didn't even turn to wave goodbye. "The change of scene will do him the world of good," Leila said. "He's been a really down in the mouth recently."

For a while my father's absence created a gap inside our house. Gradually, however, the blank space shrank and vanished, creating a subtle shift of atmosphere. Leila talked about Max often, but as a personality outside our sphere. She took total physical and mental possession of the house, pulling her horns in only a little when Max came to "visit." Max was tentative around Leila on these occasions, extraordinarily polite, as a good guest should be. It was clear that he was happy to concede the home to her completely, to give Leila free run in exchange for his freedom to come and go, and it did not seem to bother him that he had more or less abandoned me to her influence.

Leila loved ruling alone, absolute queen of her own realm. Every time she came home she sang out "Joelly? Joelly?" – the doubled syllables a self-echoing sonar of command. However, despite her obvious pleasure in her Maxless domain, she claimed she was lonely. Her friends, she said, were mostly interested in Max. Besides, she did not trust other women, and she suspected that all the men she knew had "designs" on her in her "semi-divorced" state. "I'm happy to be free of social obligations," she said primly, when I asked why she never went out with other people. "All I need to be happy is to paint my watercolors and be with you." Her high soprano trilled through the house, singing the popular show tunes and Edith Piaf songs she adored. At regular intervals she chanted *Joelly? Joelly?* to make sure I was still within earshot.

But under her superficial contentment I was always aware of a deep drag of melancholy. The old sorrow that was somehow my fault obliged me to stay home with her as much as possible, almost every night and weekend. Often in my sleep I was visited by the Weeping Woman. She was there, hovering in the background of my uneasy dreams, accusing me of a failure of sympathy that was never clearly defined. Sometimes I sensed Leila's presence just outside my door, but I was never sure if she was really there, or whether my innate culpability had conjured forth her shadow. In the morning my bones ached, for her and for me.

I longed for my father, but his stays at home were brief, and each time it was obvious he wanted to leave as soon as he decently could. He was enjoying his work and had made many new friends, he said, and I could see he was a changed man. The mocking scowl whose lines had begun to bite into the corners of his mouth had smoothed out and there was a vivid light in his eyes. He no longer referred to himself as a cripple, no longer used his wheelchair as an accusation. Formerly "The Bounder," it was now his "Royal Chariot."

One day he startled me by announcing that he would likely be living up north for years to come. Pleased with his work, the university had offered him several other projects to design, he told us, and had given him an office-cum-apartment right on campus. It had wheelchair access, a bathroom and kitchen designed for the disabled, and a wide view over the mountains. "You come and visit sometime," he suggested vaguely, but it was clear he wanted his new life to be quite separate from the old. "Maybe he has a girlfriend," Leila shrugged, and

I was surprised by her equanimity. She no longer appeared to regard my father as an intrinsic member of our tight unit. He was now simply a "provider," the sender of the monthly stipend that supported the house, a distant figure who might or might not really matter.

If my father had told me before he went away that he was planning to leave me permanently alone with my mother I would have been able to protest, or at least have time to brace myself. By more or less sneaking away he had robbed me of my right to object and I resented him for it. To punish him I ignored his letters and was surly on the phone. "It's all shit!" I blurted out one time, when he was trying to soothe my ruffled feathers. "*Mierda pura.*" Recognizing the phrase's origin, Max winced. "Don't turn into another *caradura*," he pleaded. "One hardhead in the family's history is quite enough." Mostly, though, Max failed to take me to task for my rudeness; he just let things slide, and I never quite forgave him his absence. Many years later, when we danced around the subject, he tried to offer a sort of apology, which I didn't care to hear, perhaps because I understood too well what he might say. The brute fact was that he had betrayed me, and such basic betrayals are hard to reconcile.

Mierda pura, mierda absolutamente pura – my repeated mantra, a bitter but bracing comfort. In that rough time Enrique's *ferocidad* served me better than any hope of *gracia*.

five

BUT MY FEROCITY was powerless against Leila. She always outflanked me.

Now it was her nightmares. They began to overwhelm her. She had long been plagued by "vicious dreams," as she called them, but the cycle of nightly disturbances became acute a few months after my father moved up north.

Her bedroom was a room away from mine, but I could hear her low moans and sudden shrieks through the intervening walls. Worst of all was a kind of sucking gasp, as if some creature had abruptly seized her by the throat in the midst of sleep. I imagined her wide, terrified eyes as this happened, the look of absolute fright, and my blood ran cold. She told me that her horrors happened in some mythical Paris, a city she had left when she was barely five years old. She did not want to talk about her nightmares, and that made them seem all the more fearful.

Her expression as she shrugged away my queries over the breakfast table scared me more than any description. She had strong nerves for awfulness, so if the "vicious dreams" were too appalling for Leila to speak of them, they must have been unimaginably ghastly. The harrowed, haunted look on her face at such moments twisted my gut. I wanted to take her in my arms and rock her, comfort her, protect her from her demons.

At night, hearing her cries, I often came close to running to her bedroom. But what would I do there? Crawl into bed with her? Soothe her till she fell into a dreamless sleep? The thought of it simultaneously thrilled and repelled me. I feared that if I surrendered to my mother's deepest, darkest needs I might drown, lose all sense of myself. What would happen when we woke up? I asked myself. Who would I be then? Would I turn into my father, that crippled man? These thoughts were hard to think, and harder still to forget.

To give myself some relief, I stayed late at school, coming home just in time for dinner. I did my homework in the school library, and I joined the chess club that met twice a week in the afternoons. It was run by Mr. Morales; he welcomed me warmly. I liked the game's logic, the clarity of its objectives, such a contrast to the murkiness of everything else. "This is a world in which most questions can be asked and answered," Morales said dryly.

Out of concern for my well-being, Morales tried to query me about my home life, but his conventional questions of concern made me squirm. I couldn't begin to describe the atmosphere in my house to an outsider. Most of all, I was inhibited by a fear of betraying my mother's intensely private world by discussing it with a stranger. Like it or not, I was the guardian of that small universe, Leila's only ally against aliens, and she would never have forgiven me if I were a traitor to that trust . Or was it a collusion? However that might be, I was all she had left, the one human being she loved, and who loved her.

Her love was a truly marvelous and terrible force. It came at me in waves, its tidal energies lifting me up and throwing me down day after day, night after night. It was a special thing, I knew, a phenomenon none of my school friends could ever imagine. It marked me out, shut me off from ordinary intimacy with anyone else. Compared to the intensity of that ebb and flow every other kind of human interaction seemed pale, hardly worth the effort.

I hated to go home each day, and I couldn't wait to get home. As soon as I entered the house and heard her call, "Joelly? Joelly?" my heart swelled with an indescribable feeling, a heady mix of joy and apprehension. When Leila wrapped me in her arms it was as if I had been seized by a mermaid while surfing, sucked down to some deep cave that was simultaneously in the sea and in the sky.

Sitting in my upstairs room some evenings, cocking an ear to hear her singing as she put the dinner dishes in the washer, which filled the house with its cozy rumble, I struggled to make sense of my life. I knew I would never be able to puzzle things out in my head, that my relationship with my mother was beyond rational comprehension. It was no chess problem I could strategically think my way through; its energies were too complex and too fluid. Basically, I loved being loved by my mother on the plane of intensity and need only she could offer;

in effect, she addicted me to her kind of loving. She demanded my whole soul, and I began to wonder if I would ever be able to survive her passionate affections, or even if I wanted to survive.

In my diary, I scribbled: "If Leila wasn't there to lift me up, would I fall out of the sky and fatally crash to earth?"

After writing this sentence, I stared at the words, and trembled. I had truly become her "creature" – a wonderful, frightening thought. She'd made me, inventing me out of blood, bone, and the sheer force of her desire. Without her, I could hardly exist. Or rather, I would live a miserable, low-grade life – an "average existence," in her scathing phrase.

Actually, I don't think Leila ever had any concept of what might constitute an average existence. For her, even the commonplace moments of our lives were charged with an almost biblical significance, and she dated everything that happened by the events in our shared personal history. The years before I was born were called, simply, "before." Other events were linked to my birthdays – "A month or so after you turned five" – or to the small triumphs and minor catastrophes any child suffers. The day I fell down on the sidewalk and chipped a front incisor became "the tooth time." "That was a before the tooth time," she'd say, recalling some trivial or dire incident. The conventional calendar was replaced by her own private, semi-sacred reckoning, and I, too, had fallen in with her way.

My birthdays were always major celebrations, and for my fourteenth birthday she took me out to dinner at Santa Monica's best Italian restaurant. She insisted I wear a suit and tie, and she bought herself a sleek velour evening dress in a shade of green that subtly counterpointed her eyes. She hennaed her hair to subdue the few traces of gray, swept the tresses to one side, and fastened them with a Spanish comb inlaid with mother-of-pearl. The curve of her slender neck made my heart melt, and when I walked into the restaurant with her on my arm I felt like a princeling escorting royalty.

I was so proud of her! She was a truly marvelous woman. Men kept sliding their eyes toward her, and the sly way she flirted with me as we sipped our vintage chianti made me puff up like a peacock. She talked about Tuscany, which she had visited as an art student before her marriage, and told me that we would travel there someday soon. The names of the towns she described – Siena, Florence, San Gimignano – were sheer music on her tongue. She made me feel they belonged to us in some subtle way just by being spoken there and then. There was an enchantment about her that evening, and I was immensely proud to be her son, and her squire.

"Please, no `vicious dreams' tonight, mom," I pleaded as I kissed her cheek at her bedroom door. The abrupt flash of panic that seized her face, obliterating its beauty, tore at my heart. It was unbearable to think that, after such a splendid evening, when she had been so gay and so superb, nightmares might yet claw at her spirit. Before I knew what I was saying, I murmured: "Would you like me to stay?"

Her face lit up at once. "Would you?" she cried. "Stay here, with me? Just be here, for a while?"

"Sure," I shrugged. Right then it seemed a small thing to do.

She pulled me into her bedroom and shut the door, even though we were alone in the house. While she was in the adjoining bathroom getting ready for bed I sat in her plum velvet armchair not quite sure what to do. The aroma of the pink carnation buttonhole she had bought me tingled my nostrils, mingling with her familiar scents of lavender and lilac.

Her boudoir was an elegant setting, the chamber of a fastidious woman with taste. The dressing table was a classic modern design in blond wood and black metal; the bed was raised on a wooden platform – like a sacrificial altar, I thought cheekily. In the soft lighting the drapes and carpet reflected plain, unpatterned shades of aquamarine.

The wine in my blood both soothed and excited me, inducing a mood of calm expectancy. Events had taken over and that was a delicious relief. I sat waiting for Leila to return with a slight smile on my face – "a lovely smirk," she teased, when she appeared in her dressing gown. She slid out of her gown and I glimpsed her pink satin nightgown as she slipped under the covers. "Come, Joelly," she beckoned, "lie here beside me awhile."

Kicking off my shoes, I climbed onto the bed and stretched out on top of the covers. She gripped my hand, squeezed it, sighed, closed her eyes and seemed to fall instantly asleep. Carefully, I reached across her and clicked off the bedside light, leaving only the strong moonlight shining through the curtains. In the semi-darkness the regular rhythm of her breathing was the world's heartbeat, and I drifted into oblivion to its deep and steady pulse. That night I had the best, most restful sleep I'd had in months. It was dreamless, a sweet nirvana, soothing as the touch of her hand. When I awoke it was late and I was alone in her bed. I heard her humming contentedly in the kitchen below, a sound that made me smile. A few minutes later she brought me in a breakfast tray, greeting me with a cheerful cry of "Wakey-wakey, sleepyhead!"

In the following weeks I often lay beside her on top of the covers as she slept. At first she would tell me when she felt one of her bad dreams threatening; soon I recognized the small signs of tension in her face and didn't need to be told to come to her bed. The summons was there in the tilt of her left eyebrow lifted in the glimmerings of a grimace, the tightened line of her lips, the hint of a shadow in her eyes. These were delicate signals only I recognized, but they were all I required to know she needed me. Sometimes, though, tremors of fright shook me. Suddenly my heart raced, my nape hairs tingled. I was now so deep inside her atmosphere I feared I might never emerge.

I went through the motions of attending school, playing chess, though less frequently, taking driving lessons, going to picnics with friends on the beach. Outwardly, I was a perfectly normal Southern Californian kid. Inwardly, however, I lived in another realm, a secret country ruled by a compelling queen who demanded, and received, every ounce of my love and loyalty. The truly amazing thing, to me, was that I had so much of both to offer her. However much sympathy, concern, affection and passion she needed, I found in myself to give. It made me feel so grown up, so much older than the other kids I knew. Yet whatever I had to give was never enough. Not nearly enough.

* * *

My father phoned several times to invite me to come and visit him during the summer vacation, but I resisted. I suspected it was guilt that spurred his invitation, and I resented that. Also, I didn't know how to relate to him any more. He was a stranger – a dangerous stranger, one who might ask too many awkward, unsympathetic questions about my mother and me. Just talking to him on the phone made me feel disloyal, as if he might glean private information from the tone of my voice, even though I was curt and monosyllabic. "I'm still your father, Joel," he said despairingly, and I hadn't the heart to tell him I no longer knew what that word meant.

The overwhelming event in my life just then was the apparent retreat of my mother's nightmares. By sleeping together we seemed to have driven them to the edges of her awareness. Lying beside her in the dark in my pajamas, now under the covers, a few inches from her body, I listened intently to her breathing, tensed for any sudden shift in rhythm, any abrupt intake of air that might signal inner distress. She gripped my hand as she fell asleep, tightly, at first, then easing, and that soft pressure was another gauge of her dream status. The feelings that flooded through me, of pride and fondness, masked the sexual stirrings provoked by her intensely female warmth. I could not even begin to put "the physical thing" and my sympathy for her in the same space in my head. My feelings remained "pure," untainted by the kind of fantasies I conjured up while jerking off.

Trouble was, I was randy as a goat. Crude sexual images flashed before my eyes a hundred times a day. The glimpse of a girl's thigh revealed as she crossed her legs in class sent me into a whirl. The odor of female hair, sniffed in passing, destroyed my mind. Sometimes, in a frenzy, I masturbated three or four times in a day. It was as if I had a cunt living between my eyes, as if the entire world was one big vagina I longed to penetrate.

My searing, lubricious thoughts made me shy with girls. To cover my shyness I became super-cool, affecting a worldly attitude of disdain. Perversely, this seemed to attract rather than repel the girls I knew. They whispered together as I passed them in the corridor, sent me coy little notes and flirted with me shamelessly. I itched to grab hold of them, ravish them, have them, but I simply could not let that happen, fearing it would somehow pollute the tremendous thing I had going with my mother.

Besides, what did I really have to give these girls in exchange for their favors? My mother consumed every ounce of my emotional energy and more, leaving little left over for anyone else. I lacked the arrogance, claimed by some of my male school friends, to just "fuck and run." Entering a woman's body was no trivial act, it seemed to me; it was something momentous, I imagined, almost holy. In the act of love you surely had to penetrate, and be penetrated by, a woman's personality, and that could never be a light thing. The only female person I knew intimately was overwhelming in her dangerous power; and if Leila were the measure of a woman, who was I to trifle with such energies just to ease the hot wire in my groin?

Rory's return threw all this for a loop. She had been away for months, spending time with her divorced father in Toronto, and I had almost forgotten her. Then, suddenly, she was back, and changed.

Her appearance stunned me. Since we had last been close she had metamorphosed from a plump chrysalis into a slim butterfly. Her face seemed to be longer and more womanly and the pubescent plumpness was replaced by a more slender tautness. Her eyes sparkled with a sex-amused humor, as if she had just discovered that the world was a horny joke. Her sophistication awed me, easily demolishing my false disdain. With her, my coolness melted, leaving me naked.

The first time we met she took one long look at me and seemed to know everything. I stood still, trembling, as she gauged me with her eyes. "Hi, Joel," she said, and there was affection in her tone as well as mockery. Those two words made my heart overflow. I was speechless.

Rory nodded gravely, touching my cheek with her fingertips. "I thought about you a lot," she said.

"Me, too," I mumbled, finally finding my voice.

"How's your mom?" she asked, with gentle innuendo.

"Fine," I replied, blushing.

"Ah," she said, and the period bell called us in different directions.

My head was a mess the rest of the day. After school I searched for Rory, but she had vanished. Deeply disappointed, I cycled home and ran upstairs to my room before my mother could detain me. At my desk I tried to write Rory a note explaining everything. But everything...? What was that? The words congealed on the page. In despair, I tore up the note and flung myself on bed, burying my face in the pillow.

Some time later I felt my mother's touch on my shoulder. "Joelly?" she said. "I called you for dinner. Are you alright?"

I wanted to shout *go away! leave me alone!* but I couldn't. Instead, I mumbled something about being tired and not hungry. Sensitive to my mood, she stroked my hair then departed, leaving me to stew in my own juice.

Questions pounded my brain. Why had seeing Rory disturbed me so? In the past I'd liked her a lot, even had a hot crush, but this was something else. Had I been struck by a "thunderbolt," one of those love-at-first-sight things I'd seen in movies and read about in novels? What would Rory say if she knew how I felt about her? What would Leila say!

Trying to calm down, I took a long, hot shower. The spray hitting my face eased the hammers inside my skull. Afterward, I sat by the open window staring at the night sky, trying to puzzle things out, but my thoughts and feelings were a tangle I could not begin to unravel. Finally, bone weary, I went to bed and fell into a troubled sleep. For the first time I did not care whether my mother might need me that night. She was on her own.

Rory appeared to ignore me for the next few weeks, but now and then I caught her glancing at me with an odd look I couldn't decipher. Was it derision or interest? Or a mixture of both? She was very popular, always surrounded by a cluster of male and female admirers, and I could only hover on the edge of her sphere, sweating out my inchoate yearnings.

At home I was moody, even surly. I even tried to wriggle out of sharing my mother's bed. Fortunately, her bad dreams were in abeyance and her need for me was less urgent. Still, her eyes were mildly reproachful and that gave me sharp twinges of guilt. She was my friend, my only real friend. I longed to confide in her, but couldn't for fear of hurting her, and that made me resentful. She doesn't really care about me, I thought sullenly, watching her over the dinner table. Now that I need her she's just too caught up in herself to be a real mom.

Then, one day, I suddenly found myself face-to-face with Rory in the school corridor. Late for class, we were hurrying in opposite directions; abruptly, we were alone with each other. We exchanged the ritual monosyllables of greeting –"Hi," "Hi" – then stood silent, at a loss. Or rather, I was.

"I'd like to see you sometime, Joel," she said.

My heart leapt. "When?" I croaked.

"Are you free after class today?"

"Sure," I replied, flinging obligations to the wind, though I was due to go shopping for clothes – her clothes – with my mother.

"Let's go walking in Palisades Park, like we used to," Rory suggested.

"Okay," I agreed.

The hours oozed by slow as treacle. Finally, it was three-thirty and I raced out of class to the school entrance. To my delight, Rory was there already, surrounded, as always, by some friends. She shook them off as soon as she saw me and we strolled toward the oceanfront with our backpacks slung over our shoulders.

Rory talked about Toronto, but I hardly heard the words, listening rather to the flow of her throaty voice, that seemed so wonderfully female. For a moment I hoped she would burst into song, let rip a rendering of "Anything Goes," say, as if she were serenading under my window as she used to. *In olden days a glimpse of stocking*...But I sensed she was now too grown-up for such foolishness. A pity, though, I thought ruefully.

"Tell me about you," she said as we crossed into the park, and for one mad moment I was on the verge of telling her everything. Maybe she would somehow understand, would perhaps forgive me – but for what? The words, "I sleep with my mother," formed in my throat but were choked back. The phrase "to sleep with" had a terrifyingly ambiguous meaning. It would blow her mind, destroy her sympathy, and that was the last thing I desired right then.

"My dad's left home," I said matter-of-factly. "My mom and I are alone."

She glanced at me, then quickly looked away. "Oh yeah?" she murmured.

Leaning on the concrete railing overlooking the cliff and the Pacific beyond, we shared a long silence. Her raven hair was swept back from her face by the wind. I was ravished by the vision. If only I could have shouted *I love you* in that instant everything might have changed. But I could not. The words, which I had only ever spoken to my mother, were too potent, too charged, and too sacred. The bottled-up force of feeling in my body almost made me jump over the railing and try to fly, as poor Jack had done a couple of years earlier.

I was sure Rory knew what was going on inside me. She didn't speak, and that could mean either that she felt the same way and was as scared as I was, or that she was embarrassed by my puppy-dog passion. Since it was most likely the latter, I shriveled up inwardly and kept quiet.

We strolled on until we parted at the pier. I watched her go, remembering my father's sardonic comment that you never could really know a woman until you saw her walking away. The sight of Rory walking away was a delight and a disaster, and I ran home, created and destroyed.

SIX

LEILA TOOK ONE LOOK at my face and knew I was in shock. "Joelly," she exclaimed, "what happened?" She tried to put her arms around me to comfort me, but I pushed her aside almost rudely. For one moment I felt a surge of absolute hatred for her, followed by an immediate rush of guilt. "Feel a bit weird, that's all," I mumbled apologetically. "Something I ate, I guess."

She hovered over me, offering me soothing drinks and aspirin, and I tried to endure her concern with patience while tamping down resentment. Why can't you leave me alone? I cried silently. Just leave me *alone*! The misery I felt was curdled by bitterness as I submitted to her fussing. Finally, I managed to escape and run up to my room. Ripping off my clothes, I fell onto the bed and covered my head with a pillow.

My head was splintered by thoughts, feelings, imagery: Rory walking away; the flash of hatred for my mother, that kept recurring; guilt; terror; yearning. At last, exhausted, I fell asleep as the daylight died in my window.

Later, I was wakened by the sound of sobbing. At first I thought it was Leila in distress and my instinctive response was *Oh no! Not again!* Then I realized that I was crying, the tears were my own. My face was wet and the pillow was stained as I wept without restraint. Everything seemed hopeless. I wanted to kill myself. If I'd had the energy I would have done something drastic, but I was too weak to move.

Why had life boxed me in so? I asked the air, in a pause between sobs. Had I done something wrong, something horrible, to deserve this? I derided myself for submitting to such self-pity, countering with the argument that I had good reason. I was damned by events I could not control. There was no one to blame, except maybe my dad, but he was too far away to really count in the equation. Life itself was to blame. My life. Like an octopus trapped in the coils of a net, I thrashed and flailed struggling to escape, but only tied myself up in knots.

Then someone was beside me in the bed. A warm body clasped me from behind, circling me with soft arms. Waves of warmth flowed down my naked spine, penetrated my stomach, soothing my solar plexus. A gentle hand stroked my chest, ran down my flank, circled my groin. My nerves tingled with a rising excitement yet I felt utterly serene. Maybe, after all, I had died, drowning in my own tears.

The hand moved to my crotch. Skillfully, the fingers stroked my scrotum, teasing the hairs there, making me quiver. Then they snaked up the stiffening shaft, and I shuddered. For a second the fingers departed leaving me shivering and disappointed; then they returned, wet, fondling the head of my penis. Erotic heat surged through my whole body as an almost painfully ecstatic glow charged every nerve from head to toe. All anguish was released with my ejaculation and the muffled cry that went with it. I was gloriously, profoundly happy, consumed by a powerful desire to sleep. "Good night, Joelly," a voice whispered in my ear as I blacked out.

* * *

A mockingbird trilling outside my window woke me up, and for a moment I felt like joining his delirious song. I had never felt so marvelously, simply content, as if all the stale old junk inside me had been replaced with fresh hope. Some powerful agency had come down out of the night and renewed me, body and soul. Who or what that agency was, I deliberately left undefined.

My mother was humming when I entered the kitchen and sat down at the counter to eat my breakfast. "Good morning, Leila," I said gaily. Recently, I had slipped into the habit of calling her by her name, and she seemed to like it. She glanced up me shyly, alerted by my cheery tone, and gave me a charming smile. We chatted about this and that until I planted a kiss on her cheek and left for school. Entering the school building, I felt I had aged a decade overnight. All my old friends suddenly seemed so young! A surge of newfound confidence brought a spring to my step, I was on top of the world. I knew something they didn't know: that it might be possible, after all, to survive growing up.

Seeing Rory, I marched straight up to her and kissed her cheek. She was startled, but also pleased.

"So, J," she said. "What's happening?"

Impulsively I asked her to come to a movie with me Saturday night.

"Thought you'd never ask," she replied dryly, tossing her tresses.

As soon as she accepted my invitation, however, I knew I would have to lie to Leila. But wasn't that sort of white lie an intrinsic strategy of adulthood, sprung from a civilized impulse not to hurt other people unnecessarily? What she doesn't know won't hurt her, I told myself cheerfully. After all, taking a girl to a movie on a Saturday night was a perfectly normal thing for a fourteen-year-old to do.

As it was, the lie came easily to my lips. Casually, I told Leila that a bunch of us were going to see a popular film that weekend.

"Boys and girls?" she asked.

"Sure," I shrugged.

"Anyone special?" she said lightly.

"Nope," I replied. In that instant I knew that if I had mentioned Rory – the "precocious hussy" – she would have reacted negatively. Better to lie, lie all the way, even to myself, I mused sagely. Truth was deadly.

At the movie Rory and I held hands. She leaned her head on my shoulder, and I was overcome by a sensation of pure fondness for her. I really like this girl, I thought in the flickering darkness; she's a terrific person. Her hand, bigger and stronger than mine, gripped me firmly and I knew with absolute certainty that one day soon she and I would make love.

What would it be like? I wondered. So far as I knew, she was inexperienced, and so was I. How did you go about exploring a woman's body, being *intimate*? Would I be a good lover when the time came? Maybe she would lead the way, since the girls of my age seemed more naturally mature than the boys. I wanted to have sex with Rory, but more than that, I wanted to be close. Desire, I realized dimly, was a complex business, part lust, part exploration, part self-discovery. And then there were the practical problems. Where might we go? My house was out of the question; the thought of making out with Rory under Leila's roof made my mind shy and buck like a nervous horse.

I was in the midst of all these ruminations when the lights went up, leaving me blinking.

"That was crap," Rory laughed. "I loved it! How about you?"

"Loved it," I replied. "Let's get a burger."

We bought burgers and fries at an outdoor stand on the pier and wandered to the far edge to watch the waves lapping at the piles, shoulder to shoulder. Ketchup from my overstuffed bun dribbled into the ocean and Rory teased me for being a messy pup.

Then, out of the blue, she said, "I'd like to have sex with you, J."

"Yeah?" I gulped, choking on my burger. Then I asked a truly dumb question. "Why me?"

I expected – and deserved – a flip retort; but I underestimated Rory. "You turn me on, and I like you," she said quietly. "The two things seldom happen for me, in one guy. They do, in you."

"That's—" I mumbled.

"If you want to, we can go to my house. My mom's out tonight and my brothers and sister are all out of town, so the place is ours. If you want."

"I want. Very much."

Rory took my hand. We tossed our half-eaten burgers into the sea and walked away, hurrying the mile or so to her house as quickly as our legs could carry us. My heart was pounding like a demented piston, but my mind was amazingly calm. Somehow this all seemed absolutely right. For once, the gears of the universe were in sync.

I followed Rory's lead, sensing that women knew things I didn't, marvelous things. She took a bottle of red wine from her mother's liquor cabinet and led me upstairs to her room. "Get comfortable," she said, and vanished into the bathroom.

I dithered, wondering whether she meant me to undress and lie on the bed or merely to sit in her floral chintz armchair and sip my wine. In the end I compromised by stripping down to my shorts and lazing in the chair while waiting for her to emerge. The thought of seeing her naked scared me a little, and the wine took the edge off my apprehension. I imagined the as yet unseen areas of her body would be strong and sure, like the rest of her. I didn't want to disappoint her, yet I suspected I would. But she probably knew that, I told myself. The thing was just to be together, close; as close as two bodies could be.

Minutes passed. I listened to the house's small noises and sipped my wine. Time began to drag. Glancing at my watch, I saw that more than half an hour had gone by since Rory had disappeared into the bathroom. I called her name, and heard a muffled response I couldn't interpret. When another fifteen minutes went by and Rory still had not emerged, I began to wonder if she had changed her mind. Maybe her long absence was a subtle suggestion that I should leave. I was about to start dressing when Rory finally opened the bathroom door. She wore a terrycloth robe, but otherwise the many minutes she had spent at her toilette seemed wasted. I moved to embrace her, but she slipped by me and slid under the covers, still wearing her robe. Her face was tight, no longer graced by the sophisticated ease that had entranced me.

"Should I go?" I asked hesitantly.

"Go?" she echoed. " Are you nuts? After I spent almost an hour shaving my legs? "

"Shaving your legs?" I asked, nonplussed. "What for?"

"I'm too hairy," she said, blushing. "Men are turned off by leg hair."

"Is that a fact?" I asked, more curious than anything else.

"A well-known fact," she said with certainty. She added, shyly: "Aren't you?"

"Never thought about it," I said truthfully.

Lifting the covers, I got into bed and began to remove her robe. Her limbs were stiff as boards, her skin was icy. I pulled her into my arms and gradually she warmed up and began to hug me back.

Just then I heard noises downstairs. "My mom," Rory whispered as I began to pull away. "It's okay."

Then I was inside her, not quite knowing how it happened. Her breath quickened. A soft flush spread from her cheeks down her throat to her breasts as I moved, very slowly. Her face took on an intent, almost fierce look, like a lioness stalking a prey. I sensed a flood of warmth bathing my cock. She must be coming, I imagined.

The warmth spread down to my thighs as Rory struggled against me, grinding her belly against mine. Her actions agitated me and I couldn't control myself any longer. We came together, with mutual muted growls and I felt her cunt pulse and spasm thrillingly.

"Oh my god, oh my god," Rory moaned. Shoving me aside, she threw back the covers, revealing the large pool of blood leaking from her vagina, soaking deep into the sheet and mattress underneath. "Oh my god, oh my god," she repeated helplessly.

I leaped from the bed. My knees and belly were smeared with gore, as if I'd been wounded in battle. In a panic I grabbed Rory's dressing gown and tried to wipe myself clean. She grabbed the gown and jammed it between her legs. "It won't stop," she whimpered. "I'm going to bleed to death. For godsakes do something!"

"What?" I mumbled, frozen in shock.

"Get my mom," she gasped. "Quick!"

Her mom! The very thought of bringing in Mrs. Molloy to view the disaster I'd provoked blanked my mind.

"*Move*, dammit!" Rory shouted.

Pulling on my pants and shirt, I stumbled downstairs and burst into the living room. "Upstairs! *Bleeding!*" I blurted. Appraising my panic-stricken face, Mrs. Molloy ran up the stairs with me on her heels.

Instantly, she took command, ordering me to fetch clean towels from the linen closet and bring a bowl of hot water. She removed her daughter's sodden gown, cleaned her groin and thighs, and formed an impromptu diaper out of a towel.

Rory's face was so deathly pale my heart sank. What if she dies? I thought frantically as I helped her mother ease her into a fresh dressing gown. "So sorry," I hissed in Rory's ear.

"Deflowering a girl can be dangerous," Mrs. Molloy said matter-of-factly. Surveying the bloodied bed, she gave a comic shrug. "My poor sheets," she moaned, rolling her eyes.

I must have blushed scarlet, for Rory started laughing. "Cheer up, J.," she said. "It ain't the end of the world."

In that moment I wondered what was the end of the world, and hoped to God it would happen soon. As I was washing the blood from my crotch in the bathroom another, even more drastic thought struck me. "We didn't—" I blurted, stepping into the bedroom. "Are you—?"

"On the pill," Rory murmured sleepily. "My mom put me on the pill soon as I started bleeding. Girls have a greater responsibility, she said, since we're the ones who get knocked up."

"Jesus wept," I muttered, nonplussed. "You're way ahead of me."

"Always have been, always will be," Rory retorted. Smiling, she took my hand. "God, that was good, J. I knew it would be, with you – despite the drama."

"Have you before...?" I asked tentatively.

"Never," she replied. "You?"

"No," I answered, and it was only half a lie. "Must get home," I said, moving to leave.

"Stay," she pleaded. "Please?"

"Can't," I muttered. "You know..."

"Yeah, I know. See you." She dozed off before I finished dressing.

* * *

I had to hurry home because Leila would be waiting up for me. She claimed she could not fall asleep if I wasn't in the house. Recalling this, I resentfully slowed my steps while mentally challenging her to do her worst to herself. I knew I would have to lie to her about being with Rory and that made me angry and ashamed.

I needed time to sort out all the stuff in my head. In a few days I had become sexually involved with two women – from the standing start of virginity! I didn't even begin to understand what was happening between Leila and me, but I did know I was crazy about Rory. A flush of happiness swept through me every time I thought of her. I could still smell her skin, remember the sensation of entering her body, hear her rushing sighs, see the hot orgasmic snarl on her face. The memory of that marvelous moment resonated endlessly, like the vibrant silence following an echo.

What a woman she was! And she'd made love to me. *Me!*

A sudden realization hit me like ice water in the face: I would have to lie to her, too. I could never tell her the truth about Leila, she simply would not understand. Hell, I didn't really grasp it myself. I could hardly begin to explain the potent mix of attraction and repulsion, my willing collusion and essential helplessness. Rory would never comprehend how much Leila needed me and why I had to feed that need. She was no Weeping Woman – that was what I loved most about her. She was a terrific girl, full of cheerful lust and laughter, she made my heart leap for joy. But she would never understand.

So, I would have to lie to both women I loved, for their own sakes, and for mine. Would that mean I had become a person I didn't like – a professional liar? But there seemed to be no other way, I concluded. Not if I wanted to keep both women happy. Not if I wanted them both to love me. I needed them both and they needed me, in different ways. If I was careful and a skilful fibber – I could maybe manage to keep them on separate, parallel paths. The cost would be my sense of honesty and self-respect, but that seemed to weigh little in the balance against their desires, and mine.

Walking up the pathway to the front door of our house, I anxiously searched for a light in Leila's bedroom, hoping against hope she was asleep. No such luck. Her curtains glowed like cat's eyes tracking me as I approached, and her urgent voice drifted down the stairs as soon as I slipped into the entryway: "Joelly? Joelly?"

"Mom," I responded grudgingly, reverting to a childish mumble. "It's only me."

She hurried down the stairs, clutching her robe about her chest. "I was worried," she said, "It's so late!"

"Not so late," I muttered defensively.

"Two in the morning!"

"It's the weekend," I said gruffly.

"Still," she said. "Still."

Her eyes scoured me, sensing a change in my attitude. She knew me so well I often felt she was actually inside my skull, regarding me as I regarded myself, instantaneously. I would never really get away with lying to her, I realized; not unless she wanted to be lied to.

"We were all having such a good time," I murmured apologetically. "Didn't realize it was so late. Are you okay?"

A shadow of sorrow and regret darkened her eyes. She knew I was being shady, but she chose to let it pass. "Bad dreams," she said. "Very bad." She left the implication, "and you weren't here," hanging in the air.

"Want me to—?"

"Yes. Please."

I took her hand and led her back up the stairs. From the roiled condition of her bed sheets I could see she truly had been having a bad night. I straightened the covers, plumped up her pillows and tucked her up tight. Kicking off my shoes I lay down beside her on top of the covers, holding her hand until she slipped away with a sigh.

In the darkness, listening to her breathing, I was sorry I had resented her so earlier. She did not deserve that. Her life was so hard. Not in its external circumstances, but in her own internal pain and terror. Somewhere, somehow, life had dealt her a primal injury, a blow to the spirit from which she would never truly recover. For her, each day was a struggle to survive, to claw her way through the hours. Being male, I knew I would never really understand the nature of her distress, but I was vividly aware of its intensity.

Lying there beside her, I knew I ought to give up Rory if I did not want to hurt Leila, badly. But I could never give up Rory, and I couldn't bear to hurt Leila. And I didn't want to be a liar. Finally, exhausted, I blacked out.

Opening my locker at school next morning I found a single red rose stuck into a sneaker. I laughed, blushed, and my heart swelled with delight.

"You know my combination?" I hissed at Rory as we passed in the corridor.

"Sure do," she retorted cheekily.

"See you at lunch?"

We bought tuna salad sandwiches in the cafeteria and found a quiet corner behind the wall of the gym out of the sun. We sat on the grass shoulder to shoulder, munching contentedly. Her closeness excited me and I wanted to make love to her immediately. She must have felt the same way, for she spontaneously grabbed my face and kissed me passionately, filling my mouth with breadcrumbs and greasy bits of tuna. "I love you," she said simply. "Ever since we did the naughty I can't think of anything else."

"Did the what?" I frowned, wondering if she was getting at me for all that blood.

"I heard it in a British movie."

"*Did the naughty* eh? Yeah. Well."

"An eloquent response," she said dryly.

"I didn't think it was naughty," I said stiffly.

"It was, though," she said, and kissed me again. "And I want more."

"Me, too."

"Tonight?" Rory said. Seeing a shadow cross my face, she added, "Your mom? We'll have to talk about that."

"Talk about what?" I said, pulling back an inch or two.

"That," Rory said tersely.

For one wild moment I imagined she knew everything. She was a very perceptive person, and maybe she had intuited the nature of my entanglement with Leila. But that was surely unlikely, I reassured myself; no one could possibly divine such secrets. "I can always stretch it on the weekends," I offered. "But there's still the problem of where to, you know."

"Fuck?" she said tartly.

"Make love," I countered.

She took my hand and kissed it. "What a romantic you are, J. It's lovely."

"You didn't answer my question."

"Actually, it's no problem. My mom says its cool to get together *casa mia*. She says it's better we do it under her roof than under the pier, since `young blood will have its way.' " I blushed, and Rory giggled. "Are you going to finish that sandwich?" she asked as I struggled to regain my cool.

Watching her consume the remains of my sandwich, I was overwhelmed by admiration and desire. I would give my life for this girl, I told myself, smiling inwardly at the hyperbole but not entirely disowning it. Lying to her and for her was well worth the cost to my integrity, whatever that was.

That Friday night we went back to Rory's house after the movie ended and we had consumed the ritual burgers. Rory's brothers and sister lounging before the TV treated me with an offhand courtesy, as if I were now an established family member. I was, quite simply, Rory's guy. As soon as was polite, Rory tugged me up the stairs to the privacy of her bedroom and firmly shut the door. She came into my arms and in a trice we were naked together under the covers.

"Kiss my breasts," she urged, offering one to me in a cupped hand.

Though I had been inside her body I had never kissed her breast and the thought of it made my pulse speed up. I tentatively touched my tongue to her big, dark nipple and she impatiently shoved it into my mouth. "Kiss!" she hissed. "Suck!" Opening my mouth wide, I half-swallowed her breast and suckled while she clutched at my hair and cried out in pleasure. In the midst of this I had a vision of Leila suckling me when I was an infant. Rather than dowsing my ardor, this fantasy added fuel to the fire and I kissed, sucked and squeezed Rory's breast even more passionately.

"Oh, God, you're a wonder," Rory panted. "You get me, you really get me, lover."

Her generous response, and her use of the word "lover," inspired me. I ran my tongue over her belly and along the inside of her thighs, circling her groin. "I want to see you there," I said. "I've never seen a cunt."

"You're sure you want to?" she asked, momentarily shy.

"I'm sure."

"See it, then," she said urgently. "Now!"

I gently parted her labia to reveal the pink clitoris in its sheath and the opening of her vulva, the entry to a tunnel that vanished into infinity. Boldly, I touched my tongue to her clitoris. It was firm and silky as a tiny oyster and I imagined it sliding hot and tasty down my throat. Rory made a sound I couldn't decipher – pain or pleasure? – and I quickly withdrew. But she grabbed my hair, pushed my face into her cunt, and came. This is truly a woman! I thought deliriously. A *woman*... The complex, marvelous reverberation of these fundamental syllables, the immense surge of pure emotion it released made me feel as if a hummingbird's furious, glorious wings were beating in my chest.

We made love for an hour or so, until the recollection of my duty toward Leila tugged me from Rory's bed. She would not let me go at first, half-playfully gripping my arms as I tried to escape. When I was free her empty fingers flailed the air in mock-despair. "J..." she murmured. "My J..." I kissed her lightly on the eyes and tiptoed out of the dark house.

* * *

If Leila were waiting for me, I was determined not to be guilty, I told myself as I hurried home. After all, I was getting on to fifteen years old and shouldn't have to account to my mother for every minute of my time. But my bravado melted like snow in the tropics as soon as I saw her bedroom light. I eased my way through the front door, trying to suppress its habitual creak, sure she would come down the stairs to accuse me with her eyes. But she didn't. I crept up the stair in stockinged feet, expecting her to appear at any instant, amazed to reach the safety of my room without confrontation. So as not to ruffle the surface of this surprising luck, I undressed in the dark and got into bed without brushing my teeth. Breathing a sigh of profound relief, I dropped off.

Some time later I awoke abruptly, aware that I wasn't alone. Leila was standing there, watching me, her silhouette a block of sheer darkness in the moonlight. As soon as I stirred she lifted the covers and eased into bed beside me. Her naked body, pressed against my back, was cold. For one erratically indignant moment I was about to protest her presence. The unwritten rule was that she came to my bed when *I* was distressed, not she; I went to her when she needed me. Breaking the rules was, well, just plain wrong. Then I had to laugh at myself. What foolishness, to believe there were hard and fast rules in such situations! Leila had created our game and she could change the rules any time she liked. Need was need, and that was the supreme governing principle here.

Leila tugged at my shoulder, urging me to turn around to face her. I resisted at first. My back was somehow neutral territory, but to be belly to belly with her would expose everything. She might even discover that I had been with Rory, would smell the scent of her on my body. The crazy notion struck me that maybe Leila already sensed that I had made love to another female and was deliberately staking out her territory, claiming me for her own. "Joelly," she sighed, breathing into my mouth. "My life..." She pressed her lips to mine and her breath seared my throat. I wanted to say something – anything – but my voice was choked with fright and desire. Compared to Leila's potent intimacy, Rory's recent closeness paled. I could vanish in Leila, obliterate my life, and the temptation was irresistible.

Leila reached down and took my penis in her hand. In an instant I was erect. Without a word, she put a leg over mine and eased me into her. "Joelly," she moaned softly. "My Joelly..." Her words burned a hole in my mind. I could not believe I was inside her. This was more than just cunt. It was heaven and hell, and both were the very same place.

Leila was shaken by a series of orgasms that made her hips jerk. In the moonlight I was transfixed by the rapt expression on her face: blood-red cheeks and brow, white circles around staring eyes. Her wild energy terrified and excited me together, and in the convulsion of my coming I could not distinguish between ecstasy and terror. "Mom—!" I cried out in that moment, and the childlike howl echoed back to my ears, making me cringe. For godsakes, how could I call for my mommy when I was in the act of fucking her?! My mind slid away from the sheer ludicrousness of it all.

Afterward, I lay in the dark as Leila slept, thinking. I was doing a lot of thinking those days, but it did not seem to get me anywhere. Powerful events I couldn't begin to comprehend had swept me up and were rolling me along like a loose log on a torrent and there was no way I could even begin to know where I was going. "We swim too deep in female waters," Max once said to me. Those waters were vital and fabulous, but the question was: how not to drown?

seven

WHEN YOU'RE YOUNG the context of your life seems somehow preordained. The character of your parents, the attitudes and expectations of the surrounding society appear to be the natural order of things. You are a creature of your place, time, and particularity, and whatever happens to you has the character of inevitability.

So I accepted my passionate connection with Leila as if that was just the way things were. She was my mom and I loved her, and whatever she wanted from me, I gave. I could not talk to anyone about our situation, and did not know enough about what really went on in other families to clearly judge my own. Rumors floated around the schoolyard about fathers who beat their wives and children or abused their daughters. There was gossip about philandering parents, and I knew of kids who had run away from home. Taken together, these stories engendered a sense that each person's family life was a private mystery impossible for any outsider to fathom.

All this is to say that being my mother's lover seemed to me simultaneously startling and somehow unexceptional. Leila acted as if sharing our beds was nothing out of the ordinary for a devoted mother and son. Her notion of normality was not the general rule, I knew, but in our house her view of things ruled unquestioned, especially since my father's departure. She was strong and sure of her feelings, just as Rory was, in her way, and I was weak and unsure. I did not have it in me to challenge either woman's will.

Yes, I was weak. I doubted the validity of my own feelings whenever they ran counter to Leila's or Rory's, and I could not tell either of them about the extremity of my confusions or the moments of terror and bewilderment that frequently overwhelmed me. At times I resented my mother intensely, even hated her, but that was shameful. I was crazy about Leila, but also fearful. She demanded something from me I didn't yet own – myself. My spirit was in fragments, splintered by mixed-up emotions and fundamental self-doubt. Often I wondered if I really existed at all, if maybe I was just the figment of other people's imaginations, a kind of human shadow play.

Given my own radical unsurety, it astonished me that Rory could be so sure of herself. She was my age, but she seemed so much older: a woman. And she wanted me.

Why? I scribbled in my diary, the only place I could have a real conversation. *Why does Rory want me? I feel I have some sense of Leila's motives, but Rory's are a mystery. She's so strong-minded! So maybe she finds my weakness attractive? Perhaps she sees me as putty in her paws. Or maybe molding me helps her shape her own nature. It's a puzzle…*

In my endlessly bemused state I was often caught off-guard. For instance, it astonished me when Leila asked me to invite Rory for supper. I gaped at her, blushing furiously. "Maybe next Saturday," Leila suggested amiably, as if it were the most normal thing in the world, though I'd never in my life brought a girlfriend home to sit down at our table. "Do you think she likes seafood? Maybe I'll make that crab in black bean sauce you used to like? It's ages since I prepared a really gourmet menu. Ask her, today."

My head was still reeling when I got to school and bumped into Rory. "My mom wants you to come to our house for supper Saturday," I blurted. By saying it out loud I hoped to dump the burden of it into Rory's lap. She blinked, utterly taken aback, and I was about to babble on about how weird the invitation was, all things considered. But I bit my lip, awaiting Rory's response. After all, I was just the shuttlecock tossed back and forth between the women. It was not my place to have an opinion.

"Well," Rory said finally. "What time?"

"Pardon?"

"What time should I come to your house, dummy."

"She didn't say!" I exclaimed.

"At seven, I guess. If that's okay." She shot me a sly glance. "Will you be allowed to come home with me, after?"

"What?"

"Saturday night, you know," Rory drawled. "Our assignation?" She walked away, leaving me gaping.

Leila went into high gear in preparation for the dinner. She skipped her art history class at UCLA Extension to scour the fish markets for just the right kind of Alaskan blue crab. She traveled all the way across the city to Chinatown to find authentic ingredients for the black bean sauce. On Saturday morning she set me to vacuuming the living and dining rooms and polishing the best silver for the evening. For the table arrangement she brought out her heirloom Art Nouveau candelabra, inherited from her grandmother, and burnished them bright bronze. She scattered rose petals and dried wildflowers over the white damask tablecloth, creating the effect of an indoor *déjeuner sur l'herbes*.

Her face glowed with pleasure as she invited me to admire her accomplishment.

"It's great," I said.

"Has to be, for your lady friend," she replied.

"It's just old Rory," I said, vainly trying to play down the evening's significance.

Leila smiled and lightly touched my cheek. "Just so," she said.

What would Rory make of all this? I wondered. Maybe she expected to take potluck in the breakfast nook, a deliberately casual dinner. She would never expect such elaborate and aggressive hospitality, and I thought I ought to warn her. But each time I reached for the phone I just could not dial her number. The game that evening was between her and my mother, face-to-face, and I had no license to load the dice one way or another. If I had been more relaxed I might have enjoyed a certain sly pleasure in the prospect. As it was, my overwhelming impulse was to get the hell out of the house and flee as far as I could.

The moments ticked toward seven, each one marked by a flutter in my stomach. My mind was a blur, too dazed to even begin to imagine how the evening would go. When, finally, the doorbell rang it seemed to be just one more noise in my buzzing brain. I stumbled to the entryway and jerked open the door, both knowing and not knowing what to expect.

Rory stood on the threshold clutching a big bunch of red carnations. I saw at once that she had chosen a formal mode – after much agonizing, I was certain. Her hair was swept up and twisted in a tight chignon pinned at her nape. Her eyes were highlighted with stark mascara and there was a touch too much blusher on her cheeks. She wore a green satin gown with a plunging neckline and a blue velvet choker with a pearl pendant circled her throat.

"Rory," I said huskily.

"Am I early?" she whispered, darting her eyes into the darkness behind me. As I took the bouquet from her I noticed that her neck and bosom were flushed, but the flash of panic in her eyes was not erotic. She grew even more agitated when I led her into the living room and she caught a glimpse of the dining table beyond. The candles added a Gothic glow to Leila's stage set, suggesting arcane rituals, and Rory was truly nonplussed. When Leila emerged to greet her, dressed as formally as she in a black velvet gown, Rory seemed too stunned to speak.

"*Cherie*," Leila said, taking her hand. "How nice of you to accept our invitation. It's ages since we last had a real guest for dinner, certainly not one as charming as yourself." She led Rory to the sofa and seated her close by, ordering me to fetch the white Bordeaux cooling in the refrigerator.

When I returned, Leila was conversing in her most invincibly gracious manner while Rory sat tongue-tied, nodding like a mechanical toy. As we sipped our wine Leila's words flowed over us, seducing us with their urbane rhythm, inducing a trance neither Rory nor I seemed able to resist. Rory was transfixed, holding her wine glass by the stem as if it were a blossom she was offering Leila in the hope of mercy for some unspecified felony. We moved to the table at Leila's command and enjoyed the crab at her urging, though I hardly tasted it; and, most likely, neither did Rory.

"That was wonderful, Mrs. Bajamonde," Rory murmured, rinsing her fingers in a bowl of scented water. She blushed again, for the hundredth time, as if the compliment were somehow inadequate.

"Leila," Leila corrected patiently. She leaned back in her chair and startled me by lighting up a cigarette. She seldom smoked, declaring that tobacco blunted the taste buds. "Tell me your plans," she said, blowing out a stream of smoke.

"Plans?" Rory said guiltily. "What plans?"

"For the future," Leila said airily. "College, and such."

"Ah," Rory said. "College. Yes. Well I had an idea about maybe studying medicine, or maybe architecture."

"Architecture." The word was slightly sour in Leila's mouth. "Joel's father's an architect."

"I know. I thought that maybe he could advise me, if I get to meet him. Ever, that is. I mean—"

"He hates it."

Rory and I were both taken aback. "Dad doesn't—" I began.

"*Hates* it," Leila cut in curtly. "Would you care for a liqueur with your coffee, Rory? A snifter of Armangnac, perhaps?"

"No thanks Mrs. — Leila. I'm a bit sozzled as it is, with the wine and all." Rory giggled abruptly, then clapped her hand over her mouth.

Leila looked her over yet again with a frank appraisal, as she had many times throughout the evening. He eyes were lidded, lazy as a lizard's, but glinting. "Joel is a very special person," she said slowly. "Very, very special. I treasure him."

"Leila," I protested. "Gimme a break!"

"Isn't he special?" she asked Rory, ignoring my squawk. Rory nodded emphatically. "Very, very special," Leila emphasized.

There was a charged pause. Watching Rory, I saw her take several deep breaths. She straightened her spine and stiffened her head; I noticed a vein throbbing in her throat constricted by the choker. "In what way special, exactly, Leila?" she challenged, her voice rougher than she perhaps intended.

"Good question," Leila nodded. She stubbed out her cigarette and immediately lit another. "He has a loving heart. That's rare as hen's teeth, don't you agree?" Rory mumbled a response as Leila ran on. "Such hearts can easily be savaged. That can't happen to him."

"But it might," Rory retorted boldly. "Life's a bitch."

A grimace of distaste at this crudity disturbed Leila's composure. "Kant wrote that `out of the crooked timber of humanity nothing straight can ever be made,' " she quoted. "But there's crookedness and crookedness, you know. That's the point."

"I think what Rory's trying to say—" I began, and was stopped dead in my tracks by simultaneous glares from both women.

"I never had a daughter," Leila said, after a moment. "I miss that. Please make yourself at home here, Rory, I implore you." She rose, and Rory and I followed suit. "I'm tired, I think I'll retire," Leila announced, and left the room.

After she had gone Rory and I were lost in a dazed silence.

"Your mother's a remarkable person," Rory said at last. "Very deep."

"Deep enough to drown in?" I said lightly.

"Oh yeah," Rory agreed. She gave me a long and searching look, forcing me to drop my eyes. "Take me home," she said.

At her door she squeezed my hand, kissed me lightly on the lips and dismissed me. "Not tonight, Josephine," she said, in answer to my unspoken question. "Leila's waiting up." Before I could reply she shut the door in my face.

Walking home, I was struck by the thought that it was likely both women knew exactly what was happening between me and each one of them. Rory knew I was sleeping with Leila and Leila knew of my affair with Rory. Or, more accurately, perhaps, they knew and chose not to know exactly what was going on. Perhaps that is how people survive, by choosing not to know what they know, I mused as I wandered homeward. A wise trick of the mind, but one that never seemed to work for me. Once I knew something it scratched at my brain like a burr in a sock, irritating my awareness at every step. My head was crammed with so many burrs there was only room for my own perplexities, and for the lies I told to others.

eight

Later that month I got a call from my father. He invited me to come to Berkeley and stay with him during the spring break. There was an unusual appeal in his voice and I sensed he had a special reason in asking me. "You'll like the campus," he said, "and we can spend time together. After all, it's been ages since we did that." And whose fault is that? I wanted to retort, but didn't. Recently I had been thinking about him with some sympathy and less resentment, and his invitation made me realize how much I missed him.

Leila was not too keen that I should go. "Why's he asking you now?" she said suspiciously. "You'd never desert me, would you?"

"Desert you?" I echoed, astonished.

"I don't mean physically," she said. "You'd never do that. You're my life."

My life's my own, I thought rebelliously, while hugging her to ease her worries.

In the weeks leading up to the spring break we kept a certain distance between us. Leila didn't come to my bedroom and refrained from calling me to hers. It was as if the combination of Rory's visit and my imminent departure for my father's realm served to cool things down. It was restful and normal, in the conventional sense – or as I imagined how such normality might be.

Rory, on the other hand, was pressing. She urged me to stay over at her house on a Friday evening and I did, after phoning Leila and placating her with the lie that I was out with a bunch of guys at an all-night bash; a lie she accepted with no more than a sigh. I spent the night several times at Rory's before I left for Berkeley; it was delicious to sleep beside her sweet, warm body, waking up to find her still beside me. We had a kind of easy intimacy I cherished, and I realized yet again just how much I liked her. When I kissed her good-by she clung to me and I had to prize myself loose, laughing at her comically glum, bereft expression.

On the short plane ride to San Francisco airport, where my father had arranged to meet me, I gazed down at the landscape and tried to imagine what my own life might look like if seen from such an elevation. It seemed to me that, if it were rendered physically, my life would resemble a sticky miasma with me trying to wade through the muck sucking at my shoes. I saw myself as a kind of half-formed blob subject to the tugs and pulls of forces far more coherent than I was, or might ever be. My marshy, on-high vision was discouraging, to say the least, and I wondered if I would ever get a footing on dry land. Not at this rate, I mused gloomily. With each month that passed I seemed to wade deeper and deeper into an emotional morass.

My heart leapt when I saw my father's face in the crowd at the airport gate. He wheeled toward me vigorously, beaming with pleasure, and dragged me down into his arms in a hug. I was so happy to see him after our long separation that I began to cry, and he tenderly wiped away my tears. "Me, too," he murmured. "Me, too."

I noticed a woman hovering in the background, and my father introduced us. "This is Vivienne," he said shyly. "We work together, and live together."

Vivienne held out a slender hand. She was younger than my father, I saw at once, but not that much. And tall, thin as a beanpole, as Leila would say. Her face was tentative in that moment, but there was a sweetness evident in her soft brown eyes that charmed me at once.

"Hi," I said nonchalantly.

"Hi," she answered.

For an instant I resented the fact that I would have to share my father's attention for the week, but I was too pleased to be actually there with him to hold the bad feeling for long.

Vivienne – Vivvy, as my father called her fondly – drove the old Buick station wagon my father owned up the San Francisco peninsula and across the Bay Bridge. The view of that bridge, spanning the water for miles and miles, took my breath away. In Los Angeles you were always somehow surrounded by the city, you seldom had an overall view of it from the edge, because L.A. has no edges. Seeing the Bay Bridge emerge from the mists, springing nimbly from the towers of the city to the far shore, I had the heady sense that it might be possible after all to see things whole, to escape the feeling that life forever spills over the far horizon.

"Spectacular, huh?" my father said, twisting around in the front seat to watch my face.

"Awesome," I replied breathlessly.

"Awesome's the word," he laughed. "Absolutely."

"I guess you never miss L.A.?" I queried.

"I miss you," he said promptly, reading my real question.

As we rode on I stared at his profile. He looked at once younger and older than when I had last seen him. That is, his hair was grayer and there were more lines around his eyes and mouth, but his expression was easier and more buoyant.

He's in love, I thought suddenly. My father is in love!

The perception threw me; I didn't really know what to think or feel. If he were in love with Vivienne, that really was the end of our family. Up till then the family unit had been in a kind of suspended animation. At least, its form remained even if its content had leaked away; my father, though absent and faint, was still the other pole in our magnetic field. But if he were truly in love, the basic balance would tilt permanently. The thought that Leila and I would be set adrift forever in our own roiled sea made me panic.

"You're very quiet," Vivienne teased as we came off the far end of the Bay Bridge and followed the freeway toward Berkeley.

"Oh, Joel's a very thoughtful fellow," my father said mock-gravely. "He never stops thinking, maybe in the vague hope he can make some sense out of the general insanity."

"Just like his father," she said, smiling.

"Yeah. But there's a difference," my father retorted. "I know I'll never make sense of things while Joel hopes it's possible."

"You have the advantage – or disadvantage – of experience," Vivienne countered. "Give him time."

Vivienne and my father shared a rambling ground floor apartment in a pleasantly decaying Victorian building a few blocks north of the campus. Compared to the neatness of our house, which Leila kept spotless and pristine, their place was a mess. Books, clothes, rolls of blueprints and a host of tchochkes littered the furniture, spilling over onto the floor. The living room was dominated by the padded steel apparatus my father used to exercise his upper body; it stood in the center of the space like a shrine to some mechanical god of fitness.

"Excuse the mess," Vivienne said, and I gathered from her flat, unapologetic tone that she had uttered that trite phrase often.

"We live like a pair of teenagers," my father said proudly. "Creative chaos, kind of. You'll fit right in." He paused, regarding me thoughtfully. "Wait a minute, I remember, you're a neatness freak, like your mom. This man is tidy," he told Vivienne.

"Oh dear," she said. "Can you bear it, Joel?"

"I'll try," I promised solemnly.

Despite her laconic domestic habits, Vivienne prepared a tasty lunch of pasta. I liked the way she fussed over my father, was touched by the tenderness that shone through every gesture she made toward him. But I wished she would go away and leave us alone for a while. Sensing this, she excused herself after lunch and left the apartment to go shopping.

"So," my father said, pushing back from the table. "What's up, kiddo? How's your mom."

"Okay," I shrugged. I didn't want to talk about Leila with him. She would hate that, and the whole topic was far too fraught. Besides, I wanted to be free of her presence for a while.

"What do you think of Vivvy?" he asked, in a tone that was light yet anxious.

"She's crazy about you, that's obvious."

"Nuts, bonkers," he said happily. "I'm in love, for the first time in my life."

"The first time—?" I blurted, shaken by his words.

"Sadly, yes," he murmured. "When I met Vivienne I realized I'd never loved a woman. Leila and I, well...That's another story."

"Tell me," I said harshly. "I'm strangely interested."

My father cocked his head at me. "Okay," he murmured. Taking a deep breath, he plunged in. "She was nineteen, I was twenty – two virgins. She was ravishing; I lusted for her, madly. We had this hot little affair, she got pregnant, and we couldn't bring ourselves to abort. We had you, and the rest is history."

I stared at him. "You mean it was all because of me?"

"In a sense, yes," he nodded. "Not your fault, never that," he added quickly. "But an error nonetheless. We were at odds from the get-go. Apples and oranges."

"What does that make me – a lemon?" I retorted tartly.

"No, no, Joel. No." he leaned forward and held my wrist in his strong grip. Through exercise and will, all his physical power was focused in his hands; each finger had clearly defined muscles, miniature biceps and triceps. "You're the only valuable thing to come out of our mismatch. You make it all worthwhile, in the end."

"How so?" I challenged bluntly. The thought that I was "an error" shattered me. Yet, at the same time, it was somehow reassuring. If I were an error, anything I did would inevitably be erroneous, thereby absolving me from blame.

"For years I cursed the choice I'd made in `doing the right thing' by Leila. But looking at you, I see its purpose in the scheme of things. You see, I can't imagine the world without you, Joel."

If that's the case, why have you disappeared from my life? I said silently.

Reading my mind, he nodded grimly. "I had to get away, to save myself," he said quietly. "After the accident, when I was crippled, I felt I was shriveling up. The one real connection Leila and I had left, sex, was severed, along with my lower spinal cord. It was escape or die and, selfishly, I chose escape."

"Yeah."

The monosyllable was all I could manage just then. His unbearable revelations explained everything and nothing. I felt pity for the young man he had once been, locked into marriage with a woman he did not love, maybe didn't even much like. If I hadn't been born, would I be happier? I thought, mocking my own foolishness. I felt pity for him, but much more for Leila. She did love him, I knew. A strong strain in her passionate attachment to me was a displacement of that frustrated love. He had been imprisoned but she had been condemned – a far sadder fate.

"What a fuck-up," I said. "And me, the result."

"Joelly!" he exclaimed, reverting to the childish form.

"Don't call me Joelly," I snapped.

He blushed at the rebuke, shaken by my rudeness. "Look, sport—" he began in a tough tone.

"Maybe this was another mistake, this visit," I cut in. "I'm not your accomplice!"

"Huh?" he blinked.

"Against her. I love Leila."

"Of course you do," he placated. "She's your mother."

"No – *I love her.*"

As soon as the words popped out of my mouth I wished I could suck them back. This involuntary outburst could be the proverbial straw that broke the camel's back, and mine. However, its implication passed my father by entirely, thank god. He was too wrapped up in trying to sort out my sharp reaction to his confession about my origins.

"I shouldn't've sprung all this on you at once," he mumbled apologetically. "You're only a kid. Why should you bear the weight of adult errors? You have your own life to live."

"Right on, Max," I said.

"'Max'? I like it," he smiled. "Do you call mom Leila?"

"Yep."

"Far out," he said. "You are growing up." He cocked his head at me shrewdly. "Maybe you already understand more than I do, or ever will? You're a better person than I am. More scrupulous."

"I don't understand diddly," I retorted. "Never have. Never will."

"Well, then, join the club," he laughed, toasting me with his coffee cup.

Later that afternoon, after his siesta, I wheeled him down to nearby Euclid Street for afternoon tea at a popular local teashop. We ordered English muffins – "crumpets," the waitress called them – and a pot of Earl Grey. The pale tea, served with a slice of lemon, tasted like warm piss to me, but I pretended to like it, to please him.

"We've never had a regular father-son sex chat," he said with a twinkle. "I guess by now you know about the birds and the bees...Is there anyone kind of, well, serious in your life right now?"

"Yes. Her name's Rory."

He asked me to tell him about Rory, and I offered the bare facts. However, something in my tone alerted his antennae. "You don't go all the way yet, do you?" he enquired. "I mean—"

"Sure we do."

He reared back slightly. "Good grief, you are precocious! I thought I was a hell of guy when I began sleeping with Leila, at twenty. You're not yet fifteen!"

I regarded his amazement with some amusement. If he only knew... Suddenly, I understood something about my father: for all his air of sly knowingness he was essentially an innocent. He could never have imagined or begun to comprehend the complexities and intricacies of my relationship with Leila, its temptations and its terrors. That is, he could never really know me or help me sort out my perplexities. Despite his Spanish heritage, he lacked his father's tough-mindedness, that clear-eyed acceptance of hard facts and Enrique's glorious gift of fury. In that instant I missed my grandfather intensely. If he had been here I could have told him anything without causing shock, but Max was simply a softie.

In a way, this realization made it easier for us to be friends. If my expectations of him were eased, I could just relax and enjoy his company. He had a ready wit and a lively mind and was fun to be with. And I liked his new lady, who doted on him. In his innocence he had found happiness, and I envied him. But in my heart of hearts I placed him at a far remove from crazy creatures like Leila and me.

* * *

Leila phoned me every evening while I was away. Promptly at eight, just we were sitting down to dinner, the shrill ring interrupted our conversation, provoking a grimace from Max and an apologetic shrug from me.

Her urgent voice leapt out of the receiver into my ear. "Joelly? How are you, sweetheart? I miss you horribly."

"Hi, Leila," I replied coolly, aware that Max and Vivienne were listening.

Leila described every detail of her day in a rushed and breathless monologue punctuated by my inarticulate grunts. When she asked what I had been up to, I made a series of brief responses that exasperated her. "You must've done something exciting, surely?" she insisted. "Or is your dad ignoring you?"

"Not at all, we're real buddies," I replied, to annoy her.

When she finally rang off she was furious with me, and I felt rather shabby, as if I had played to the Max-and-Vivvy gallery.

Later that evening, when Vivienne had gone to bed and Max and I were sitting on the terrace sipping late night beers, Max began to ruminate about "the Leila phenomenon." His train of thought wound in upon itself, a tangled twine that soon lost any sense of where it began or ended. As he rambled on I realized with a kind of shock that he had no real notion of who the woman was that he had lived with for all those years. Yet just as it seemed that Leila had eluded him completely, now and in the past, he made a shrewd comment that struck to the heart. "Leila's lost in a kind of dream of herself," he said quietly. "The dream may be pleasant or unpleasant at times, but the point is, it's all her own."

I was mute, trying to absorb the implications of this remark, which seemed so amazingly apt. If she were lost in a dream of herself, where did that leave me? A figment of her fantasy, perhaps? But what a fantasy! Leila's dreams were sheer sorcery and I was lucky to be in them.

"I was never included in her dream," Max said, a trifle ruefully. "But you are – and that can be either marvelous or dangerous. Know what I mean?"

"Sort of," I murmured, mainly to placate him. Since he was "outside" Leila's dream, he would never comprehend its power, and I felt I had to protect him from knowing just how ignorant he was.

As we headed for bed I bent down to kiss his cheek, and he gripped my hand. "I'm here," he said forcefully. "Always. Okay?"

"Okay," I said. "Thanks, Max."

He rolled away toward his bedroom and I watched his back until the door closed. In that moment I knew that our roles had essentially reversed. In terms of grasping the truth of things, I was now the adult and he was the child. Or rather, Max had come to the end of his narrow road and I was just starting out on my open highway that I hoped would run on far beyond anything he could ever imagine. It was a liberating perception, but also sad. It meant that, effectively, I no longer had a father that counted in the emotional equation of my life. From now on it was Leila and me. And maybe Rory.

nine

LEILA WAS SULKY when I returned from Berkeley and it took me several days to coax the pout from her face. She suspected that my father had "seduced" me, as she put it, and I had to demonstrate that it wasn't so, that I was still "her boy." She meant it when she said I was her life, her only life, and I could not leave her feeling in any way betrayed. After all, she had made room for Rory, and that was more than enough to ask of her.

Ultimately, the visit with Max brought me even closer to Leila. We were two of a kind, she and I. He was another species, neither better or worse, just different. Our species was rare, I suspected; certainly, I'd met no one else who might possibly understand the way we were.

Rory belonged to that other species, and maybe that's why Leila allowed her to get close to me. Perhaps she thought I should experience dissimilarity and discover its limitations for myself. But it did not work out quite that way. Instead, I split my life in two separate and self-contained parts, between the Leila-world and the Rory-world. The nights I was with Leila had nothing to do with the nights I slept over at Rory's, and the two women seemed to connive in this disjunction. However much each one may have resented my attachment to the other, neither of them provoked a showdown.

After the awkward dinner party, Leila never mentioned Rory's name again. Rory was more naturally curious, and more troubled by a situation rife with ambiguities, but she nonetheless carefully avoided probing too deeply. The most she would venture was to remark that any woman I ever took up with would have to share me with my mother. But what exactly that sharing implied, she left vague. At times I feared these parallel realms might collide, creating an emotional meltdown that would surely damage us all. A chance remark, a slip of the tongue, perhaps a circumstance that might reveal everything could explode my little universe and blow me into outer space.

Occasionally, there was a devilish glint in Leila's eye that scared me, a hint that she expected, even welcomed, calamity. She had an inclination for an intimate *Götterdammerung*, and she was sure that her life and mine were always at risk, along with life itself. "You don't know the half of it, Joelly," she said many times, "not the half of it," and the look on her face was both touching and scary. It was up to me to keep her from vanishing into the darkness of her spirit – her "black hole," as she called it – since, she claimed, no one else in the world seemed to care whether she lived or died.

I could not bear the thought that she might just quit. To me she was unique, a rare, marvelous, dangerously selfish spirit I'd give my life to defend. Not that she ever overtly threatened suicide; such vulgarities weren't her style. I suspected that, if she ever decided to give up the ghost, she would just sink into a fatal melancholy, an embrace with easeful death. I was her one vital attachment and she needed me as a leaf needs sunlight, to make its own green energy. She drained me, but she also drew stuff out of me no other human being ever could. She was a remarkable woman, and she was my mother.

Keeping Leila and Rory separate in my mind was made easier by the very different ways I experienced them physically. Where Rory's body was a solid contour in the landscape of my life, Leila's presence was a charged cloud, an erotic climate, all atmosphere and sensation. I could conjure up a clear picture of Rory's breasts or back or thighs anytime I chose, but actual images of Leila's figure eluded me. Put another way, I could wrap my mind around Rory, but Leila was wrapped around me.

Rory's body excited and delighted me. I spent hours tracing its outlines with my fingertips, lips, and eyes. It was so female, so very much its own shape and no other, like a tree. She complained that her ass was too big, her neck too short, her breasts too "droopy," but to me she was perfect. One day I showed her a photo of the Neolithic Venus of Wilendorf – a stone figure with pendulous breasts and a swollen, fertile belly – and told her I thought it was magnificent. She slapped my face and called me a shit, but I meant the implied comparison as a compliment.

I never actually caressed Leila because, in a fundamental sense, her physical form was never really there. When she crept into my bed, or I slid into hers, it was as if a powerful wave of pure feeling reached out and enfolded me, a disembodied intensity enveloping my spirit, stirring my blood, sucking me up into her intimate heat. My breath came in gasps, my bones melted, my cock swelled to meet a fabulous female immensity. At the same time she was my child, a vulnerable little girl seeking safety in my arms, curling up so close I felt her heart pounding in my own chest. When we came to our shared climax it seemed as if the circle of life was closed, returned to some original completeness.

Leila and I were never just "lovers." We were mates, linked in a connection that was absolute in itself. The conventional phrase, "making love," applied to what I did with Rory, but not to what happened with Leila. She and I made something other than love; we made magic.

Perhaps this sensation of sorcery was just my way of sidestepping my awareness that most outsiders would likely be shocked to learn that I slept with my mother. ("Sleep" was another slippery locution. The deep doze Leila and I fell into after orgasm was way beyond mere sleep; it was a kind of nirvana, a divine forgetfulness of everything outside our embrace.) But the fact was, I felt remarkably unashamed. However much Leila's emotional necessities overwhelmed me, I was seldom troubled by the sense that we were doing anything "unnatural." In truth, our act of love seemed the most natural thing on earth. After all, we were mother and son.

With Rory, things were so much easier. For instance, when we weren't cuddling, she would begin to nag me about college. We still had several years of high school left to get through, but she fretted that we might end up in different towns far apart. "I couldn't bear that," she said. "It'd be too awful."

Her questions aroused a host of disturbing thoughts, apart from our possible separation. Firstly, I had no clue as to what I wanted to do after school. My impulse was to wander around for a couple of years, to catch my breath and see some of the world, especially Europe. Through Grandpa Enrique and Morales, I had become fascinated with Spanish literature, and I had a notion to travel to La Mancha and see Quixote's hard, entranced landscapes where serving wenches were damsels in distress and dragons lurked behind every rock. I also wanted to visit Granada and maybe find the house where Enrique's family had been murdered by Falangists.

But what about Leila? Could I ever leave her alone for long? Obviously not. That meant I would have to go to UCLA and live at home while at college, maybe for as long as she was alive. Or she could travel with me. Not hitchhiking and bunking in student hostels, of course; the price of her companionship would be rented autos and comfortable hotels. It could be fun, though. But what if Rory wanted to travel with us? I could hardly imagine such a *ménage-à-trois* knocking around Europe. Still, all that was a good three years away and I tried to put it out of my mind. But it was clear a watershed was approaching, one that could provoke some painful resolutions.

* * *

Max was also concerned about my future. He had urged me to do a B.A. at Berkeley, and then maybe go on to graduate school, but the prospect did not excite me. However, he seemed more troubled by the unexpressed ambivalence of our recent meeting. In one of his rare letters he wrote: "After your visit here I was left with the feeling that you were somehow disappointed in me. Maybe you came with certain expectations I did not or could not fulfill. Or perhaps it's that I feel so guilty for having in effect abandoned you to your mother's tender mercies..."

I bridled at this tone and almost crumpled the letter and tossed it aside. I'm not your accomplice! I thought hotly. And yes, there were expectations you didn't fulfill – like being a real dad!

Relenting, I read on. In the next few paragraphs he elaborated his need to make a new life for himself after his unhappy marriage, and how much Vivienne meant to him in that regard. "In the process, I sacrificed our relationship," he wrote, "and that just tears me apart. I'd do anything to make that up to you, now that I've remade my own life. Anything."

Like what? I asked silently. Return home? I gave a bitter chuckle and immediately felt mean. The poor guy was trying. He had a bad conscience about "sacrificing" me to Leila's "tender mercies," but he didn't begin to grasp the implications. The blunt fact was he was way out of his depth. Stick to your sweet Vivvy, I wanted to tell him. Be happy. Reading his letter made me come to terms with an obvious fact: that, in truth, I had less and less connection to Max, apart from a residual fondness, and the remains of a yearning for the father that might have been.

I was struck by a ludicrous thought: maybe I had really sired myself! If anyone was or could have been a mate to Leila, it was me. Her spouse had to be of her own making, her own flesh; no "other" would do. It was a weird notion but it stuck with me. In its crazy way it explained a lot.

This idea led to a disturbing but fascinating fantasy, one in which Leila and I had a son or daughter of our own. It was perfectly possible, of course. She was still a relatively young woman, in her mid-thirties, and I never asked her whether she "took precautions" when we made love. In my imagination, our child was alternately male or female. Either way, it looked a lot like Leila, as I did. She was crazy about the kid, and sometimes I was very jealous. We went on adventures in the Santa Monica Mountains or Catalina Island, camped out in the Mojave and Joshua Tree, had evenings at home when I read aloud or taught the child to play chess under Leila's fond eye. In age-jumps, I was at one moment watching Leila suckling the baby as she had suckled me; then I was traveling with my "son" in Spain and France. At times Leila was my wife, at other times she was my daughter. The fantasies were thrilling, in a threatening kind of way. I never quite knew what to make of them, and they were much too real for comfort.

I filled my diary with these hectic imaginings, composing a kind of episodic novel of our "family." Oddly, though, I never gave the imagined child an actual name. Any names I tried out – Jillian or Ruth, Jake or Robert, say – seemed too prosaic for such a mythical being. The only name that seemed appropriate was Shakespeare's Ariel (in class we were studying "The Tempest"), a creature of the air.

One evening at dinner Leila startled me by announcing that she would love to have a baby. "A little baba, to cuddle," she said, moist-eyed. "Wouldn't that be lovely, Joelly?"

I gulped. For one horrible instant I suspected that she had discovered my diary and my cheeks reddened with shame. Then, recovering, I asked the prosaic question: "Who'd be the father?"

"Oh, anyone," she said airily. "Maybe a sperm donor?"

I pulled a face. "You'd mate with just any sperm, then?"

She regarded me gravely. "Max wants a divorce," she said. "So's he can marry his woman."

"Divorce—?" I exclaimed. "Well, I guess you two already are divorced, in effect."

"He says he's willing to go on paying the bills, as he damn well should. Including your college."

"College?" I echoed.

"That's a topic we need to discuss."

"Years away," I mumbled.

"Not so many. What are your plans?"

"Don't have any," I said, getting surly.

"I have one," she announced.

"What's that?"

"We sell this house and move to Paris. You could go to the Sorbonne. Me, too."

"My god!" I cried, knocked right off my perch.

"We'd be students together, you and me. What do you say?"

"No!" The primal cry burst from my mouth, startling us both.

"No?" Leila said. Her lips trembled. "You don't want to be with me?"

"I don't want to leave L.A.," I said quickly, covering my tracks. "I like our life here."

"Ah," she sighed. "So do I. Okay. No Paris. But it might've been fun. So long as we're together, that's all."

"Yeah," I muttered. "Exactly."

This brief conversation turned my head around. It brought home to me full force the reality that, in a few years, my life would enter a new phase. And that gut cry – that fierce *no!* – shone a harsh light on my confusions. It revealed that, on the one hand, I wanted my current life to continue indefinitely; equally, I hoped it would end some day and that I would emerge into some undefined but radically different emotional scenario. But would Leila allow things to change in any real way?

And then there was Rory...

These questions loomed large. I had no answers.

* * *

"You're scowling a lot lately," Rory said one day over lunch in the school cafeteria. "What's up?"

"Nothing," I said irritably. "Just stuff."

She studied me shrewdly. "It's seldom 'just stuff' with you, J. Don't you trust me enough to confide in me?"

"I'm tired of all these lies!" I burst out.

"What lies?"

"You know," I mumbled. "Just lies."

Rory nodded. A friend of hers, Angela, passed by and favored us with a knowing smirk. "Hi, lovebirds," she called out cheerily.

"'Lovebirds'!" I snorted. "Dumb bitch!"

"Hey, cool it," Rory admonished.

"How many people know about us?" I demanded angrily. "Has it been on the fucking evening news, or what?"

Taking me firmly by the hand, Rory led me out of the cafeteria and walked me around the schoolyard till I calmed down. She sat me on a bench and held my face in her hands. "Talk," she ordered.

"It's this college thing," I shrugged. "Decisions, you know?"

"Sure. But why get so pissed off? Is it about leaving your mom?"

I blinked, startled by her insight. Yet I shouldn't have been so surprised. In many ways Rory was a lot more mature than I was, and a great deal more clearheaded. Taking a deep breath, I stuttered: "Can't leave her. Ever."

"Every boy has to cut the mommy cord sometime," she said, gently mocking. "I know you're very attached to her, but all the same..."

"You don't understand," I said desperately. "I'm all she has. I'm her life."

"That's crap," Rory retorted. "No one is ever anyone else's life."

I hung my head, gazing into the Grand Canyon of incomprehension between us. Part of me wanted to try and leap that divide, tell Rory everything, bring it all out into the open. I yearned for her understanding, to crack the cocoon of my lonely lies and secrets. Confession was a hot ache in my chest. But the risk was too great. She would have been shocked out of her socks by my revelations. I could lose her. Worse, the details of my relationship with Leila could become common knowledge and she might end up branded as a – what? "Whore"? "Child molester"? "Statutory rapist"? "Incestuous monster"?

Judging her from outside, on the basis of "normality," Leila could be considered monstrous. But if you viewed her from inside, knew how bone-deep sad she was, how hard it was for her to survive her days, understood that she truly loved me, saw that she was the complete captive of her own passionate nature, any condemnation would just have to be discounted. But Rory wouldn't understand. Maybe nobody could, outside of Leila and me. This realization, coming home to me yet again, made me draw back from opening up to Rory.

"Aren't you worried about leaving *your* family?" I asked, lowering the heat of our dialogue. "You love your mother, don't you?"

"I can't wait," Rory said. "And, frankly, neither can she. We've reached the stage where we constantly get up each other's noses. Everything I do gets her mad, and her attitudes drive me up the wall. These days we spend much of the time bitching at each other. She's a strong person and I know I'll never truly be myself until I get the hell out of the house."

"You're a strong person, too, R."

She picked up on my nuance instantly. "So are you, J., in your fashion. Maybe you don't know it yet, but you are."

"I don't know who the hell I am!"

She took my hand and squeezed it. "My dad once told me something very wise. He said everyone has his or her tempo, the pace at which they come into their own."

"What's that mean?"

"That simple natures, like mine, find out who they are, what their strengths are, early on. Complicated characters like you take longer, but the result can be a lot more interesting, though maybe more confusing, in the short run." She nodded sagely. "I may seem to be more, well, resolved than you are now, but you'll outclass me one day, by far. That's why I want to hang onto you as long as I can, while I still have the edge."

Her tone was serious, free of any mockery I could detect. I looked into her eyes and saw a certain regret there that I had never noticed. I leaned over and kissed her full on the mouth. She sank down onto the bench, folding me in her arms. We hugged and kissed for a several moments, and I felt closer to her than ever. She was a very dear person and I loved her. But she knew and I knew that we would soon move in different directions, along trajectories we could not help but follow, that would launch us into separate orbits. The pain of it cut right through me as I hugged her close, and I could feel her anguish in the harshness of her breath.

ten

ONE MORNING A FEW WEEKS LATER I awoke with a humungous itch in my crotch. Scratching made it worse, and when I examined myself I found several small and rather scary blisters on my penis. Rubbing hand lotion on the area only made it worse and by the time I got to school I was maddened by the prickling sensation. I hurried to the nurse's office. She took one look at my crotch, told me I had some form of herpes, and suggested I go to the local clinic for sexually transmitted diseases to get tested and treated.

The horrifying fact that I might have a venereal disease shoved the actual itch to the back of my mind. In answer to my nervous questions, the nurse answered that only "sexual contact" could be the cause of my complaint. "No other way to get infected with this kind of herpes," she said bluntly. "Forget about toilet seats or whatever."

The only possible source of the herpes had to be Rory. The thought that she might have been having sex with others shocked me to the roots of my hair. It changed my view of her radically, and I was appalled. She had claimed she was a virgin when we first made love, and I believed her, so the possibility that she had been infected previously was out. Anyway, we had been lovers for well over a year, and I doubted that herpes could persist that long. (I was mistaken, I later learned; herpes can last a lifetime.)

Rory! *Fucking around!*

Slowly, my shocked surprise metamorphosed into anger. She must have done some pretty dirty things on the side to get a STD. Hey, she was a free woman, I argued; still, her sexual and emotional disloyalty was hard to swallow. To tell the truth, it knocked me for a loop; I didn't really know what to think or feel. It seemed that Rory was indeed a "hussy," as my mother had declared. On the other hand, she was clearly far more worldly than I was, and I suddenly saw myself through her eyes, as an unsophisticated, mixed-up kid. No wonder she needed other guys; there was no way a mere stripling like me could fulfill her mature needs.

And then there was Leila to consider. What if I had passed this thing on to her?!

Later the same day I went to the local STD clinic. A nurse examined me, took a urine sample, gave me an injection of antibiotics and some pills, and told me to keep clean and dry "down there." She told me the infection would pass in a few weeks, but that the itch would come and go for years and years – "a friend for life," she said cheerily. She also insisted that I had to inform all my "sexual partners" and tell them to be tested.

But that was too shaming, I decided, and the next time I met Rory I was so embarrassed for and by her I couldn't look her in the eye. I tried to avoid her, but she followed me down the corridor until I was trapped in a corner. "What's up, J.?" she asked. "You look weird."

Remembering the nurse's injunction, I swallowed hard and whispered, "I have herpes."

Rory's jaw dropped. "Herpes? You must be joking!"

Nice try, I thought, mocking her assumed innocence. "You ought to get treated, if you aren't already."

Her face froze. "If I'm what?"

"Getting treatment."

Her eyes flared with fury. "You think that I—?" she broke off, choking on the thought. "You shit!" She hauled back and slapped me so hard I slammed into the wall behind me. Without another word she turned on her heel and marched off.

My cheek stung like hell, but my head was reeling for other reasons. Was Rory denying that she had been sleeping around? Was her outrage a ploy to throw the blame on me? It seemed so out of character for one so forthright. Having been found out, she should have just been straight with me, and we might have worked things out. After all, we were both almost adults, no? In a couple of years or so we would both be out in the world. It was time to grow up and shed the shell of false innocence adolescents often cling to.

But if Rory insisted on denial, I would have to be the mature one, forgiving her her trespasses, overlooking her betrayals, moving on. Such imagined generosity of spirit gave me a glow, allowing me to bear my itch gracefully. Trouble was, Rory refused my forgiveness. She cut me dead when I offered to ride home with her after school. Her face was frigid, and when she walked away her spine was stiff with rage. Give her time, I told myself, feeling rather superior.

Rory did not talk to me for a week. Then, one day, she cornered me in the schoolyard. The look on her face was grim. "Let me get this straight," she said roughly. "You're accusing me of giving you a dose, right? Well, let me set you straight, amigo. One – I've never screwed anyone but you. Two – I've just been tested, and I'm clean. So that leaves you as the culprit. Only you."

"Me?" I gasped. "Impossible! I've only made it with you, Rory. Only you."

"Well, then, it's a mystery," she said tartly. "Since you can't get genital herpes from anything but sex, you must've been contaminated by an alien. Maybe you were cast in an episode of 'Star Trek'?"

"I don't know what to say," I mumbled. "Sorry. Sorry."

She eyed me suspiciously. "You're a dark one, J. Maybe more than I know. Maybe we ought to cool it awhile until we sort this out, okay?"

"Okay," I agreed miserably.

"Don't look so glum," she chided. "*Toute passe, comme la vie même*," she quoted, practicing her schoolbook French. She walked off with a flounce of her head, leaving me stunned. For the life of me I couldn't fathom the situation. If she had not been unfaithful to me, how on earth could I have gotten infected? It was a riddle that threatened to crack my mind.

I was walking in the door of our house after school that day when it struck me.

Leila!

She was the only other possible source. But the thought was monstrous. My mother didn't— Couldn't— Surely?

I stood in the entryway, poleaxed. Leila's customary crooned, "Joelly? Joelly?" came at me from an infinity. This can't be, I cried inwardly. Can it? The house seemed to fall about my ears, crumbling wall by wall, dropping the ceiling on my head.

Leila. Oh my god...

Jealousy burned me like hot coals, singeing my soul. At that moment I passionately desired to die. There was no way I could go on living if Leila had betrayed our intimacy. Absolutely no way.

"Joelly?"

Leila came toward me, cocking her head quizzically, arms outstretched to hug me. In a rush of revulsion so hot it burned my throat, I shoved her aside and fled up the stairs to my bed, burying my head in the pillows.

A minute later she was there, close by, stroking my back, murmuring my name in a soothing litany, *Joelly, Joelly, Joelly*...Her touch made me shiver, it was ice and fire, alternately chilling and searing my skin. A flame of pure hatred flared in my gut, I was consumed by a passionate hostility. She was a bitch, a demon, a whore who had corrupted and betrayed me. Worst of all, she had gone outside the family. This phrase, "outside the family," hammered in my head. She was a traitor of the worst kind! If only she'd go away.

Instead, Leila stretched herself beside me. Her slender figure, now almost a foot shorter than mine, pressed against me. The touch of it was unbearable, a torture of desire and disgust. Paralyzed with horror and lust, I wanted to simultaneously strangle and fuck her. She was my "sink of sin," as the Old Testament has it, and the stiff phrase kept pounding in my skull, degrading into an idiotic "sink or swim" – but swim to what? There was no longer any safe shore on the horizon. Everything in my world had melted into mud, leaving me flailing frantically, trying not to be sucked down into a black pit.

Leila's nimble fingers slipped under my sweatshirt, tripping lightly up and down my belly. Her touch was agony; an agony I deserved. I merited torture for ever having believed this woman would be faithful.

Didn't she know the whole thing only worked in a context of fidelity? What I meant by "the whole thing" remained vague but fervent, a whirlwind of feeling. Unfaithful bitch! I shouted soundlessly as her fingertips probed my groin.

Suddenly, with a roar of pure rage, I sprang off the bed, out of her embrace. Her empty arms reached out to me, hands grasping air as I backed away. "Joelly?" she cried.

"Honey..." Quivering with a revulsion so potent I thought I'd puke, I ran from the room and out of the house into the open air.

I ran and ran, down to the oceanfront, across the pedestrian bridge over the Pacific Coast Highway leading to the wide beach. I loped along the water's edge, letting the sea lap at my shoes, heading into the sunset whose golden glow seemed to offer absolution, forgiveness for the sin of having been born, for having been born of *that mother*. I hated her and I loved her, and the more I hated her the more I loved her. My chest split as I gulped the salty air, ripped by irreconcilable emotions. My feet pounding the sand seemed to belong to someone else; someone who, unlike me, knew where he was going.

Finally, exhausted, I fell full-length on the beach. The sun had set into dusk, leaving me several miles up the coast, almost in Malibu. I clawed at the sand, trying to bury myself like a turtle. The image of myself as a turtle struck me as ridiculous and I rolled over and stared up at the stars. I had to think, but I couldn't think. This was beyond thinking, beyond me. "I'm only a kid," I mumbled piteously, then mocked myself for such self-pity. I was only a kid, barely sixteen, but I had already been intimate with two women, one of whom was my mother.

The sheer precocity of it struck me full force. For the first time I allowed myself to clearly confront the reality that I loved Leila as a son and as a man, as a child and a near-adult. The son-love and the man-love were fused currents in my soul; I couldn't begin to separate their flow. It was glorious and horrible, and I did not know how to continue, how to face her, how to go on living in her house now that she had so grossly betrayed our intimacy.

For a moment I considered phoning my dad, pouring out my heart to him, asking if I could come and live with him. But when a picture of my father and Vivienne in their Berkeley apartment flashed before my eyes, I shuddered. There was no way he would ever understand my feelings. In truth, there was only one person who could, and she was now my enemy. The circularity of all this made me desperate and I looked longingly at the darkening ocean, wondering if the waves could swallow me up in their black embrace.

Suicide seemed to offer the only way out. It was an attractive offer, I mused, shivering in the night chill. The damp air made my shirt stick to my skin, but my thoughts were stickier. I imagined the waters clinging to my body, gluing up my eyes and mouth, clogging my throat, dissolving my fears in their liquid generosity. To me, the sea's embrace had all Leila's maternal intimacy without her troubling sexuality. At that moment I wanted nothing more than to curl up in that eternal mother's arms and sleep forever. My actual mom was deadly; but the ocean, mother of us all, was welcoming and serene.

Compelled by the suck of the tide lapping the shore, I took off my shoes and waded into the water. In an instant, my feet were blocks of ice and I turned and fled back to the safety of the sand. Defeated and cold, I realized the bitter truth: there was no place for me but at home, with her. How that would play out, I had no idea. I put my shoes back on and trudged to the highway, and waited for a bus to take me back to Santa Monica.

Leila was waiting for me on the sidewalk at the bottom of the path leading to our front door. As soon as she saw me walking disconsolately down the street she let out a cry of pure joy. I brushed her aside when she tried to grab me and headed for the house.

"What—?" she began, closing the front door behind us. The click of the deadbolt struck me like the snap of a prison cell lock.

"Don't want to talk," I said sulkily, cutting her off. "I'm starving."

"Go change your damp shirt and put on a sweater while I make dinner," she fussed. I obeyed meekly, happy to be a boy again, bullied by his mom. It was just too damn hard to be anything else.

Magic Time

eleven

In the year I turned sixteen I found it was too damn hard to be anything but a run-of-the-mill high school sophomore, and Leila seemed to understand my need to be "normal." We never discussed it, but she sensed that I couldn't handle too much intensity right then, and for a while we played at being straight-up mother and son, and knew we were play-acting, and enjoyed knowing it. For both of us it was a relief, though I suspect I relished the temporary suspension of our compelling intimacy more than she did. At the same time my need to be "average" was a declaration of independence, and she implicitly acknowledged it as such.

Since I had led the way, this low-key mode marked a change in the balance of power between us. As a consequence, her manner toward me became slightly more formal, as if I were now also an adult with my own will, not just her boy. Her somewhat polite attitude implied that, having always loved me, adored me, admired me, desired me, she now also respected me. Her "Joelly," altered its tone, became less charged and yearny; sometimes she even addressed me simply as "Joel."

At times, though, I missed the old intensities. Being average could be pretty boring. Often I blamed myself for not being able to measure up to Leila's level of being. The shaming thought struck me that I was inferior to her in this regard, a disappointment. No one but me had ever been able to endure Leila's passionate complexity for very long. Yet in the end even I had to withdraw from her, temporarily, and I was troubled by the thought that I might be essentially commonplace.

It seemed that, for a while, her emotional energy had lifted me into a more extraordinary kind of existence, one I could not sustain on my own. It was a sobering realization, and humiliating. However, it struck me that if I were indeed merely average my relationship with Leila was a perversion of my true self, a psychic distortion that might damage my whole life. If I were essentially prosaic, I had been exposed to a force of feeling I could never integrate into my personality, and that could kill me, or twist me permanently out of shape. I am articulating this now, all these years later; back then these perceptions were mere shadows on the edge of my awareness. But Leila's passionate necessity, coming at me full on, forced me to question myself far more acutely than most kids my age. Perhaps that was her true gift to me, and the source of her grip on my soul.

True, I loved Rory, in a "normal" way. But, after Leila, could I ever be satisfied with a Rory alone, not just as a counterpoint to Leila? Had Leila given me a taste of something I could never forget, that might haunt me forever? Perhaps I'd loved too much too soon, and that, I dimly realized, could be fatal.

* * *

Rory continued to cut me dead for weeks after our herpes confrontation. She treated me as if I didn't exist, sliding her eyes over my face whenever it came into her line of sight, as if I were just a blank space, a blur in the air. I was glad, for I knew I could not meet her eye, not then, perhaps never again. But never's a long time when you're sixteen, and the new semester, with its new faces and new teachers, gave us both a sense of fresh beginnings. One day she actually looked at me. Next time, she smiled, faintly. By the end of the week we were talking again.

"You were shitty," she said, more or less amiably. "But I missed you, you dork."

"Sorry, Rory."

"'Rory'? What happened to 'R.'?"

"Sorry, R."

"Did you clear up that 'mystery'?" she asked forthrightly.

"My mistake," I mumbled. "Sorry."

"Herpes can be contracted in other ways, you know," she asserted, offering us both a graceful fib.

"Sure. Many ways."

"You're clean now?"

"Pure as the driven snow."

"You were never that, thank God," she laughed. "Wanna date sometime?"

"Please."

"I'm free Friday."

"Thanks."

She took my hand and squeezed it painfully. "Don't ever shit me again, you hear?" she said harshly. "Not ever!"

We went to the movies that Friday and walked home arm-in-arm. But she did not invite me up to her room, and I was glad. Post-herpes, our lovemaking would have been more self-conscious, less lovely and innocent, and we both required some time to adjust to the now more adult reality. Or, as Rory put it, we needed to grow up a little and think about what we were doing. "No longer babes in the wood," she said with a wry grin.

Six weeks or so into the semester Mr. Morales startled me with the suggestion that I might consider making Spanish literature my major in college. He said I showed a real sympathy for the subject and offered to tutor me after school for free. There were summer courses in Spanish literature at the University of Granada, he told me, and with his help I could prepare to attend after high school graduation, and maybe get a subsidy from the State Department.

Like my grandfather, Morales's family came from Granada. He told me he was born in Los Angeles a year after his parents immigrated. The Spanish he spoke was Andalusian Castilian, in contrast to the sing-song Mexican variety of most local Latinos, and I loved its crisp, hard sounds, so much like Enrique's. The Andalusian poets he admired, particularly Lorca and Góngora, wrote with the same lyrical clarity and it was a thrill to hear their rhythms roll off his tongue. The refrain of a Góngora ballad, "*dejadme llorar/ orillas del mar*" – "Let me weep by the shores of the sea" – seemed to echo the resonant melancholy that had touched me so often in Enrique's voice. This now seemed a way to go, to plunge into a different culture, one that was simultaneously familiar and strange, a link with one branch of my ancient family. There was a pleasure in it, and a kind of honor I seemed to have lost.

When I suggested to Leila that I might want to study Spanish literature in college, I thought she might object that it was an impractical course to pursue. Instead, her eyes lit up. "What a fabulous idea!" she exclaimed. "Something really worthwhile, not like some stupid profession." She pronounced the word "profession" as if it were slightly disreputable.

Her reaction abashed me. On the one hand, I was pleased she was so taken by my suggestion. On the other hand, if she welcomed it so warmly, might that not signal that I was following a fantasy? Leila's attitude toward the so-called real world was a mixture of contempt and incomprehension, I knew, and my choice of something other than "some stupid profession" might be truly dumb.

Nonetheless, I accepted Morales's offer of tutoring. Twice a week, after school, I went to his office and we studied Spanish novels, plays, and poetry, and made conversation in Castilian. He had a penchant for jaunty multilingual puns, flipping French *c'est la vie* into homophonic Spanish *se la ví* – "I've seen it;" or English "embarrassed" into Spanish *embarazada*, meaning "pregnant." We chatted about Cervantes and Calderón, about the Moorish kings who had built the Alhambra, and the Arab and Hebrew poets who had sung the praises of the Red Citadel.

"In the eleventh century, the Jewish vizier, Yusuf ibn Naghrallah, began to build on the hill that later became the Alhambra," Morales explained. "Muhammad ibn-al-Ahmar, founder of the Nasrid dynasty, continued it two hundred years later. It was the last symbol of the Golden Age of Arab Al-Andalus, that the roughneck Castilians called Spain – a monument to an era of greatness," he added, eyes shining. "The Alhambra is the human spirit as an architecture of the soul, celebrated in the Jewish poet Ibn Gabirol's description of it as a *dome like the Palanquin of Solomon hung above the glories of the chambers...*"

As he spoke I could see the glorious Red Citadel rise behind his head, a beckoning shadow that enthralled me. In my imagination, Spain became a territory of intensities, a land that offered a replacement for the fervid passions I had retreated from in Leila. Far safer to love a country than a woman, especially if she is your mother… Nations have impersonal histories, at least for a foreigner, and it would be good to be a foreigner, for a while. *La vida es un soplo y hay que soplarla* – "Life is a breath that must be sighed" – Enrique used so say, " and I was beginning to believe him.

But sometimes sighing just can't cut it.

* * *

Walking down Wilshire Boulevard one afternoon, on my way to a department store to buy a new pair of sneakers, I saw a man and a woman kissing in a doorway. The woman's face and body were hidden by the man's bulky form, but one white arm circled his neck. There was something disturbingly familiar about the arm, but I dismissed the thought; an arm was an arm, after all. However, when the embracing couple turned slightly in the midst of their ardor, I instantly recognized Leila.

I felt as if a bolt of iron had been driven through my skull, down my vertebrae, into the cement sidewalk. The cold iron riveting my spine fixed me to the ground. If I tried to move, I was sure I would shatter.

After an eternity, Leila and her companion sauntered away arm in arm. Gradually, my body recovered its mobility, and with it came a flood of shame. Leila – *kissing in the street!* Like, like – I couldn't think of the right word, but whatever it was, her action was shockingly improper. What if anyone had seen—? And with another man, maybe the one who—?

Somehow, it was my fault; that was the residual feeling as the successive hot flushes of shame and anger cooled into misery. *It was my fault.* My fault that she behaved like a loose woman in full public view. My fault that she needed other men. My fault that our intimacy complicated her life, making it difficult for her to have other relationships. Most of all, it was my fault that I just wasn't enough for her.

I walked on in a trance, the guilt-bees buzzing in my brain. Moving like a zombie down the street, I saw nothing, heard nothing. The brute fact, one I had to again accept, was a realization that I could never be enough for a woman like Leila. "I'm nothing!" I said out loud. Compared to her, I was transparent, you could see right through me; there were no depths, no compelling darkness. But then, she must have always known that. And knowing it, why did she let things happen? She was the adult after all, and my mother. Why didn't she protect me from myself? Guard me against ever knowing just how shallow I was?

It was devastating to glimpse something so beyond me, to taste it and know it would always be unreachable. If my mother and I had never been lovers, I might well have been happy with the Rorys of this world. Rory was a terrific person, but Leila was something else, an absolute in everything, including selfishness. Selfishly, she had taken me as a lover when she was desperate, and ruined me for any other woman.

Was this melodramatic? I asked myself, brought up sharp by an abrupt view of my situation as it might be seen from the outside. An overwrought teenage drama? But hell, I *was* a teenager, after all! My vulnerability was no act. Leila had ripped away my clothes, stripped me to the skin, a tender skin that had not yet hardened into a protective adult hide. She had shown me to myself in all my lacks and limits, and that was horrible.

I despised her. No, I adored her. Quite simply, she had me in her thrall, forever.

I sat down on a bus bench and racked my brains for answers. I had never thought so hard in all my life. After a while it seemed clear that I had two basic options. I could create a scene when I got home, blow up in a rage, shame her into sharing my unbearable guilt. Or I could try to win her back, bend every nerve to recapture her attention. After all, I had lately scorned her bed, and discouraged her from coming to mine. Perhaps, it was time to coax her to return.

But as I rode the bus toward home, forgetting sneakers and everything else, I knew with cold certainty that I hadn't the will, experience, or self-assurance to follow either of these courses. I was too old to throw a convincing tantrum and too young to be calculating. Besides, Leila outmatched me. I loved her and had to take my chances. It was as simple and as scary as that.

After getting off the bus, I turned away from the direction of home and went toward Rory's house. My head was numb and I had to talk to someone, and she was the only person I really trusted. Not that I could tell her everything, but I felt I could lay my miserable mood at her feet, like a dog offering a chewed old bone to his master.

When she opened the door Rory took one look at my long face and threw her arms around me in a hug. She took my hand and led me upstairs to her bedroom. Sitting me in her chintz armchair, she said, simply: "Tell me."

"It's, well, Leila..." I began hoarsely.

Rory nodded, a gesture that spoke volumes. But, mercifully, she was silent, sensing that any comment might send me scuttling from the room. I stared at my shoes, wondering how to begin, how to find a thread in that tangle that could be pulled free without unraveling the unrevealable. "She's deep," I muttered. "You know? Deeper than me. Much." Rory made a vaguely sympathetic sound. Glancing up for a second, I saw her bright brown eyes were shrewd; too shrewd, perhaps, since she had no idea just how "deep" Leila really was.

A long silence followed. I did not know what word to utter next. It was all too inexplicable, too painful, and I sank into a pit of despair. The only way to go was down, down to the center of the earth where there was no sun or moon, day or night, just everlasting, soothing nothingness.

"You know, J.," Rory said gently, "your mom's an amazing person. Awesome. I mean, I'm totally in awe of her. But..."

She let that "but" hang pregnant in the air, and I seized it greedily. "But too much for me!" I cried. "Just too much!"

Suddenly, I began to sob. Hot tears stung my eyes and rolled down my cheeks. Rory came close and pressed my wet face into her bosom. She stroked my hair, murmuring soothingly. "You're such a baby, Joelly," she said. "That's what your mom calls you, isn't it – `Joelly'? A baby name."

"I like it," I snuffled, snuggling deeper into her stomach. "It's sweet."

"Sure it is, but babyish."

Rory stepped back, kneeled down, and took my face in her big hands. "I'm going to talk to you like a Dutch uncle," she said solemnly.

I giggled. "You're not my uncle, and you ain't Dutch."

"All the same. Sometimes it's hard to cut the cord, you know? Especially if the mother is strong. I fight my mom tooth and nail. I'm crazy about her, but right now she's my worst enemy, know what I mean? Maybe the same is true for you and your mom?"

At that moment I loved Rory with all my heart. She was so good! But her struggles with her mother were worlds away from what was happening with Leila and me. Between Rory's experience and mine there was an abyss, a gap so deep and wide I couldn't begin to think of jumping across it. The cruel irony was that the only person I could talk to was Leila herself. She would understand at once what I was saying, whereas Rory never could, not in a million years. But I loved her throaty voice, and to keep her talking I asked a host of questions about her relationship with her mother. She spilled it all out, alternately wise and wounded, coolly sage and bitterly hurt. At the end she kissed my hand and thanked me for my sympathetic ear.

At the front door, however, she grabbed my sleeve. "You tricky devil," she exclaimed. "Making me spill my guts, to avoid spilling yours!" She shoved me out and slammed the door in my face.

Leila was home when I retuned. "Hey, honey," she said, kissing me lightly on the cheek. "Did you buy sneakers?"

"No."

She looked at me askance. "Couldn't find the right brand, then What's the word in sneakers these days?"

"Sneaky."

She focused on me, sensing undercurrents. "Isn't that what sneak ers are all about? Sneakiness?"

"Sometimes."

"I bought a pineapple upside-down cake. Want some? With a glas of milk."

"That's kids' stuff."

"Yeah? Well, I'm having some. Join me, if you like."

She drifted into the kitchen, humming. I heard the clatter of th kettle, the spurt of the faucet, the flare of the gas ring on the stove. Sh refused to buy an electric kettle, claiming it would pollute the water sh boiled up for tea. We had argued this several times, but she was stub born. Putting a kettle on the fire was a primitive act, she said. It mad her feel close to those old cavemen she suspected still haunted the edge of modern life. "If they don't see me using fire they'll get peeved," sh said, "and that's not a good idea."

Lord, how I loved her then. My heart welled up inside me, drowr ing me in feelings I could not contain. Whatever she wanted from m I would give her, however limited my offerings might be. She took m way beyond my limits, sucked out emotions I never knew had, and swelled up with the sheer privilege she conferred upon me. But she wa also a wicked woman, one who kissed her lovers in public, contracting disgraceful diseases, which she passed on to me. I wanted to view her as a man might, harshly and honestly; but, listening to her humming, I realized I would always see her through a boy's dazed eyes.

I would never manage to alter that primal perspective.

We drank tea, nibbled cake, and chatted about this and that. "You know, I've really missed our cuddling," she murmured at one point. "Haven't you?" I nodded dumbly, my heart in my throat. She fondly stroked my cheek. "You're my man, Joel," she said. "My one and only."

I blushed, but she seemed oblivious that I had caught her in a blatant lie. In her mind, though, she wasn't meretricious. The current of her inner truth carried many different strands of veracity, and so it was no lie for her to call me her "one and only," just as it was no lie that she made love in the street to other men. In the country of the heart all lies are true.

That night I crept into her bed and we made love. We made love face to face, frankly. We made love as a man and a woman, male and female, seeking ecstasy and pleasure in each other's bodies. It was the most glorious night I had ever spent in her arms.

At one moment, staring into her luminous eyes as my cock slid into her cunt, her raven hair fanned out on the pillow, her face beneath me brilliant with desire, I felt I was staring straight into the blaze of creation itself. Could anything in the world be more amazing and superb than this marvelous woman, I wondered. As the hot wire of orgasm began to sear my groin I knew the answer was a clear and emphatic *no!*

twelve

WHAT FOLLOWED was the sweetest winter of my life. Leila and I slept together many nights, sometimes in her bed, sometimes in mine. Every sense I had was drunk with her. Whenever we were apart her absence shadowed my mind.

There was a subtle evolution in our passion. Where, before, Leila had led the way, cloaking me in her sexual enchantment, she now drew back a space, allowing me room to be. More and more we became two adults, a woman and a man, exploring each other's erotic imaginations. At the same time she quite deliberately showed me how to please her, how to do the many and varied things that gave her pleasure. She taught me what she called The Golden Rule: that a man's deepest delight derives from a woman's pleasure. "Go slow, give me time to feel," she whispered, showing me how to run my tongue lingeringly around her breasts and their large pale aureoles. Squeezing her breasts in her fists, she rolled first one and then the other over and under my tongue while a series of soft moans heralded her preliminary, gentle orgasm. Other times she directed my fingers to the backs of her knees or the edges of her groin, or led my tongue to the side of her small, high breast where it folded into her armpit. "I'm very sensitive there," she murmured as I kissed the shaven skin.

Whenever we were close my nose sucked in the scent of Leila's skin, drawing it down into my chest, suffusing the female smell of her through every fiber of my being. It was a complex and ravishing fragrance, compounded of a subtle muskiness and the always slightly musty odor of her hair, the trace of her lavender and lilac perfume, and the underlying tang of the minty bath soap and bubbles she favored. As I breathed her in, the balance between these various delights shifted from moment to moment, depending where my nose was moving. At her neck sweetness ruled; her armpits were more earthy; the underside of her breasts, the inside of her thighs and the backs of her knees of fered an erotic undertone of sweat. Her warm cunt was all these aromas together in full flower, plus a pungency of the slightly spermy odor of her arousal.

Night after night Leila revealed the basic rhythms of loving. She told me when to be quick, when to be slow; when to be gentle, when to be bold; how to rein in my puppy-like excitement, how to hold back the orgasm that seemed to rush at me the moment I touched her magical body. "It's all about rhythm, sequence, surprise," she emphasized. She made me curl my forefinger up just inside the roof of her vagina, o stroke the soft wet tissues there that, she said, were especially sensual. Unusual places, like the inside of her ankles, the crook of her elbow, esponded to caresses as avidly as her mouth, breasts and cunt. Blowing ightly on the silky down at the base of her spine made her shiver deliciously, and she could find pleasure in a subtle scratch or a strong tug at her hair at the right moment. In my erotic delirium it seemed to me hat some inspired sexual deity had devised Leila's entire, erogenously endowed, quicksilver body for my loving.

The right moments were everything, she insisted. "Just listen for hem, with your ears, fingertips, eyes, nose, tongue. That's the key to making love." And yes, now we were truly "making love," cherishing each other's enjoyment, pursuing the kind of rapture only possible between two people whose hearts have no reservations. Mine was so open because I was so young and because Leila was my mother. Her heart was open because I was her son and because she was forever and only herself. In that mutual sense we were utterly naked to each other.

And naked, literally. Leila invited me to look at her cunt full on. Propping a pillow under her buttocks, she opened her legs wide and pulled her labia apart with her slender fingers. Shyly at first, but with increasing fascination, I knelt by the side of the bed and stared at that glorious female landscape. God, it was magnificent! – the plump, hair-shrouded outer lips, the tiny clitoris bulb peeking out from its silvery sheath, the silken inner folds, sliding down into the wet pink tunnel. Gazing in awe upon that marvelous sight I felt I truly was looking into God's own eye.

"Touch it," she murmured. "Lick it. Start lightly, flicking, tip of he tongue. Then let your tongue go soft, roll it around all over, slide it n, kiss it!" She guided my lips and fingers over the inside of her thighs and around the tight muscles of her ass, leaving me with a haunting aftertaste of the ocean in my mouth. "Don't forget the button," she commanded, pulling apart her buttock cheeks to display her anus. Sometimes, overcome, she'd push her own fingers into her vagina and bring herself to a hip-jerking climax.

The diversity, force, and subtlety of her sensuality staggered me. Rising from soft sighs to fierce shouts, harsh grunts and wrenching cries, her responses seemed to flow from some inexhaustible fount of desire. Compared to my blunt orgasmic outburst – the conventional male *Oh God!* – the range of her rapturous expression was truly symphonic.

It was as if she were revealing to me the secret language of life, an essentially female idiom, allowing me to worship at the altar of her erotic glory, leaving me stunned and humbled, often more excited than I could bear. She said I was a "natural lover," and remarked that such men were rare, but I was never under the illusion that I was or would ever be her sexual equal.

In those marvelous nights I learned the ancient magic of the flesh Reentering the womb that gave me birth, I was initiated into its mysteries. Sometimes, when I was inside Leila, I looked down at her transformed, glowing face and thought, *this is my mother*. The mingled thril and guilt of it was an ecstasy all its own.

Sometimes, after making love, we lay in the dark, talking, giver license by our intimacies to say anything.

"I fell in love with you the first moment you were put into my arms, all slimy and slippery from the womb," she told me one evening Her voice was soft in the dim light of the bedside lamp behind her as gazed at the profile of her delicate yet strong face with its expressive lip and slender jaw and neckline. "A kind of dam burst inside me. Sure I was your mother, and mothers have this rush about their newborns But there was an extra thing, an excitement, you know? Having you li so vivid and male on my breast made me horny."

The use of the vulgar word in that context simultaneously shocke and intrigued me. Surely it must be some kind of primal transgression – a "sin" – for a mother to be erotically turned on by her infant Or did the surge of feelings in a woman's heart at the extraordinary mo ment of birth run over the edges of all the formal boundaries between categories of loving?

"It wasn't just that you were my very own creature, made in my body, but that you were my very special sweet male babe. I loved licking you all over, breathing in the warm smell of your head, your tummy, your knees, your toes. In that time, when I was suckling you, even your dirty diapers smelled sweet." She chuckled softly. "During the year I was breastfeeding, I only had to imagine suckling you any place or time and I'd start giving milk, making great wet patches around my nipples. Max made fun of me. But you know, I had orgasms while suckling you, gentle spasms in my womb, the deepest sensations..." Her voice trailed off dreamily, and I was silent, caught in the spell of her reverie.

Shifting into a different tone, she continued. "All the men I've known, including your father – especially him! – are other people. I mean that they're, well, *other people*...But you are me. Not that I own you," she added quickly. "Nobody owns anybody, maybe not even themselves. But you and I are part of the same reality, a particular way of being alive." She turned her face toward me, throwing it into shadow. "Does that make sense?"

I nodded. We certainly were "part of the same reality." I knew it in my blood and bones, and that recognition both thrilled me and scared me.

Leila was supremely uninterested in "facts," and her answers to my specific questions about her childhood and her early life with my dad were perfunctory. "That's all history," she said dismissively. "Just things that happened. There's no clue there, I assure you. All the real history we need to know is right here, now, in this bed." "But what about Paris?" I insisted. "Don't you remember anything?" "Only that I was miserable," she replied, and that was it.

"Will we always be – close?" I asked. As soon as I had said this I wanted to bite back the words. Asking such a question could destroy everything, breach the willing suspension of disbelief protecting our extraordinary connection.

"I want you to know me," Leila said quietly. "That's all."

"I'll never manage that!"

"First you'll know me, then you won't," she answered cryptically. "But then you always will."

I stared at her shadowed face, trying to bring it into focus, and failing. No matter how hard I looked I could not really grasp its true character. "You'll always be inside me, Leila, that's for sure. You'll always be right there, in my gut, under my guard."

"Well, after all, I'm your mom," she replied serenely.

* * *

Despite our intense intimacy, it was an unspoken aspect of our more mature connection that Leila would have other lovers. Though I spent the nights she was away from home sobbing helplessly into my pillow, I accepted, in all humility, that a kid like me could never be everything to her. Perhaps, with those others, she was trying to put a little air between our glued souls, for both our sakes. Yet she told me over and over that none of her "friends" meant anything near as much to her as I did, and that was some comfort. But it tore me up inside all the same. The brute fact was that I'd given Leila everything I had, and it just wasn't enough.

She talked to me about her other lovers, tentatively at first, then openly. She never brought them home and I was grateful for that, but I felt I knew them from her vivid, sly descriptions.

There was Henry, the UCLA law professor, cheating on his wife while jealously having her followed by a private detective to find out if she, too, was unfaithful. "His nose twitches like a rabbit's when he's in heat," Leila laughed. "Maybe he really prefers carrots." There was Carl the salesman who pitched her a line in a bar, "As if he were selling sex," Leila said. "He almost offered me a discount!" There was Dapper Dan the snappy dresser, "never without a compliment, mostly for himself." There was Jerry the assistant football coach at Pepperdine – "He calls out the plays," – and Gary the horticulturalist who worked miracles in our garden. Gary was the only one I had seen close up: a small wiry man with a charming, lopsided smile and a wart on his cheek.

The subtext in all this was her tacit declaration that she was coming out of her shell, exercising her sexual power in the wider world. My father, she implied, had made her believe her sexuality was somehow "whorish." Maybe he had also been afraid that Leila was too much for him and needed to keep her on the defensive – a cowardly ploy.

hoped that I, at least, was man enough to accept her as she was, not make her feel guilty for being such an amazing woman. "No one will ever be as close to me as you are," she told me, and I was filled with joy to hear her say that.

Many winter evenings before we went upstairs we sat beside the fire I made of pine logs, the air filled with the smell of tangy resin as the rain slashed at the windowpanes and the drafts billowed the drapes. Again, I pestered Leila with questions about her childhood, wanting to know everything about her. She was coming into focus for me, as a person, not only as my mother-lover, and I was greedy for every detail.

Despite her disdain for "history," Leila grudgingly revealed some fragments of her past. She told me her father had deserted her mother before she was born, leaving Leila at the mercy of her mother, a woman she described as "selfish and silly, a deadly combination." Her father disappeared, she never heard from him, and that had left a huge hole in her emotional life. "My mother went from one man to another, from Paris to L.A., dragging me along like a bag of dirty laundry, a burden she couldn't quite bring herself to shed." When Leila was older, her mother forced her to pretend to be her sister so that her lovers wouldn't know she was old enough to have a teenage daughter.

"I was a kind of orphan," Leila said. "My mother ignored me and prevented me from knowing any of my relatives, including all my grandparents, claiming they were `crocodiles.' To this day I have no idea where any of them live." Leila's mother, my grandmother, had died of a stroke in her mid-forties, when I was four years old. All I remembered about her was a woman who smelled of expensive lotions and powders and wore scarlet lipstick.

Leila's only good memories of her childhood were the times her mother farmed her out to Mama Richard, an old, French-born countrywoman living in Santa Barbara, who had once cleaned house for her family in Montparnasse. "She was strict but loving," Leila said, her face dreamy with recollection. "I had to make my bed and always be polite, but she often cuddled me, called me her *petit chou,* and let me hide in the folds of her apron when something scared me. I begged my mother to allow me to stay with Mama Richard permanently. I wanted her to adopt me, but my *maman* – I never called her `mom' – was stupidly jealous of my feelings for the old woman. She condemned her as `peasant,' and claimed that Mama Richard's aim was to sell me if ev she got legal possession of me!"

Listening to her, I conjured up a wrenching vision of little Lei being torn from the arms of her beloved Mama Richard by her ev mother. It was like a fairy tale, and even if she were dramatizing, I kne her story was emotionally true, rendering the real feelings of the sa child that she had been, and essentially still was. I yearned to go bac in time and protect her from her mother, make her happy in retrospec I wanted nothing more than to smother her with love.

Leila was born to be loved. Her nature was as thirsty for passic and affection as a rose is for sun and water. Yet all she'd ever had was dash of loving from her old woman and a short-lived dribble from m father. She was the archetypal Weeping Woman and it was up to me dry her tears and nurture her spirit. It would never be enough, I knev but at least I could try to make up for some of her lifelong depriva tion.

"Sometimes I feel I'm sucking out your spirit, like some kind c vampire," Leila said one evening as we watched the flames lick the fire back. "Am I?"

"That's silly," I replied. "Maybe it's me who's sucking out your spi it?"

"You're such a tender thing," she murmured, gazing into my eye "How could something so nice happen to someone like me?"

"You deserve it!" I cried.

"But there are dangers."

"Why?" I demanded, heart hammering. I feared that if we eve openly examined our relationship we would surely lose our nerve.

"You're such a tender thing," she repeated.

"Oh, balls," I said rudely. "When it comes right down to it I'm whole lot tougher than you are, Leila. Like dad. Look how he's sur vived."

"Maybe that's true," she murmured. "I see him in you, sometime The part of him I fell in love with back then."

"What part's that?" I asked tartly.

"He was always very grounded, even at twenty. I liked that a lot."

"Opposites attract," I said tritely.

"Guess so," she nodded, and an impish smile danced across her face. She looked away and I watched her profile lit by the firelight, thinking I had never seen anything so entrancing and so moving. "This thing we have...It can't really go anywhere," she said softly. "You know that, don't you."

A wave of fear choked me. "Guess not," I said hoarsely.

"It's too – circular. Self-enclosed, a snake biting its own tail." She turned to face me, her eyes stark. "There's an old alchemical symbol like that. I think it means wholeness, completeness."

"That's a good thing, isn't it?"

"For symbols. People are untidier."

"Oh what the hell," I said crossly. "Let's have some coffee, Leila."

I followed her into the kitchen and watched her put on the kettle and spoon instant coffee into two cups. "You don't mind instant?" she asked politely. She poured boiling water into the cups, added sugar and milk, and handed me a cup. "Careful," she said, "it might scald you. Blow before you sip."

We drank in silence for a while standing up, awkward as strangers. The coffee hit my nervous stomach like a jolt of acid.

"Next year you'll have to think seriously about college," Leila said. I shrugged sulkily, and she took one of my hands in both of hers and stroked it gently. "What we have now is the best thing that's ever happened to me, or ever will," she said in a low, quiet voice. "It's like..." she broke off, searching for a metaphor. "Like a golden bubble in a black sea. But bubbles burst, and this will, too. It's the nature of things."

"What `things'?"

"I'm older than you are. I'm your mother." She paused, as if reminding herself of these facts. "If anybody ever found out about— Well, you know. They'd damn me to hell, hang a big red letter around my neck, like poor old Hester Prynne. But she was merely an adulteress, and adultery's no longer a crime. Incest is."

"For god's sake—!"

"That's what I'd be forced to wear, a big red `I.' "

"And me?" I cried. "What would I wear?"

"Nothing. You're the victim here."

"Not true."

"In the eyes of the world."

"Please stop talking this way, " I pleaded. "It makes me feel cheap, and I'm not. We're not."

"The eyes of the world are very unforgiving." She shivered, feeling their hard gaze upon her, and I wanted to put my arms around her.

"Look," I began desperately, "nobody else has anything to do with what we have. It's just you and me, me and you. Maybe it is a `bubble.' If so, it'll burst and we'll move on." To what? I asked myself silently, unable to imagine a world without Leila as my lover. "Just now, let's leave others out of it, okay?"

"Okay," Leila agreed promptly. She smiled. "What the hell do they know, anyway?"

"Zilch," I answered. "Zilcheroo."

"Zilcheroo," she echoed, laughing.

thirteen

IN THE SPRING following that mythical winter Rory dropped hints that she would like to sleep with me again, but I pretended not to notice. Hurt by my deliberate obtuseness, she began dating other guys, making sure that I knew. Since my feelings for her had subsided into friendship, her attempts to make me jealous fell flat, which chagrined her even more. She slipped me a note, saying "Ships that pass in the night, eh?" and I began to feel I owed her an explanation about why I had cooled off. I couldn't tell her the truth, however, so I let it slide.

But she did not. "I don't like it when people treat me as if I don't exist," she declared, approaching me in the school entry one morning. Softening, she gripped my arm. "I thought we had a good thing going, J.," she murmured.

"Yeah," I shrugged.

"Well, that's articulate," she retorted. "Meet me after school today, okay?" I nodded and she hurried away.

In the afternoon we walked to Palisades Park as we used to do, and sat on a bench overlooking the Pacific. I had no idea what to tell Rory. I certainly did not want to offend her, but the fact was that there was simply no room in my world for any woman but Leila.

Rory was silent for a while. Having confronted me, she clearly wasn't quite sure what she wanted to say. How can anyone, male or female, ask another person why they are no longer desired? There can be no question more excruciating.

"Got any plans for college?" I asked at last, for want of a better topic.

Her head jerked back, as if I had slapped her. "College?" she said. "What's that got to do with anything?"

"It kind of looms," I said apologetically.

She glanced at me askance. "You're in a weird space these days, J. I can't figure you out."

"Join the club," I replied, trying for a chuckle.

"How's your mom?"

The abrupt, loaded question rocked me. "Fine," I said curtly. "Just dandy."

"Will she ever get her claws out of your skin?"

I recoiled at her crudeness. "Never," I said coldly.

Rory reached for my hand, but I jerked it away, furious at her presumption, and her face tightened. "You have to cut the cord sometime," she said.

Struggling to control my anger, I recognized that Rory was speaking out of her hurt. "Look," I said as calmly as I could, "you know how much I like you. But right now I need a friend more than I need a – well, you know. I'm sorry if you feel slighted."

"'Slighted'?" she cut in. "Who's slighted? You fancy yourself, don't you, Mr. Perfect."

"You know what I mean, R. I need a friend. Really."

"Put an ad in the classified," she said curtly.

"Can you discuss everything that's happening in your life right now?" I cried in desperation. "Do you even know what's happening? Hell, you're just like me – neither a kid nor a grown-up. So gimme a break, okay? Give *us* a break."

Rory gazed at me. "It ain't easy to hate you," she drawled. "God knows I've tried."

"I've never hated you, R."

"That's because you've never really loved me," she retorted shrewdly.

"Not true. I did, once."

"What happened?"

"Nothing lasts forever, I guess. Lesson Number One in Growing Up 101."

"I'm going to study medicine," Leila said. "Be a doctor, maybe a gynecologist."

"Spend your days fiddling about down there?" I teased.

"Why not? You used to dig it, before you got all mixed up."

"I still like it."

"Just not with me, eh?"

"Just not with anybody right now," I lied glibly.

"Well, sport," she said, flicking my chin, "when you get the urge again, forget my number."

"Already have," I said lightly, matching flipness for flipness.

She flushed. "Well, at least that's clear," she said with a brittle laugh.

* * *

There was a surprise waiting for me when I got home that day. My father was sitting in the living room. He was weeping.

It was so long since I had thought of my father as part of the family that the sight of him in his wheelchair in our house gave me a jolt. It was as if a character from one novel had jumped into another, by a different author. For a moment I could not find a word to say, and the odd expression of sly triumph on Leila's face was no help.

"Dad!" I exclaimed at last. "Are you okay?"

My father wiped his smeared cheeks shamefully and held out his arms for a hug. I embraced him warily, not knowing what this was all about. "Vivvy left me," he whispered in my ear. "She just walked out."

"He wants to come back home," Leila said behind me. "What do you think?"

My head lurched. Events were happening much too fast. "Home?" I blurted. "This isn't his home!"

I was instantly ashamed by my outburst, but Leila turned to Max with a wicked smile. "See?" she said, the hiss of that one syllable slicing the air.

My father slumped even further in his chair and literally wrung his hands, a melodramatic gesture I'd thought did not exist outside Dickens. "I've got no one. Nowhere," he said in a wobbly voice.

"You gave up your apartment?" I asked, amazed. "Your job?"

He looked at me, disappointed by my lack of understanding, and shook his head. "No, no, nothing like that," he muttered.

Well then, I wanted retort, but bit my tongue. "Nowhere" was a metaphor, I recognized belatedly.

"You can stay here for a day or two, while you get your head straight," Leila said. "If that's okay with Joel. He's the man of the house."

"Sure," I shrugged. "Why not?"

"Thank you," Max said humbly.

At last, a flow of sympathy for him broke through the dam of my astonishment. I hugged him again, warmly. "How'd it happen?" I asked softly.

"She got tired of his bullying," Leila said crisply.

"Tell me, Max," I said, ignoring her.

"It's true," he said. "I drove her away, just like I did your mother." A tear gathered in the corner of his eye and ran down his cheek. He wiped it away with the back of his hand.

"Where did she go?" I asked. "I mean, is it permanent?"

"She was so good to me!" he exclaimed. "No one was ever so kind." He stared at me, stark-eyed. "What's the matter with me?" he asked plaintively. "Am I a monster? Am I a real cripple, here?" He pounded his chest over his heart. "Am I?"

"I would say so," Leila said calmly. "If you asked me."

"Please," I pleaded, "let's all be friends."

"If you're willing to face the truth about yourself at last, that'd be something," Leila continued relentlessly. "Otherwise, you'll just careen from one misery to another."

I was getting angry at Leila's meanness, and for an instant I wondered if she were willing to face the truth about herself. The ugly word incest jumped into my head. I had looked it up recently in the dictionary and found it derived from a Latin word meaning "sexually impure." Anyway, I thought, watching Max's miserable face, she has no cause to be so self-righteous.

With her acute antennae, Leila sensed my shift in allegiance and softened her tone. "You're welcome to stay here awhile, Max, to collect yourself," she said graciously. "Joel and I are glad to have you as our guest. You can sleep in your old room. I got rid of your stuff, but it's quite cozy."

"Thank you, Leila. And Joel," Max said humbly.

"But don't expect us to fetch and carry for you," Leila added. "We have our own lives, you know."

"Of course. I'll be meek as a mouse."

"That I'd like to see," Leila laughed, but with an edge.

"Actually, I've taken a week's sick leave," Max said. "Is that okay?" Before Leila could reply, he rushed on. "It'll be a chance to play catch-up with my son. You've grown so tall, Joel! And you have the beginnings of a beard."

"Just fluff," I shrugged, pleased that he had noticed this mark of manhood.

"You must tell me everything," he said warmly. "All about school, about your love life, the girls whose hearts you're surely breaking. I'm dying for details!"

I did not know where to look, but Leila stepped in suavely. "A young man's secrets are his own," she declared.

"You look so tired, dad," I said.

"Old, you mean," he countered. "Yes, I'm an old man, at forty. Maybe I was born ancient? A palmist on Venice Beach once told me I had the hands of a very old soul, one that had been used up by many previous lives, and I sometimes feel a million years old." His shoulders slumped, as if exhausted by the weight of all those lives.

"I'll make the bed and you can take a nap before dinner," Leila said briskly.

Left alone, Max and I were suddenly awkward with each other. It had been a long time since we had effectively been father and son. I had grown up a lot in those years; I had too many secrets I did not want him to know. For his part, Max no longer quite knew how to treat me. He'd never had much gift for the paternal gesture and his lack of practice hampered him. In the silence that followed Leila's departure I could almost hear him rehearsing and rejecting fatherly ploys in his mind.

"Leila tells me you've maybe decided to study Spanish literature," he said finally, stiffly. "That's very interesting."

"Foolish, you mean," I smiled, moved by the clumsiness of his approach. Max the uncertain was a lot more likable than Max the adamant.

"Well, maybe so, in some view," he replied staunchly. "But if it's what you want to do."

"I think I may go on to be a journalist," I declared, startling myself with a notion that had never previously entered my head.

"Indeed?" Max said eagerly. "What attracts you about journalism?"

At that moment I had no idea; but, once articulated, the notion gathered surprising force. "It gets you to meet a lot of people, go to a lot of places," I replied vaguely, realizing that my knowledge of the actualities of the profession was woolly, to say the least.

Max asked if I liked writing and I said yes, thinking of all the pages I'd filled in my diary. Almost everything I had said, thought, and done since I was twelve or so was meticulously recorded. However, until that moment, I had not thought of my diary as "writing" in the literary sense. To me, it was just stuff I scribbled down to keep track of things, not a coherent narrative. Now Max, unwittingly, provoked the possibility that it might be something worthwhile.

"I'm glad you're visiting, " I said. " I've kind of missed you." Meant as a polite lie, this was truer than I had imagined. Another male presence in the house restored a natural balance. I felt as if I had been walking on a slant for years and now was coming upright, and I liked it.

While Max took a nap, Leila and I found ourselves at a loss, distanced by a sudden awkwardness. Maybe she resented my newfound sympathy for Max. For my part, my father's reappearance had thrown our household back into an earlier, more conventional mode, and that was something of a shock.

Leila compounded the stiffness between us by launching into a vehement attack on Max and his bullying. Suddenly, she was overcome by bitter memories of her long struggle to overcome his defensively contemptuous idea of her. Furiously, she detailed the endless nitpicking criticism and carping that Vivienne, "that poor girl," must have suffered. She described what she suggested was a typical day in their lives, from the not-quite-right breakfast toast to the inevitably painful business of bathing the cursing, self-pitying, semi-paralyzed man. "Why would any self-respecting woman put up with such crap?" she cried.

I kept silent during this tirade, but I did not like it. It seemed mean-spirited in the light of Max's genuine distress. He had come to us for succor and it was ungracious of her to attack him so viciously. He was only a poor, battered human being, a bird with a broken wing that had crawled inside for shelter. And I didn't care for Leila's ugly expression as she ranted on. Her face lost its natural grace, collapsing into a bitchy dissonance. Finally, unable to bear it, I made an excuse about doing my homework and escaped to my bedroom.

At my desk I opened my diary and wrote this sentence: *My father came home today, crying.* I stared at the words, trying to decipher their meaning. As a sentence, they formed a coherent sequence; as a statement, they made no sense. Rather, they made too much sense.

* * *

Temporarily, with Max's presence, our house became a conventional home, with a mommy, a daddy, and a teenage son. The contrast between this situation and the other staggered me. It compelled me to some hard thinking.

Sure, I reasoned, my life with Leila was unusual, to say the least. It was likely unique, at least in my neighborhood. Maybe, if Max had stayed home, we would have been more of an ordinary family, at least outwardly, and ordinariness helps you fit into society. As it was, I felt very much an oddity. But when all was said and done, the gains outweighed the losses. Leila was leading me in a singular adventure, one no conventional family could begin to imagine. My adoration of her flooded my heart, sweeping me along on a current of desire that made every nerve in my body electric. Put simply, Leila had addicted me to her kind of loving, and I was hooked on that female sorcery, perhaps forever. And glad of it. Maybe she had spoiled me for all other women; but that was a price I was happy to pay right then. In the end, the renewed contact with Max only served to reaffirm my total attachment to Leila.

Once I had sorted all this out in my head, I could relax and enjoy Max's visit. At the dinner table each evening I was bubbly, overriding the pervading awkwardness with irresistible good cheer. At first Leila was mired in her old-new resentments, but she was soon seduced by my gaiety. Max set aside his recent humility and entertained us with witty, snide anecdotes about his colleagues. It turned out that he loved his job and was eager to get back to his drafting table. Vivienne's dereliction was ultimately bearable, he hinted. After Leila, she was "kind of dull," he admitted ruefully. "Then all women are dull, after you, L.," he said simply, winning a wry smile.

Later, I helped Max wash himself and lifted him into bed. He weighed much less than I did, and that shocked me. But the deadness at the center of his eyes shook me even more. Catching my expression, he gripped my hand and whispered: "I'm living out my life sentence, Joel. Day by day by day..." He closed his eyes. I switched off the light and left the room.

Every evening after school that week I took Max for a walk in Palisades Park, as I used to. He waited eagerly for me to come home, saying our time together was the high point of his day. Leila provided his meals, but otherwise she acted as if he wasn't there. Any attempt to talk to her, he told me, met a blank wall. "Not that I blame her," he said, rueful as a boy whose mother snubs him for good reason.

We strolled the length of the park beside the crumbling cliffs several times, from the pier to San Vicente Boulevard. Max drank in the sights avidly, like a man whose days are numbered, eyeing the Russian women in their bulging track suits, the slim joggers pumping wrist weights as they ran, the kids skating skillfully along the pathway, the Latino families picnicking under the palms, and the supine drunken derelicts baking grizzled faces in the sun.

He talked obsessively about Leila. His tone was a complex amalgam of regret and self-justification, as if he were simultaneously blaming and excusing himself for misdeeds he could not quite define. At times an inturned bitterness burst through, transfiguring his face with an almost demonic glow.

"I can't forgive myself for failing to grasp who she is," he said in a low, harsh voice. "For not seeing how ruthless she is. No," he corrected quickly, "I mean, how absolutely true to herself she's always been. True but deadly, the man said, and that's what she's meant to me. My fault though. I wanted her too much." He turned his haggard face to me. "Do you know what it's like to want a woman too much? It's a hell, of your own making. That's what's so hard to swallow."

I said nothing, shaken by the intensity of his words, that were such a contrast in tone and substance to the ironic bitterness of his past statements about Leila. In truth, I had never seen him so passionate as he was in these confessional outbursts. As he spoke his eyes came alive for a moment, blazing with heat, before subsiding back into dead coals.

"Maybe I'm making all this up, to warm my old bones," he said with a dry laugh. "I have a theory that imaginative people invent the stories of their lives, to create the psychic atmosphere they feel they need. You take the lumber of your mundane existence and assemble it into a personal, ramshackle little temple filled with fables." He paused, gazing sightlessly at the sea. "In my case, maybe I've needed to invent a Leila to lift me out of the common rut. Maybe, in the end, she's just another self-obsessed woman with conventional shtick. Or perhaps she's both: Leila-the-boring and Leila-the-amazing. Who the fuck knows, eh?"

I nodded, not quite knowing what I was agreeing with.

"One thing's sure. In all her life she's only ever loved one person – you," Max said. "What a gift that is! And what a responsibility."

"Yeah," I muttered noncommittally.

He laughed. "An apt comment. Home, James, and don't spare the horses."

On Max's last night in our house Leila prepared a dinner of roast duck a l'orange followed by a lemon soufflé. She set the table with her wedding silver and crystal. When Max was summoned to the table his eyes grew so wide I thought they might pop right out of his head. "Wow," he whispered, deserted by fluency.

Leila, every inch the gracious hostess in an ankle-length green velvet gown and swept up coiffure, smiled benignly. "This could be the very last time we three sit down as a family," she declared. Max blinked, wandering what she might mean, but let it go.

After dinner we lolled at the table, relishing full bellies. "I forgot what a grand chef you can be when you try," Max murmured. "When we were first together you used to surprise me with some new menu every Saturday, remember?"

"Until you told me to `try simplicity for once,' "Leila retorted.

"I'm a meat-and-spuds man at heart," Max apologized. "You were too rich for my blood."

"Or something," Leila shrugged.

"Talking of too rich," Max said awkwardly, lowering his head. "I may have to make some cuts in the alimony." Leila's eyes flared, and Max hurried on. "It's a recession, the college is cutting back, including my pay, so supporting two households is a stretch. Temporary, they say. Just for a while." Max shot a worried glance at Leila. "Maybe you can get a job?" he suggested tremulously.

"`Get a job'? Are you out of your mind? I'm a mother! That's my `job.' "

"Just for a while," Max mumbled. "Till things pick up."

"No."

"Can't you give an inch or two? Please?"

"I can get a job, after school or weekends," I cut in, desperate to head off a bruising confrontation. "There's a burger stand on Arizona that hires high school kids."

"You'll do no such thing," Leila replied. "I won't have my son slinging burgers in some street joint. It's degrading."

"Truly, I don't mind," I pleaded.

"But I do," Leila retorted crisply.

"Well, I guess I could do some moonlighting," Max said wearily. "There's a company in Oakland that farms out drafting chores. Tedious, low-grade stuff – but what the hell?" He raised his wine glass. "*Salud y pesetas*," he toasted. "*Leche en las tetas y fuerza en las castanetas*."

"That sounds gross," Leila said, but she drank her wine.

Later, when I was putting Max to bed, he asked me to get a packet from his bedside table. "It's for you," he said.

I opened the package. Inside was a fading cheap silver-coated sports plaque mounted on a shield-shaped wooden block. Under a pair of crossed tennis rackets an engraved inscription read: "University of California at Los Angeles, 1963, Men's Singles Championship, Won by Max Bajamonde." "To remind you I wasn't always a cripple," he said lightly.

I hugged him, hard, and tucked him in for the night. He was snoring gently before I reached the door. Next morning he returned to Berkeley.

fourteen

"FOR AS LONG as I can recall, my most intimate things were my nightmares," Leila said. "Now you are my most intimate thing."

"Am I, really?" I queried, swelling with pride.

We were lying naked in bed after lovemaking. Since Max's departure, Leila's passionate need for closeness had intensified. For weeks after we slept together almost every night.

"You're the only person in the world who really knows me and still likes me," she said, stroking my cheek. "You're my one-and-only very special friend."

I wanted to say, lots of people would like you if you let them, but I knew it wasn't true. People had strong reactions to Leila, and she to them, so simple liking was seldom possible.

"I don't like myself much," she went on, moving her stroking hand to my chest. "All in all, I'm just not a likable person."

"Don't say that," I countered. "I like you very much."

"I know, and that's precious," she said. Her fingers slid over my belly, tracing the contours of my navel. "You're a real sweetheart."

Her fingers circling my groin distracted me from her words. Sensing something extraordinary was about to happen, my blood began to race, driven by my hammering heart. Leila leaned over me and took my penis in her mouth.

A shivering excitement riddled me from head to toe. In an instant my cock was stiff, conjured into rigidity by her licking tongue. Looking down, I saw Leila's dark head resting on my belly like a furry animal. I clenched my fists and stared fixedly at the ceiling, trying to pretend I wasn't about to explode with feelings so delirious I could not bear to have them either stop or continue. Drowning in the wetness of her mouth, my penis became all of me, compressed into one tense column. The orgasm when it came sparked at the nape of my neck, shot down my spine, and leapt into her throat.

Leila raised her head and turned to face me. Her lips looked swollen, her eyes glistened. "I love you, Joel," she murmured. "Now you know how much." She smiled beatifically, rested her cheek on my stomach, and closed her eyes. In a moment she was asleep, her warm breath tickling my skin.

Shattered, still panting, I struggled to grasp the significance of her act. Clearly, we had breached a new dimension of intimacy, a core of brazen closeness. Now she owned all of me, and I was overjoyed, and a little scared, fearing that nothing was left of me that was purely my own. I could not think it all through, and didn't really try, so I just pulled the covers up over us both and dozed off.

My mind was numb for days after. I felt as if I had fallen into a hole in the fabric of the world, dropped through a sudden gap in the ground. I stumbled through the hours as if a spotlight were picking me out, running its hard brightness over my bare skin, exposing every nerve to public view. And then, in yet another twist, I was swollen with a huge pride, as if I had conquered the stars.

Schoolwork was a blur, and several times Mr. Morales pulled me up sharply when I gave an unfocused or messy answer to one of his questions. My befuddlement reached a nadir when he asked me, abruptly, why Don Quixote chose Dulcinea del Toboso as his damsel in distress, and I answered, "Because he loved her." In punishment, Morales had me write out Chapter One of "Don Quixote" in Spanish and English, underlining the passage that begins: "At last, when his wits were gone beyond repair..."

Where Leila had entranced me, she now possessed me, totally. Her consuming presence filled every crevice of my brain and body, and for the first time I really understood the phrase, "you are my life." I gave my existence over to her keeping, wandering around with a moonstruck expression, my face glazed with inwardness. My wits were, indeed, gone beyond repair. Leila was greedy for sex and love, and I was swept along in the tides of her desire. At times I felt I was turning into mush, my sinews and muscles made muddy by streams of lust. I no longer knew where I ended and she began. Wherever I turned she was there, filling my mind's eye.

However, despite our extraordinary intimacy, we were still shy with each other in some ways. For instance, she refused to let me wash her back when she was in the bath, or observe her when she was at her dressing table making up her face and combing her hair. She claimed that bathing and doing her toilette were essentially private rituals, something a woman needed to do alone, without anyone else watching, even me. “That's when I really let my hair down,” she said, and though she was smiling I knew she was serious. As a child I used to love watching her comb her jet-black locks, that always reminded me of Rapunzel in the fairy tale, who let down her hair for her lover, and I missed being allowed to share this voluptuous moment. All the same, I was awkward when Leila came into the bathroom to scrub my back, as she used to when I was little. When I protested the unfairness, she claimed “maternal privilege,” and I had to let her have her way in this, as in everything else.

Given our absolute intimacy, the announcement she made one evening over dinner was a bombshell. “I'm going to live in Paris,” she said, deliberately casual.

“Paris?” I said, barely comprehending. “For a visit? Can I come, too?”

“To live,” she repeated. “Alone.”

“I don't—“

“It's all arranged. I've booked a room in a small pension in Montparnasse, I have my plane ticket. In ten days, I'm up and away.”

Noting my dumb, blank stare, she continued. “Max is moving back to L.A., into the house, with you. He lost his job in Berkeley, but there's an opening in the campus architect's office at UCLA. It's an economy measure, you see,” she went on chattily. “He'll give me an allowance, and save money by supporting one household only. Paris is cheap, so everyone wins.” She brushed my cheek. “When you graduate high school, you can come and spend a year with me over there. Won't that be fun? A great adventure!”

I was speechless, so robbed of voice I felt I might never say another word. The million things I wanted to say congealed in a messy ball inside my skull. “Paris?” I repeated, as if the city's name held a clue I was missing.

“Paris,” she echoed dreamily. “I've always wanted to live there again. Maybe try to paint, seriously. There's an artist in me somewhere, I know there is."

"But you said Paris made you miserable!"

"That's history," she shrugged. "Isn't it wonderful? Aren't you happy for me?"

I gaped at her helplessly. As the impact of her decision began to hit home, I struggled to hold down the dinner that threatened to rise up and choke me. *Be a man*, I hissed inwardly. *Be a man!* But it's hard to hang onto manhood when your life is being trashed.

What truly shook me was the discovery that Leila had been secretly scheming this betrayal while we were lovers. Suddenly, everything she had said to me, done with me, was turned to dust. Our very intimacy was discredited, degraded into a great big lie. For weeks, maybe months, Leila, in collusion with Max, had been stealthily contriving all this, both of them leaving me completely in the dark, as if I were a goddam baby. A surge of childish resentment reinforced my rage as it dawned on me that I had been nothing but a dumb dupe. A real *dope*. Lost in my erotic pipe dream, I'd trusted Leila with my life, forgetting that she was a self-obsessed, utterly selfish woman – a sorceress with her own diabolical schemes. I felt like a character in a bad folk tale, an innocent seduced by a witch seeking fresh blood for her foul stew. An innocent all too willing to be seduced.

How could I have been so gullible? Worse – how could I have se myself up so eagerly for deception?

Tides of shame and anger washed through me, clashing and confusing, leaving me shipwrecked on a desolate shore. Most desolate o all was the realization that, in ten days, Leila would be out of my life vanished from my world. *In ten days Leila would vanish*... The idea wa unimaginable. Didn't she know that, without her, I didn't exist? So ho could she just disappear?

None of my agony seemed to impinge on her awareness, however Blithe, consumed with self-delight, she chattered on about her imag ined routine in Montparnasse – the life of an expatriate with artsy pre tensions, or so it seemed to me, even then. She was giving up the gol of our intimacy for the dross of an idiotic "adventure," and her mon strous stupidity and selfishness struck me dumb. In truth, her word were so shallow and so stupid I was ashamed of and for her. Abruptl in the middle of her chatter, I rose and hurried to the bathroom to puke my guts out.

I washed my face, staring at my reflection in the mirror. My life was shattered but the glass was still intact, showing me a pale visage that seemed to have aged in an instant. Yes, I am a man, I told the reflection. Her callousness has made me one. Maybe that's her going-away gift to me? I thought miserably.

Determined not to show weakness, not to her, I wandered back into the dining room and poured myself a glass of wine. "*A votre santé*," I toasted.

"*Bien sur!*" she cried delightedly. "Are you happy for me, Joelly?"

"Absolutely, Leila," I replied.

She ran to kiss me on the cheek, tousled my hair fondly, and began to collect the dinner dishes, humming. *Mierda pura*, I muttered under my breath as I watched her. *Mierda absolutamente pura*…

Lying in bed later, I wondered if Leila would have the gall to come to me that night. Would she be so self-absorbed that she could ignore my resentment and revulsion at her imminent desertion? The sheer astonishment of it all alternately chilled and heated my blood, and I resolved to tell her to go to hell if she so much as put her nose around my door. Yet I yearned with every nerve to have her close.

In the dark I felt my heart shriveling into a frozen capsule filled with rancor, a radioactive core radiating enough animosity to poison half the world. Now Leila had confirmed a lesson that Max, in his stumbling, shamefaced fashion, had tried to impart for years: that bitterness and disappointment were more reliable life companions than love and hope. But in Max, such pessimism was watered down to mere sourness. Enrique's black-hearted ferocity was more richly venomous, it seemed to me. His favorite quote echoed in my head: "Silly fool, learn that the blind man's boy has to know one point more than the devil…" I had certainly been the blind man's – or rather, woman's – boy, and now it was time to beat the devil.

Leila had just given me the gift of fury, I told myself, trembling in the night shadows. In the space of a few hours one form of intensity had displaced another, a newfound fierceness usurping the passionate loving I had foolishly imagined would last me a lifetime. Yes, I resolved, I'll loathe Leila furiously and forever; *ferocidad* rather than *gracia* would drive my future.

Still, I wondered whether I really possessed enough passionate disgust to detest her forever, with the necessary ruthless fervor. Maybe, when it came right down to it, I was by nature more compelled by grace than fury. At last, exhausted, I fell into a dead man's sleep, hoping I would awake from the nightmare to a loving past rather than a lonely future.

"I know I've disappointed you, " Leila said next day at breakfast.

I glanced up from my cereal bowl at her earnestly concerned face. "But you forgive yourself, eh?" I said. It was a nasty retort, a spasm of spite that gave me a strange frisson of pleasure.

She sat down opposite me at the kitchen counter. "I have to explain something, something you already know, I guess."

"What?" I said rudely.

"All my life I've felt unloved and unloving. Then you showed me I could love and be loved, wholly, with all heart. That's your gift to me, Joel, and I'm eternally grateful. Now I have to move on, become my own person, don't you see?"

I wanted to tell her that what I saw before me right then was a woman who had killed me. But that would have been too cruel. Worse, it would make me vulnerable to her pity, and that would be unbearable.

"Do me a favor when you're in Paris," I said in an even tone.

"Anything," she asked eagerly. "Tell me."

"Please don't phone or write to me, ever."

Her jaw dropped. Before she could recover, I snatched up by bag and ran off to school.

* * *

I hardly remember the actual events of the following week. My head was too charged with rancor to register much else. Max moved in and Leila packed; at least, I presume she did, since the day came when her bags were piled up beside the front door as she waited for the cab to take her to the airport.

She tried to confront me several times, but I always avoided her. I could not bear to look at her perfidious, hateful face. When I focused my mind on her the one word *bitch* repeated over and over – *bitch, bitch, bitch* – like the needle scratch of the old Edith Piaf discs she liked to play. It occurred to me that those songs might have been the genesis of her idiotic yearning for the Parisian boulevards and brasseries in whose mythical milieu she hoped to become her "own person."

Then, suddenly, she was gone. I hid in my room with my pillow over my head so as not to hear her calling my name in farewell. An hour later I went downstairs to find Max ensconced in the living room, like a prince who has just reclaimed his rightful realm. "Men only, eh?" he said, grinning. We ordered Chinese take-out for supper, gorging ourselves on moo shoo pork and crab with black bean sauce. Afterward, we left the dirty dishes on the table and swilled beer from cans while watching NCAA basketball on television.

"This is the life, no?" Max said, belching happily. "Footloose and female-free."

I shrugged. To me, we were mimicking a beer ad, badly.

As the cans piled up on the coffee table and Max grew more tipsy, he began to reminisce about the topic that obsessed us both: life with Leila. Once again, he told me the story of how he and Leila met and married. "A simple case of force majeure," he said. "Act of God, excusing us from sense." He seemed to have forgotten his previous confession of passion. I listened to his ramblings with half an ear, stupefied by alcohol and anguish.

"Funny thing was," Max rolled on, "she always seemed pissed off with me after we made love, even though she seemed to enjoy it at the time. Maybe she was faking all the while? Or maybe she just resented being aroused?" He shook his head. "A mystery, like everything else about that peculiar woman."

Bored and angry, I was on the verge of blurting out the story of my love affair with Leila. I wanted to shock him, hurt him, hurt myself, sting myself to death with the venomous truth. Instead, I viciously imagined his expression if I were to tell him I had been screwing my mother. Then, in a burst of drunken remorse, I accused myself of becoming a victim of my own self-pity, and being a victim wasn't good, as Leila had pointed out. In the end I was reduced to the security of that cold raft of rage Leila had bequeathed me as her going-away present. I clung to it like a drowning man.

"I should've given you a better mother," Max was saying. "Not that she neglected you. She always kept you well nourished and clean. She has clean habits...But all that comes from willpower, for she's not really maternal."

I gaped at him, bleary-eyed. "You're joking!" I exclaimed.

He shook his head. "Not really maternal," he repeated solemnly.

Wild laughter bubbled in my chest, bursting from my mouth in a hilarious howl.

Max reared back, taken by surprise. "What's so damn amusing?" he said, thick-voiced.

His bemused expression provoked a paroxysm. I rolled around on the couch, clutching my stomach, lashed by laughter.

Offended and concerned, Max shushed me. When I was quiet again, I looked him straight in the eye. "You know, Max," I drawled. "You don't know diddly, and that's a fact."

"Is that right?" he retorted pugnaciously.

"Neither do I, come to that. Let's face it, dad, we've both been screwed by the same woman."

"Don't be vulgar."

"You don't know the half of it," I said grimly.

Rising unsteadily, I grasped his wheelchair and rolled him to his ground floor bedroom. I helped him out of his clothes into his pajamas and eased him into bed. "Sleep tight, don't let the bugs bite," I murmured, kissing him on the forehead. He was snoring before I left the room. Drifting back to the living room, I collapsed onto the couch, lying transfixed by the muted TV and its flickering foolishness.

Since Leila's departure, the atmosphere in the house had immediately altered. I racked my brains, attempting to pin down the difference, but its quality eluded me. It just wasn't her place any longer, and the room's still air carried that quiet, fateful message.

Who am I without her? I silently asked the air. And the answer came back in a whisper: *nothing...*

Ferocity & Grace

fifteen

For months after Leila abandoned me, my dreams were full of murder. My nights were charged with gory images and fantasies of mangled corpses. In these nightmares I never actually saw myself committing such crimes, but my collusion was obvious, and I was racked by waves of guilt and shame. These nighttime orgies were supplemented by impromptu daytime reveries in which I planned Leila's death in detail, relishing her agony as I plunged a knife into her chest or struck her with a steel pipe and beat her senseless. Night and day my mind was stunned by ferocious, bloody visions that brought me no comfort.

Alternating with these ferocious dreams were moments of vivid recollection of our lovemaking. The memories were so intense I could smell her skin and actually feel myself penetrating her body. These episodes happened suddenly, anywhere, instantly drowning me in desire and a helpless, hopeless yearning.

God, how I hated her! God, how I wanted her! It was agony.

Questions plagued my head: How had I failed her? Why had I made her need to run away?

Why??

The fateful syllable resounded over and over. When I struggled to think it through clearly, I recognized yet again that an adolescent like me could never have satisfied a woman like Leila for long. I was a mere kid, I knew nothing. All I had to offer was my total heart and soul, and that was clearly not enough.

But it should have been.

Surely, I reasoned, no human being could ever ask more of another than to offer every fiber of his being. Maybe more mature men could have given Leila things I couldn't, but none of them would ever love her as I did. No one has ever loved as I do, I told myself, and though I knew it was foolish to say so, I believed it all the same. Yet she had simply turned her back on me and walked away.

The pain of it split me from head to toe. Sometimes I felt I was about to crack in two, like a tree struck by lightning. Guilt, fury, shame, yearning flashed along my nerves, and at times my hatred for Leila was so pure it was almost spiritual, a kind of holy rage. I did not want to go on living, but I lacked the will to kill myself, to fling myself off the Palisades cliff edge like poor Jack, and I cursed myself for a coward.

Marvelously enough, Max seemed to notice none of this. He was so happy to be home, so pleased with himself for having reclaimed his domain, that my miseries escaped his attention. At supper, prepared by Clara Ortiz, a housekeeper he hired, he chatted cheerfully to me about his day at the office and the people he had encountered. Sometimes he asked about my schoolwork, but absently, assured that I was an excellent student. Other times he blithely conjectured about Leila's life in Paris, unwittingly tormenting me with images of her strolling the boulevards arm-in-arm with some suave swain.

For a long time I never opened any of the many letters Leila wrote me. Just the look of the envelopes made me shudder, and I tossed them aside or threw them in the trash. I did not want to read her excuses or know any details of her life over there. Or rather, I did want to know the details, if only to drive them like nails into my flesh. But I resisted this urge to self-flagellation. The dreams were bad enough.

The one time I weakened and actually opened one of her letters it left me so riled up I wanted to jump right out of my skin.

A photo fell out: Leila in front of the Coupole, a perky black straw cloche tilted way over on the side of her head, a la Piaf. The inscription read: "To My Darling Joel, With Love." The cheeky insouciance of it made me scowl.

The letter in her spidery, sloping hand covered one page.

Dearest Joel,

I am writing this on the terrace of La Coupole. When I look up I see a magical world, one that has lived up to my dreams more wonderfully than I ever hoped. I am in Paris! Alone...Alone. That word must hit you hard, coming from me. I did many marvelously terrible things to you, my dear, things a mother should never do to her son. Worst of all, I abandoned you when you needed me most. But you see, it was your life or mine, and in the end we're all selfish monsters.

You remember that story I used to read to you when you were little? The one about Big Worm. You loved it, especially the part where Big Worm gobbles up the whole world, to fill his alimentary canal with everything that exists. "I'm just a bowel with legs on!" he says, gulping away. A strange story for a kid to love, unless you figure that kids know people. I swallowed you whole because I had to, to survive. That's me, Big Worm to the life.

This is not an apology. I make no apology for saving my own life. Neither can it really serve as an explanation, for such things can never be explained. They just are, that's all.

I could say I love you and it would be true, but irrelevant. I needed you. I took you. I left you. End of story, except for the consequences. However, I think there's a part of you that can grasp what I am saying: the part that was crazy about Big Worm. The part that sets you apart, as it does me. But remember this, always: you are and forever will be the most important person in my life; no man will ever mean as much to me as you do. You are my son, my blood – at least, half of you is. Whether you choose to deny that part or honor it is up to you.

I wish— Well, everything, for you, my lovely boy.

A bientôt, Leila.

"You bitch!" I shouted, bouncing the hard word off my bedroom walls. After that one time, I left Leila's letters unread.

* * *

Adolf Hitler claimed that he went the way Providence dictated with the assurance of a sleepwalker, and for years after Leila departed, I, too, was a sleepwalker, but without the guidance of Providence or any sense of assurance. I hardly remember graduating high school, and the following three undergraduate years at UCLA majoring in Spanish Literature remain a dim blur. The energy generated by my aborted passion for Leila seemed to have burned out my nerves, leaving me stunned and emotionally bankrupt. It was as if I had concentrated all my real life into those few intense years, living way beyond my means, way overdrawing my spirit. Through those years Max and I lived like a couple of lonely guys growing old together – "a couple of Leila-survivors," in his ironic phrase. Max spent his evenings playing chess at the local chess club, and sometimes with me, living out his life sentence.

It occurred to me sometimes that perhaps Leila had cut me loose so brutally not only to become her own person but also to allow me to be myself. Perhaps there was an undercurrent of maternal compassion in her abrupt cruelty. After all, there was likely no real future for us anywhere, except maybe in heaven, or hell, and no easy way to resolve our erotic connection. Maybe she had used a sharp knife to cut the cord for my sake as well as hers. Perhaps there was a certain grace in her ferocity.

All the same, I still hated her. She had left me fundamentally crippled by that old desire, and everything I felt and knew after she went away seemed essentially a postscript to my real life story. Leila – my mother, my lover – had touched me with magic. A damaging, deadly magic, to be sure, but magic nonetheless. A kind of emotional *cojismo* seemed to be the price I had to pay for having experienced more than I deserved – the Faustian bargain fate had prepared for me in all its malicious generosity.

Sometimes I fantasized about traveling to Paris to surprise her, confront her, find out what she had done with her precious freedom that had cost me so much misery. Her address, written on the backs of her envelopes, was given as 13 Citè Falguière, Paris 15. In the local library I found a street map of Paris and located the address as a narrow alley in Montparnasse, in the same district as her beloved Coupole. In a guidebook I read that the artist Chaim Soutine once had a studio in the Citè Falguière in the 1920s, and in my mind's eye I saw Leila's place as a bohemian hideaway.

Leila-in-Paris was all Frenchy, I surmised, rolling the word's crunchy, bitter taste in my mouth. Her kind of hardheaded selfishness was very French, I decided, remembering Madame Bovary, and Jean Renoir's movie, *The Rules Of The Game*. I decided that she had reverted to her origins, clothing herself in an armor of savoir-faire, grown mean in the glamorous way the French have perfected. I imagined myself standing before her Paris doorway, narrowing the physical distance between Leila and myself from around six thousand miles to less than a couple of meters. The arc between us was dramatically contracted, to the point where a single spark could leap across the narrow gap and ignite old agonies and desires. Does she sense my proximity, I wondered? Is there a relic of our old connection that may alert her to my presence? When that door cracked open – what?

At that point in the fantasy my mind recoiled. I just could not bear the thought of actually setting eyes on her.

* * *

When I completed my B.A., Max generously offered to send me to Granada to attend a course in Spanish literature at the local university for two semesters in the fall and spring. It would be my first trip to Europe, to the town Enrique was born in, to the continent of my mother's birth, and her image flashed through my mind the instant Max suggested it. Does everything in my goddam life have to be Leila-centric? I told myself testily. Is she the navel of the world? But whether I liked it or not, she was, and always would be the heart of my life.

Mr. Morales was delighted. As I said goodbye to him he pressed a map of Spain into my hands, marking the places I should visit on a literary pilgrimage to the regions that gave birth to Cervantes, Machado, Quevedo and, Góngora. Excitedly, he reminded me that Granada was the home of Lorca, and also many marvelous medieval Arab and Hebrew poets from the time when the caliphs ruled Andalusia. "If you want to understand the unique Spanish soul you'll have to visit La Mancha most of all," he said. "And you'll have to see a *corrida*." The bullfight, he explained with shining eyes, was the epitome of the Spanish soul, which he described as "a hard acceptance of life's brutish nature, balanced by a brave style."

I touched down on Spanish soil that October with my head resounding to the tune of Morales's fancies, my heart measuring the distance between Madrid and Paris. Plunging eagerly into a world orchestrated by the hard consonants and sharp music of *Castellano puro*, I rushed around the capital for a few days, trying to see everything at once.

In the Prado, shuffling through cavernous rooms populated by Velasquez, Bosch, and Zúburan, I turned a corner and came face to face with Goya's sequence of etchings, "The Disasters of War." Those small works, most of them no larger than seven inches by four, stunned me. Suddenly I was confronted by an absolute ferocity of terror matched by an equally absolute ferocity of disgust. In one etching, titled "That is Worse," Goya showed mutilated and dismembered men impaled on trees. An armless and legless victim had a branch stuck up his anus. The depiction was political and particular, provoked by the atrocities committed by Napoleon's troops in Spain, but the revulsion was cosmic and almost exhilarating in its unflinching contemplation of naked horror.

After "The Disasters of War," I was transfixed by Goya's canvas, "Saturn Devouring one of his Children" – the depiction of a horrible, hairy god caught in the act of tearing a headless human corpse limb from limb with his bloody, gaping maw.

Something about Saturn's naked ferocity reminded me of Leila. For a moment I imagined her face skulking behind Saturn's. As I stared at the canvas I seemed to see her in the Titan's image, equally voracious, equally unappeasable, as possessed as he was by a primal darkness of spirit. Both of them had consumed their own children.

Staggering out into the harsh sunlight, I was overcome by an urgent need to escape Madrid's hectic atmosphere. Suddenly, the capital city seemed noisy and pompous, essentially artificial, and I wanted to get the hell out, into the "real" Spain. And the real Spain, as Morales had said, was La Mancha.

The next day I took a bus to Quixote country, to visit the spare little cottage that Quixote's Dulcinea is supposed to have inhabited in the hardscrabble hamlet of El Toboso. I stopped by the ruined Venta de Quesada, where the Don had himself dubbed a knight by the innkeeper and two loose "lasses of the district." I walked up the windswept, garbage-strewn hillside outside Campo de Criptana to see the host of conical, black-capped windmills the old knight had taken for the flailing giants he had challenged to combat. If ever a landscape epitomized the Spanish fusion between a radical harshness and a graceful spirit it was La Mancha's rocky, treeless steppes rolling away to the edge of eternity – a blank horizon under a serene blue-white heaven, a timeless territory where peasants still squeezed survival from stones.

Garbed in a nun-like black, the La Manchan women obsessively swept their whitewashed thresholds and cobblestone sidewalks with straw brooms, while out in the fields corn farmers cracked their plows on stubborn boulders, or broke their backs in dusty vineyards to produce a harsh Valdepeñas which scoured my throat and heated my stomach. At dusk, when the sun relented, the old men tossed iron *petanca* disks at wooden pegs while the priests slid like lizards toward the oversized church in the plaza, whose steeple was home to scruffy stork nests. In this stark landscape, in his lonely middle age, Quixote had conceived "the strangest idea that ever occurred to any madman in this world." Giving up a tranquil but boring life, the skinny, skew-witted country gent set out to try the caliber of his soul against the terrors of the world. Could there be any more poignant instance of one man's struggle to bring grace to this hard life?

In one La Mancha village I watched an impromptu *novillada*, a pick-up bullfight put on by teenage would-be matadors in the central square. An improvised barrier of wooden cafe chairs and tables was set up around the plaza's perimeter. The angry young bulls, as immature as their opponents, were let loose one at a time, and the *novilleros* went into battle taunted by a jeering crowd. In their bravado the boys took risks their more seasoned and wary seniors would never have essayed. They flung their capes at the bulls and leaned right in over the animal's horns to place the barbed *banderillas*. Their attempts at mock killing were inept and several young men ended up skewering themselves, much to the crowd's glee. But they were treated like heroes afterward, and plied with wine until they puked.

A sow was slaughtered for the feast that followed – a savage public act performed with surprising delicacy. Before he slit it from gizzard to groin, the butcher covered the sow's sex with a clean white napkin, to preserve the beast's modesty. The sharp blade split the sow's belly as if it were an overstuffed sausage, spilling gore and guts into the zinc tub below, and the animal whimpered like a woman as it gave up the ghost. The butcher skillfully dismembered the pig without once removing the napkin, leaving the sow the grace of her dignity to the very last moment.

As I watched this elegant butchery, I wondered what the old Don would have made of it. He might have tried to rescue the sow, imagining it to be yet another damsel in distress. Or he could have admired the butcher's skill, appreciating his decency in regard to the animal's public exposure. Perhaps he had seen female heretics immolated at an auto-da-fé, and might have compared the pig's respectful treatment to the rude way those unfortunate women were handled.

In the same village I first came face to face with that prime fusion of brutality and grace: the image of Christ on his cross.

Until that day I had never entered a Christian church nor seen a Crucifixion, other than in art books, where the religious aspect of Jesus' agony was subsumed by aesthetics. Max had inherited Enrique's anti-clerical prejudice toward the Church, born out of the fires of the Spanish Civil War and his *marrano* lineage, and their antipathy had filtered down to me. Besides, my very Jewish revulsion against the notion of a Son of God in human form had long since prejudiced me against such icons. In truth, the whole idea of showing a holy savior nailed to a piece of wood seemed utterly barbaric. So when I wandered into that small, white, empty building, seeking shade on a hot summer's day, and found the representation of a crucified man, I was taken by surprise.

The wooden sculpture suspended over the altar was about my size. The carving was blunt but powerful, as if a naive artist had instinctively simplified the crucified body's form into a pure rendering of pain. Hung from nails driven through his palms, the figure slumped against the wooden beams, his potbelly like a ball of iron weighing down his arms and torso. Under a faded gilt loincloth was a pair of skinny legs, dangling from work-worn, bony knees that could have belonged to a peasant or artisan who had exhausted his body and spirit in hard labor. Chips of blue paint resembling drool dribbled from the corner of Jesus' mouth. His head, surrounded by a scalloped halo, was a dead weight dragging on the scrawny neck.

In that quiet, cool room, with its black-beamed, pitched ceiling, its walls washed by the raw color of crude stained glass windows, its oaken pews rubbed smooth by generations of worshipful bottoms, the nailed-up man made a potent point. The La Manchan carver who had created him seemed to say that, if Jesus had died quietly in his bed, a retired carpenter living at home with his wife and children, he would have been no more than a minor prophet in a time and place in which such self-proclaimed messiahs were a dime a dozen. Instead, the violence he had suffered and transcended had generated a lasting faith.

"Señor, quería Usted confesarse?"

The voice jerked me from my long reverie. Swinging around, I saw the village *cura* watching me. His priestly black gown had the purple sheen of a garment washed a thousand times, and his lean face had something of the hallowing-through-pain aspect of the Christ over his altar.

"*No gracias, padre,*" I replied. "*Soy Hebreo.*"

The priest's eyes widened in shocked disbelief. "*Hebreo!*" he gasped. "*Con pezuña?*"

At first I didn't understand what he was asking me. The word, *pezuña*, was unfamiliar. But the way his eyes were fixed on my feet gave me a clue as to what he was after. If the country priest had never encountered a Jew before, outside of the folklore demonizing us as Messiah-killers with cloven hooves and forked tails, I reckoned he would want me to prove I was Hebraic by showing him my diabolical heels.

This perception was confirmed by his next command, "*Móstreme sus pies!*" - "Show me your feet!"

Caught between anger and amusement, I decided to accommodate the old man's simple-minded curiosity. Solemnly, I removed my Nikes and my socks to reveal my naked feet. The priest stared at them avidly for a full minute, searching for the devilish hooves.

"*Pezuña no hay,*" he muttered, deeply disappointed. "*Hebreo no es.*"

My Jewishness categorically denied, I could only shrug, pull on my socks and shoes, and leave the church.

sixteen

Returning to Madrid, I bought a train ticket for Granada. I wanted to travel slowly through southern Spain, through the first fall rains, watching the raw landscape roll by the windows.

Searching for the right platform in the chaos of Atocha Station's echoing iron cavern, I was startled to hear a woman shout my name. Though the voice was distorted by the general uproar, I instantly recognized its distinctive lilt. Swinging around, I saw Rory rushing toward me. The next moment I was clutched to her bosom in a fierce hug. Then, shoving me away a pace, she gazed avidly at my face. "J.," she murmured, and a glaze of tears smudged her eyes.

"R! What are you doing here?"

"Backpacking around Europe. And you're heading for Granada."

"You knew?"

"I knew."

I stared at her, openly amazed, realizing that she was the one person in the world I really liked to see just then. It had been more than three years since we had last met, at our high school graduation, before she went to Stanford. Gazing at her lovely, open face, I was overcome with an intense, belated sense of loss.

"I love you, J.," she said. The quiet words, reaching my ear through the surrounding racket, made me shiver.

"Yes, Aurora," I said, using her full name for the very first time.

"'Aurora' – I like that!" she giggled. Taking my hand, she said, "Let's go."

"Go? Where to?"

"Granada."

"Just like that?"

"Not really. I was lying in wait for you. Your dad told me you'd be traveling by train, so I've been coming here every day for the past week. Look, I even have my pack, ready to go."

I gaped at her. "Aren't you—?"

"Scared? Shitless! But I love you. So what can I do?"

I had no answer to that.

The train ride lasted all day, and all day Rory sat glued to my side, gripping my hand. We passed through rainy squalls into gaps of hard sunlight, the wheels on the old RENFE car clicking the miles through silvery olive groves and patches of barren earth. With an effort the ancient engine chugged up the incline toward the Sierra Nevada and Granada's high plateau. All the way we hardly spoke, thinking our own thoughts, relishing our mutual rediscovery. It was as if we had uncovered a lost treasure we had misplaced.

The rain was pelting down when we reached Granada, and, dripping wet, we ran to a shabby pension near the station and took a room for the night. In the huge, cold chamber, its floors and walls lined with cracked Moorish tiles, we immediately stripped naked and crawled under the covers of the rickety iron bed. The moment I took Rory in my arms the warm memories of our long-past lovemaking heated my flesh. As I entered her I pushed my tongue deep into her mouth to complete our connection, and we came together with shuddering sobs.

Afterward, I lifted the covers and gazed at Rory's body, reviewing it from neck to knee. "What're you doing, J.?" she murmured sleepily. In response, I quoted Lorca's line: "*Verte desnuda es recordar la tierra...* 'To see you naked is to remember the earth.' " Indeed, seeing her there was a remembrance of something fundamentally female, something I had sorely missed these past years.

* * *

Our first view of the Alhambra was through mist. As Rory and I walked up the wooded slope toward the Moorish palace silky vapors shrouded the high stone walls, isolating the hilltop fortress from the town below. Moisture streaked the citadel's crude red ramparts, and the jagged complex resembled a giant geode whose rough skin conceals an inner crystalline brilliance. We strolled the Alhambra battlements alone, feeling like lords of the sky as we looked down upon the damp rooftops of Granada. We took shelter from wild winds under the dome of the Hall of the Two Sisters, in a cave of golden honeycomb vaults with melting stucco stalactites and whirling tile patterns. In sunny interludes between showers we wandered through the Court of Lions, following the water channels cut in the floor, admiring the light-footed structure floating on lacy porticoes as fountains bubbled with sweet whispers beneath the intermittent roaring of rain and wind. It was an enraptured realm, a transcendent elegance suspended between earth and heaven, gracc incarnate.

Yet there was a melancholy resonance inherent in the architecture, a sense of paradise lost in that marvelous museum of a palace where Arab poets once sang of glory. Moved by this underlying strain of sadness, I recited Lorca's elegy: *" 'Nadie comprendía el perfume/ de la oscura magnolia de tu vientre./ Nadie sabia que martirizabas/ un colibrí de amor entre los dientes....'* 'Nobody grasped the perfume/ of the dark magnolia of your womb./ Nobody knew you martyred/ love's hummingbird between your teeth.' "

"Ah," Rory nodded. "Always that lady."

It took me a moment to interpret her remark. "You mean, *Leila?*" I exclaimed. "What's she got to do with it?"

"Everything. Tell me about her."

"Nothing to tell. Haven't seen or heard from her in over six years. Haven't wanted to."

"I'll tell you something," Rory murmured. "She made you a terrific lover."

That night, snuggling in the dark after making love in our cold pension room, Rory gently led me to talk about Leila. Softened by the close warmth of her body and the lovely female huskiness of her voice, I gradually opened up. Soon everything spilled out, every last detail of my love affair with Leila.

I could not make out Rory's expression in the dim light of the streetlamp coming through the chamber's grimy window, but the frequent catches in the rhythm of her breath suggested both deep sympathy and profound shock. Right then, however, I didn't really care how she might react. I simply wanted to say it all, not only for the relief of confessing, but to lay everything out before her. If we were to be real lovers she had to know it all.

When, finally, I ran out of words, Rory was silent for a while. Her face was shadowed but the shifts in the pattern of her breathing revealed the intensity of her thoughts. For an instant I regretted my honesty, fearing it might have been too much for her. After all, how could anyone else understand how much I'd loved Leila, and how much I hated her for abandoning me.

"I'm surprised," Rory said at last.

"Well—" I began.

"What I mean is – you should've been badly damaged by all this. Emotionally impaired," she added, slipping into the jargon of a premed. "Incest victims usually are psychologically crippled, but you're remarkably intact. I know that from the loving way you are with me."

I tried to say something, but she put a hand on my lips to silence me, and I waited while she grappled with her thoughts. "What astonishes me is that I have no sense that you actually are the victim in all this. You're not a basket case. On the contrary, you're a real lover. A wonderful lover...How can that be? How can you have come out of such a potentially crippling experience without being twisted totally out of shape? Or," she added quickly, "are you so twisted that I just can't see it?"

"I don't feel 'twisted.' But I do feel—" I broke off, searching for the right word. "Kind of, well, suspended."

"Huh?"

Rory's query hung in the air expecting clarification, but I did not know how to continue. The word, "suspended," had surprised me, too, yet it seemed somehow right.

"I think I understand," Rory said.

"You do?"

"That extraordinary, intense, amazing, dangerous time with Leila must've left you hanging. I mean, after that, how do you learn to live and love like the rest of us low-key mortals? You know stuff," she rushed on, "that I will never know, could never know, don't want to know. Leila led you to places I can hardly imagine – hardly want to imagine!" She drew a sharp breath. "You and she – a different order of being. I guess I'm way out of my class."

"I wasn't her match. Not ever."

"But you visited those extraordinary places, for a while. So what can your life be, after?"

Rory fell silent. I struggled with the debris of feelings surfaced by our talk, my brain overwhelmed with a barrage of images, sucking me back into Leila's world, that realm of absolute desire. For me, Leila had been, and still was a climate, a condition, a total state of being. As Rory implied, the old question was: how could I live an essentially "average" life after such an absolute experience? Perhaps it wasn't possible. At the very least it might take me a lifetime to find my feet.

"Maybe you and I don't really have a chance," Rory said grimly.

"Don't say that!" I pulled her close, belly-to-belly, flooded with panic. "Please?"

"How can you ever be happy with a lump like me?"

"Lump to lump," I replied, hugging her hard.

"I've always loved you, J. When we broke up, I was shattered."

"You didn't show it."

"Female pride. Besides, I sensed I was outclassed."

"You were."

Rory pulled back. "That's honest!"

"So was I."

"Ah." She came close again. "And now?"

"No."

"So you think you're my match, eh?"

"I think I love you. No, I do love you. What more can I say?"

"What if..." Rory began. "What if I bet everything on loving you and it turns out that you really are messed up?"

"Then we're both in *mierda pura*."

"Yeah." She rolled over, turning her back to me, pressing her ass against my cock. "One thing though," she said over her shoulder, "you just have to go to Paris. "

"What?!"

"See her. See how you really feel about her now, face to face."

"No."

"Yes. We'll go together."

"I don't even know where she lives! The last address I have for her is six years old."

"The phone company office here will surely have a Paris telephone book. We can look her up. How many Leila Bajamondes can there be?"

"She may have left Paris. She may be remarried, changed her name. She may be—"

"We're going. That's all there is to it." The finality in her tone brooked no argument.

seventeen

"I WONDER WHAT BEING WITH YOU cost *her*," Rory said, as the plane to Paris settled into level flight.

Though she would say no more, her words echoed in my head. What had our time as lovers cost Leila? It had never occurred to me to ask that obvious question, and it was shaming to realize that, just like any child, I had been totally obsessed with my own feelings.

Now the questions tumbled out: Did she feel guilty about having "sexually abused" me, as the conventional view would surely have it? Had the experience also left her "suspended" between an absolute intensity and what she often derided as the "average"?
Had Leila been able to find other lover or lovers to match her extraordinary erotic energies?

"I guess, for you, I'll always be second best," Rory said, breaking into my reverie.

My impulse was to deny the truth of this, but that would have been dishonest. I was too fond of Rory to lie, so I said nothing. She nodded, acknowledging the implication of my silence. "Perhaps, for her, too, every other man is only ever second best," she murmured. "You're were her son *and* her lover – can there be a more potent mix than that? How does any woman manage her heart after such a thing?" She nodded, involved in her own thoughts. "You think of her as having been in control of the situation. A manipulator, perhaps, who used you when you were vulnerable and innocent, then dropped you like a hot potato. But what if she simply couldn't help herself? What if she just loved you too much to resist temptation? After all, you were delicious back then. You certainly seduced me."

Tongue-tied, I could only stare at Rory's intent profile. She smiled at me, a sad smile that twisted my heart. "Innocence is the ultimate seduction," she said, "and you were, and are, an eternal innocent." She turned her shoulder away from me to gaze at the clouds.

Left to myself, I tried to make sense of Rory's comments. Slowly, with great concentration, I managed to bring Leila's face into focus, as I remembered it. For years I had not been able to do that, hadn't really wanted to; any time I had tried my mind's eye slid away as if from slippery surface. What did Leila look like now? I wondered. Had she aged much in the past six or so years? Would seeing her again overwhelm me with a chaos of desire and resentment? And a scary thought – did she hate me as I'd hated her? Her hatred would be deadly.

In our first try, in Granada, we had found no listing for Leila in the Paris telephone book. Rory's call to Paris information, conducted in her high school French, had also failed to locate her. All the same, Rory had insisted that we hop a plane and try to find her, gambling that she was still in Paris. "You have to lay that ghost, as it were," she said slyly. Right then, though, I wanted nothing more than to turn the plane around and return to Madrid as fast as the aircraft's jets would carry me.

It was raining when we landed at Orly. After negotiating the lines for customs and immigration, we took the train to the Montparnasse Metro station. The Cite Falguière, Leila's last known address, was in the district, according to the map we had bought in Spain.

On the subway ride the sucking sound made by the opening and closing of the train's pneumatic doors siphoned away the last dregs of my courage. By the time we emerged into the Boulevard Montparnasse my insides were hollowed out, leaving a shuddering vacuum. While Rory consulted a nearby taxi driver about "*un hôtel moins cher*" in the vicinity, I stayed frozen to the sidewalk, clinging to our bags as if their ballast was the only weight keeping my empty spirit from floating away.

Gradually, the blankness within me was filled with dribbles of raw panic. Leila's presence loomed, soaking the drizzle falling on my head, charging the neon crackle of the boulevard in that strange, dark city with its solemn Beaux-Arts buildings, so much more ponderous than the Alhambra's delicate architecture. This is Leila's place, I muttered under my breath, shivering in the evening damp.

"Joel!"

Rory's shout made me almost jump out of my skin. For an instant it sounded like my mother's call – a preposterous notion, given the total contrast in their tones of voice. But they were both women, and they both wanted something from me, I thought sulkily. My instinct was to turn and flee, to run for my life away from Rory and her all-too-adamant insistence that I be there, in this thoroughly unpleasant foreign city. In a surly, defeated mood, I dragged the bags over to the taxi and got in. Rory chatted away to the driver, an irritable Algerian, who delivered us to a drab small hotel on the Rue du Vaugirard. I hefted the bags up the stairs to the room assigned to us by the concierge. "No palace, but it'll do," Rory said cheerfully. I grunted something noncommittal, and she cocked her head at me. "What's up, J.?" she demanded.

"What are we doing here?" I exclaimed. "What?!"

Registering my mood, Rory hugged me, and gradually the warmth of her flesh penetrated the layers of clothing and seeped into my chilled skin. "We'll have a pleasant meal in a nice bistro, with a bottle of wine, and go to bed early, get rested. Tomorrow we'll go to that place, okay?"

"No. Now." As soon as the words popped out of my mouth I realized that I could not have borne a whole night dreading the coming encounter with every breath. "Now," I said again. "Let's just do it."

Rory nodded. She took my hand and led me downstairs. On the street she hailed a cab and gave him the address. The place turned out to be less than a five-minute ride distant. Before I knew it, we were standing on the sidewalk at the entry to a narrow alley, a tunnel of blackened, rain-soaked brick whose far end appeared to vanish into infinity. The darkness within seemed to reach out and swallow me up body and soul. I sensed Leila's smoky green eyes hovering in the shadows, a demonic presence lying in wait for my shivering flesh. When Rory took my arm to lead me down the alley, I shied away, nervous as a horse approaching a slaughterhouse. "Come, sweetheart," she murmured gently. Trusting her voice, I let myself be tugged into the dark.

A blue and white street sign indicated that Number 13 was off the alley itself, approached through a narrow passage leading to the even deeper gloom beyond. By now my apprehension had solidified into a ring of cold iron squeezing my brow. I was doomed and I knew it, and helpless – astonished that it was Rory, my lady, my love, who was actually dragging me to my doom.

The interior passage opened into yet another alley lined with double-story studios. A dim lamp gave the place the aura of a Victorian enclave hiding lurid vice, and I had a ludicrous premonition that Jack the Ripper was skulking in the shadows. Rory found Number 13 and knocked hard on the door. I shuddered each time her knuckles hammered the wood. We heard a shuffle in the interior. The door opened, and my heart came close to exploding.

An old woman stood silhouetted in the light behind her. "Leila—?" I gasped, and bit my lip before blurting, Can you be so *old?* In the tumult of my thoughts it seemed that, like Oscar Wilde's Dorian Grey, Leila's sins had finally caught up with her.

Rory was talking to the woman in French, a fact that slowly dawned on me. Had Leila gone native, then? Forgotten how to speak English?

Suddenly it hit me – this woman wasn't Leila!

"*Merci* Madame," Rory said as the old woman shut the door. "It seems that your mom moved away several years ago," Rory explained as we retreated down the alley. "She didn't leave a forwarding address and the old lady thinks she might have left town, maybe returned to the States."

"Thank God!" I cried. All at once I wanted to shout and sing, to waltz Rory down the pavement in a delirium of relief. The discovery that Leila had disappeared turned my world right side up. Waves of joy washed the fright from my bones. Suddenly Paris truly was *la ville lumière,* the vaunted City of Light. The rain ceased and the glistening windows of the cafes lining the boulevards were beacons of bliss. "Now let's go have that pleasant meal in a nice bistro," I said. "I'm famished!"

We ate ourselves gloriously silly at a gaudy tavern decorated in a cheap imitation of the Belle Epoque. After the second bottle of *première cru* Montrachet – "Damn the expense! This is the Liberation of Paris!" – I felt the town belonged to me. For years Paris had been a hovering black shadow, a dangerous country of the mind. Now it was just another place and I was just another tipsy tourist. At first, Rory regarded me askance, unsettled by my exhilaration. Gradually, though, my jolly mood subsumed her reservations and she started to laugh, her throaty chuckles leading to outright hilarity as the excellent wine fired her blood.

As were sipping our after-dinner espressos and cognacs, she leaned across the table and gripped my wrist. "Fuck me!" she demanded. "Now!"

I paid the bill quickly and we hurried back to the hotel. As we climbed the stairs, hastening to beat the *minuterie*, the timed, thirty-second light switch, she stripped off her coat, sweater and shirt. While I bent down to fumble with the key in the lock, Rory loosened her bra and pushed her breasts into my face. Still searching for the keyhole, I took her sweet, squeezed-together nipples into my mouth. She was naked by the time I opened the door and we reached the waiting bed. She lay back on the covers, drew up her legs, and opened her labia with both hands. As I tore off my clothes my eyes were riveted on the wet pink hole waiting for my cock.

Kneeling beside the bed, I put my fingers over hers and opened her cunt completely. For a moment I bowed my head to gaze at the wide open vagina of a woman waiting to be fucked, the woman I loved. Then I climbed on the bed and eased the tip of my cock into her cunt. Rory gurgled softly, the sound of a baby suckling, and her eyes flared. Grasping my ass, she drew me deep into her body.

We stayed motionless for a long moment. My cock was pulsing, nosing her cervix, eager at the entry to her womb. Her vagina responded with subtle pressures, barely perceptible claspings, gentle urgencies that made my blood race. Her face, staring up at me in the dimness, seemed to rise out of some deep female sea, calling me to a glorious oblivion.

Rory swung her hips, swiveling slowly around the fulcrum of my cock. Intently restrained, holding back the hot rush blazing in my balls, I followed her momentum, lightly emphasizing each motion of her groin. Her nails began to cut into my forearms as she struggled to delay her ecstasies. Then, screaming, she plunged into her final orgasm, taking me with her.

In the breath-catching, resonant silence after, I recognized that this night was a pivot in my life. Now I knew I loved Rory without reservation, purged of past shadings of hesitation, qualification, or reserve. Whatever had belonged to Leila now belonged to Rory. Whatever my mother had taught me about loving a woman now reinforced my love for Rory. Whatever fears left by Leila's lingering ghost were banished from the feeling I had for the woman lying beside me. All trace of hatred seeped away, leaving me free.

* * *

"Thanks, Leila," Rory said next morning as we sat a cafe sidewalk eating croissants washed down by bowls of *café au lait.* Sunshine made the wet street glitter, and the pungency of fresh-roasted coffee hung in the air. When I raised a quizzical eyebrow at her words, she added: "You really know your way around a woman's body."

"Were your other boyfriends that clumsy?" I teased.

"'Clumsy' ain't the word. For most guys a woman's body is foreign territory, something to be mastered rather than relished. Mostly they come on like panting elephants trying to learn the piano. It never occurs to them to listen to the melody."

" 'The Golden Rule: a man's deepest delight derives from a woman's pleasure,' "I quoted.

"Her?"

"Her."

"Clearly, she taught you to listen to the melody. And you have a superb ear, sweetheart."

"I love your body."

"What's that Lorca line?"

"*Verte desnuda es recordar la tierra...*"

"I may be earthbound, but you make me fly." She shook her head in lingering disbelief. "Wow, do you ever...But tell me – if she happened by now, what would you do? Think? Feel?"

I took a moment before answering. "Actually, I'd be glad."

"Truly?"

"Last night was my crisis. I almost crashed. But now I'd just like to see her. See how she's getting on, and such." A thought struck me. "You know, it never occurred to me! My dad still sends alimony checks. Maybe to her new address, maybe to a bank. I could phone him and find out."

"Well..." Rory said doubtfully. "You have to ask yourself – will she want to see you?"

"Dammit, she's my *mom*," I retorted.

Rory smiled. "True enough."

That evening I phoned my father in Los Angeles. "Joel!" he exclaimed. "Great to hear your voice. How are you? What's happening?"

"I'm in Paris, dad."

There was a silence filled with telephonic crackle. "Paris, eh?" he said softly.

"I'm trying to find Leila, but she's moved from her old address. Do you know where she is?"

"I only have the name of her bank. That's where I send the checks." He told me the name and branch of Leila's bank. "Are you sure you—?"

"It's okay. I simply want to say hello."

"Nothing's ever that simple with that lady," he warned.

You don't know the half of it, I thought. We chatted for a few minutes longer. I promised to write to him soon with all the details, and we said goodbye. "Please be careful," he added as the phone clicked.

The branch of the Banque National Populaire my father had indicated was in Saint Germain. Since the day was warm and sunny, Rory and I strolled toward the Seine to find it. As we entered the bank Rory was more nervous than I was, and I squeezed her hand reassuringly.

All I wanted was Leila's address or phone number, but in France nothing is that simple. The assistant manager I approached, though fluent in English, regarded me with a profound suspicion that seemed generic to his function. Even when I showed him my passport, and explained that I was Leila's son, he refused to reveal anything. All he might do, he said, was contact Madame Bajamonde and ask her if she indeed had a son, and if she wished to meet me. "Family affairs are often very complicated," he murmured, smug in his own discretion. I asked if I might phone him later that day to find out if he had managed to contact Leila.

"Are you very disappointed?" Rory asked as we left the bank. She herself seemed relieved.

"It's in the lap of the gods," I replied with an elaborate Frenchy shrug.

eighteen

THAT EVENING, as we entered the hotel lobby, the concierge said something I didn't follow. "She says there's someone waiting to see you," Rory translated, nodding toward the far corner of the lobby.

Turning my head, I saw a woman take an awkward step toward me. But I did not realize who she was until Rory's whispered exclamation – "*Leila!*" - exploded in my ear.

I froze, utterly at a loss. We all three were immobile, each one struggling to integrate the fact of that momentous moment. "Leila—?" I croaked finally.

"Joel."

Spoken in that voice the double syllable sounded simultaneously odd and familiar. Yet the woman coming toward me with a shy, apprehensive half-smile and a tentatively stretched out hand had the aspect of a stranger. My first thought was, *this isn't Leila.* Not the Leila I remembered. Something vital was missing.

"Joel?"

There was a clear question mark the second time she said my name. Startled out of my paralysis by Rory's sharp nudge, I repeated her name. We came together in a hug that was more a small collision than an actual embrace.

"You remember Rory?" I said, my voice still hoarse with surprise.

"Hello Leila," Rory said, bridging the other woman's momentary incomprehension.

"Rory – of course!" Leila exclaimed. She held out her small hand timidly, and Rory clasped it in her broad palm.

"How did you—?" I began, still off-key.

I barely listened as Leila explained that the bank official had called her on her cell phone to ask if she wanted to meet me. "I live in Dijon, now, in Bourgogne, but I happened to be in town just today, for business."

There was something truly nerve-racking about this Leila, something both strange and familiar. Maybe it was the anonymity of her trim navy-with-white-piping business suit or the unfamiliar, bland perfume. Perhaps it was the false note of a foreign intonation in her English, or her rather theatrical Frenchy gestures. Perhaps it was the sleek aspect of her face, its very Parisian hard-eyed chic, or the absence of that old vividness that once alerted her green eyes. Or maybe it was the instantaneous perception that this new Leila had suffered a fate the old Leila would have considered unbearable: she had become, in a groomed, Continental manner, utterly "average."

"You look – good," I said roughly.

Leila blinked, registering the ambiguity of my remark. "Women get old quickly," she replied, lifting her chin in a gesture at once hurt and defiant.

Taking charge, Rory led us toward the far end of the lobby, to an enclave populated with faded plush sofas and overstuffed velour armchairs. The place had that stale, discouraging odor that seems to seep into the bones of cheap old hotels. We all made a fuss about sitting down, and I fought back an impulse to simply walk away from this half-stranger. To me, Leila seemed shriveled. In place of the semi-mythical figure who had once possessed my life I saw a nervous woman struggling to hold aging at bay with a brittle stab at stylishness.

In my unkind mood, I said bluntly, "So this is you?"

Rory gasped, Leila flinched. "Yes, Joel. This is me. All that's left." Her mouth trembled. "And this is you, a fine young man."

"I've survived, if that's what you mean?"

"I see that you're a true *bonhomme*. A fine person. Always."

"And you, no *amantes*?" I said tartly, irritated by her tone and manner. I used the Spanish word but she got my drift. For an instant a truly sad look clouded her face. "After you, every man is second best," she murmured. "I know it and they know it." She glanced at Rory. "No one likes to be second best."

A flash of anger at the implied slight to Rory made my eyes flare, and Leila tucked in her head like a scared turtle. For a moment I almost felt sorry for her, but the impulse passed quickly. Who is this person masquerading as Leila? I wondered. How dare she presume to be my legendary mother? Then it struck me: this "Leila" was an impostor, truly a stranger. As such, she deserved a cool *politesse* rather than raw anger.

"What do you do in Dijon, Leila?" I asked in a tone of polite enquiry.

"I manage a boutique. We sell accessories allied to the wine trade. You know, fancy corkscrews, credenzas, and the like. It's quite engrossing, and very profitable, though I am just an employee. A friend of mine is the *propriétaire*." With a spurt of pride, she added: "I'm a very good *vendeuse*, you know. Saleswoman."

"I'll bet you are," I retorted.

"I know all about you," Leila ran on. "Max keeps me informed."

The thought of my father "informing" on me raised my hackles, but I let it go. "I'm in Granada for the winter."

"A fabulous city. That Alhambra..." Leila seemed about to launch into a touristic eulogy, but caught herself short. "And you, Rory? Also in Granada."

"No, I'm just traveling, before I buckle down to med school."

"Rory and I are together," I cut in. "Together."

"That's wonderful," Leila said.

For an instant the old Leila was there in those eyes, and I tried to guess what she was thinking. If she had spoken I imagined she might have said something like: You at least have come away from our connection with your heart whole. This perception maybe delighted or disappointed her – I wasn't sure. No one really likes to be survived, I thought maliciously.

Leila rose abruptly. "Please excuse me, I have to catch the express train back to Dijon. Here's my card. You'll come and visit me?" I slipped her card into my shirt pocket with a noncommittal shrug. "I have a lovely apartment close to the cathedral. Our Notre Dame is finer than the famous one here, I think."

She held out her hand. I took it, then pulled her toward me in a clumsy hug. "Take care," I mumbled, suddenly at a loss.

Stepping back, Leila lightly brushed my cheek. Her fingers were icy and I could not help recoiling a little. She nodded as if to say, "just so," and walked away.

"God, you were rough!" Rory exclaimed even before Leila disappeared. Her eyes glazed with sympathy as she keened, "Poor Leila."

"That wasn't Leila," I said curtly.

"Huh?"

"An impostor. Didn't you get it?"

Rory gaped at me. Then her shocked expression eased into a dawning comprehension. "She did seem strange. Not quite as I remembered."

"A counterfeit Leila, trying to pass herself off as the genuine thing."

"And where is the `genuine thing,' d'you think?"

"Up in smoke, floating in the ether, a spirit of the air."

"She seemed so – beaten."

"Don't waste your sympathy on her. She got what she wanted, and walked away."

Rory's eyes focused on me, sharp and knowing. "I never realized how ruthless you can be, J. Will you just cut me loose when you're done with me?" Before I could respond, she added, "But that's a risk I'll just have to take, I guess. Like her."

"Please don't lump the two of you together," I retorted irritably. "To me you're as different as night and day."

"A risk I'll just have to take," Rory repeated.

"I wish that woman had never reappeared!"

"But she did," Rory said. "She did. Poor thing."

* * *

On the return flight to Madrid Rory barely said a word for the first hour or so. With her shoulder turned against me, she stared intently at the clouds as if trying to decipher a divine message. My own thoughts were preoccupied with Leila, struggling between a residual anger and a rising regret.

Yes, I had been hard on her, even quite brutal, leaving Leila to fumble for a graceful posture under my barely concealed scorn. In my mind I began a letter I might write to her, a hard-headed, honest but gracious few paragraphs in which I said I was sorry I had been cool toward her but I was clearly still very hurt by the abrupt and selfish way she had dumped me years before. *You let me in so deep, into your heart, into the hot heart of everything, then cut me off at the knees, crippling me...* But the truth was, I didn't feel crippled, just betrayed.

Yet it seemed to me that the Leila I'd seen in Paris had paid an even higher price than I had for the glories of our ruptured connection. She had shriveled into someone essentially commonplace, and didn't seem to know how to survive in that condition without becoming more and more diminished. Or was I being too high-flown? Was Leila always fated to be a successful, corkscrew-selling *vendeuse*, despite her original and extraordinary vividness? Like me, she'd had to find a way to live a life after having known marvels. But I hoped I would manage to do it with more spirit.

What staggered me more than anything was the way her soul had dimmed. The marvelous, rare spark of life glowing at the core of her character had lost its light, leaving us both in the dark. Is this the woman who had once turned me inside out? I wondered. Is this the face that launched a thousand ecstasies? Who, for a while, made me "immortal with a kiss"? *Her lips suck forth my soul; see where it flies!* Marlowe's resonant phrases, remembered from high school, echoed ironically in my head, leaving traces of amazed regret tinged with a terrible sadness. It seemed the old Weeping Woman had passed beyond her damp landscape into a dry-eyed desert no tears could make green. An archetypal icon had desiccated, leaving nothing but a dry husk, hollowed out by – what? No matter how I racked my brains I could not begin to grasp quite why and how Leila had, in six short years, become so cruelly contracted. Why and how the magic of her being had so completely drained away.

With a sharp stab of nostalgia I remembered how, at the height of our passion, the whole world had seemed galvanized by an erotic energy. Everything was electric, from the sensational sunsets over the Pacific seen from the Palisades to the fragrance of the night-blooming jessamine filling our yard on summer nights with a sweet sexual scent that gave me goose pimples. Whatever I touched had seemed to crackle with a thrilling static, and ordinary objects – a spoon, a shoe, a clock – would surprise me with a sensuous halo, as if they had been infused with a godly glow. Everything living was astonishing back then. The air itself throbbed voluptuously, quickening my pulse, sharpening my nose, recharging my spirit with every fresh breath. I had never since felt so totally alive.

"I'm going back home," Rory said suddenly.

My heart contracted. "But surely—?"

"Things are more complicated than I thought," she said, her voice squeezed through a tight throat. "Perhaps it's all beyond me. I'm essentially a simple girl and I want a simple man."

I wanted to cry out, *I'm simple! Really I am!* but that would've been totally fatuous, and untrue. Instead, I asked: "Do you dislike me all of a sudden?"

"It's not that," she replied unconvincingly. "It's just that I realized that you really are quite tough. Much tougher than I thought. Or maybe it's that, after all, the psych textbooks are right. Maybe you are damaged, and that damage makes you cruel." I said nothing, and Rory gave me a look as if to say, no argument? "Perhaps it's best to take a year or so to think about things," she said. "Anyway, I have to go back to Stanford, and I guess you'll be staying on in Spain."

"Guess so."

In the subsequent long silence I began to perceive some hard truths. First truth: Rory and I were over. Our recent love affair was an end rather than a beginning, more a coda to our adolescent connection than the overture to an adult relationship. The second truth, proceeding from the first, was that she and I really did live in different dimensions. For Rory, love was about loving pure and simple. For me, along with fondness, affection, and tenderness, love would always be charged with the electricity of absolute desire. Third truth: I would have to seek a more complex and confusing way to be in the world than Rory would ever find comfortable.

It might be that I would never be able to resolve the tensions that my passion for Leila had bequeathed me. Perhaps a conventional view might regard me as a victim – "After all, the psych textbooks are right" – but I'd be damned if I felt like one. Despite what some "experts" might think, my early sexual connection with Leila was no emotional short-circuit, no infantile urge to return to the womb. Rather, it had been a version of Adam and Eve in the original Garden, a brief but rapturous time in Paradise, abruptly cancelled. What I'd had with her was an opening to a kind of original glory, something to set against all the dull, dirty, everyday stuff that slowly grinds you down.

If there was a victim in this story, it wasn't me but Leila; she certainly seemed "damaged." In truth, her collapse into such a cramped middle age had badly shaken me. Perhaps that is why I had been so hard on her, out of panic at the prospect that I, too, might just dry up into a tight little ball. However, I hoped I was made of sterner stuff, that maybe I really was "tough." Tough enough, that is, to live permanently stretched between heaven and earth.

I slowly came to realize a fundamental fact: Leila's old betrayal was now essentially irrelevant. It began to dawn on me that if there was any magic around it now lived in *me*, not in *us*, and it was therefore foolish to keep on damning Leila for her past desertion. Her failures governed her fate but they need not govern mine, and forgiving Leila would be releasing as well as gracious. In the light of that reflection I quietly let all my lingering resentments go; they had clouded my view and warped my spirit long enough. I fingered Leila's card in my shirt pocket, thinking I would write to her some day soon, to make amends for the antagonism of our last meeting.

"I'll always love you, J.," Rory said. Her eyes darkened with tears. "You'll always be the love of my life."

I took her hand. "You're a terrific woman, Aurora," I said. "Truly."

"Maybe, one day, you and I...?"

For a moment I was tempted to play along with her, but that would have been dishonest. Better to be brutal and break clean. "No," I said. "I think we've discovered that we're very different people, and always will be. A fact of life, that's all."

At that moment the attendant announced in Spanish, French, and English that we were about to begin our descent of arrival. The crackle of her tinny voice over the public address system covered our awkwardness as we buckled up for the landing. When the tires hit the tarmac I squeezed Rory's hand and she squeezed back.

"*Adiós*," she murmured, barely audible over the roar of the reversing engines. "*Adiós amor mío...*"

nineteen

WITH RORY GONE Granada became a darker, more wintry place. The mists that shrouded the Alhambra's battlements seemed to seep into my head, clouding my mind with a vague, wet sense of absence. I wasn't sure where I was or why I was and I drifted with the rainy days that darkened the sky and dragged the horizon down low.

I holed up in the cold white room I had rented in the house of Paco Guiterrez, a carpenter whose combined home and workshop nestled on the edge of the Albaicín, the ancient Moorish district on the hill-side facing the Alhambra. The quarter's steep, cobbled alleys, running down to the Darro River housed hidden *carmenes*, villas whose walled, lush gardens scented the evening air. From my french window I could see the blunt, crenellated thrust of the Alcazaba watchtowers at the western point of the Red Citadel. When I wasn't attending lectures or seminars at the university, I lingered in bed, studying literary texts or lazily rereading favourite passages from "Quixote." I fancied that the buzz of wood saws across the courtyard was counterpointed by echoes of a fourteenth-century muezzin chanting *Allah-u-akbar* in the ghostly minarets of vanished mosques.

Paco's place was a few streets over from the house on Carnero where my grandfather was born and raised, and where his mother, father, and little sister Rafaela had been murdered by Falangists. Staring at the narrow house, squeezed into an alley opposite an old convent, I imagined my great-grandparents and great-aunt as a trio of hummingbirds uttering their last sharp cries as the looming buildings on either side squashed the life from their bodies; just one more layer of victims in the ancient city's long and violent history.

My only true companion was Moro, a skinny, jet-black mongrel who accosted me one evening in a neighborhood bar. Black as night and miserably scruffy, Moro had created a unique survival strategy in a society where stray dogs were treated worse than rats: he had taught himself to dance. The animal had learned that if he reared up on his hind legs and made a few wild jumps in the air with his front paws dangling, some compassionate stranger – usually a foreigner – might overlook his ugly mug and patchy hide and toss him scraps of food.

Moro's act was both pitiful and touching. His dancing was clumsy and he often overbalanced, landing with a thump and a howl on his back. Yet he doggedly persisted, clambering back onto his unsteady rear pins to hop around with his head cocked in a panting appeal, his dangling pink tongue slavering drool in a desperate eagerness to amuse. With this inept appeal, the poor beast hoped to rescue himself from the hell of his origins among the packs of half-starved dogs which haunted the local alleys. Moro was a "self-made dog," as one local wit dubbed him, and his will to survive was an inspiration. If he could endure, despite the crudity of his cockeyed ballet and the hardships of his origins, I could surely find the grit to rise above my own small troubles.

Moro's survival dance epitomized the dynamic tension between ferocity and grace I saw in so many aspects of Granadan life as the winter drifted into spring. At every level, from the personal to the public, ferocity and grace were woven into the texture of the world I witnessed in that very Spanish city.

The evidence was everywhere. On the ferocious side, there was the dark smear on the fountain in the neighborhood plaza, a mark made by the squashed testicles of the local priest, mutilated by Republicans early on in the civil war in the 1930s, before the fascists took over the city. There was the beautiful small red fox, its bloody mouth bound with barbed wire, which Pedro the local barman made drunk with cognac for the amusement of his patrons. There was the terrible beating inflicted on little Paquito, my landlord's oldest son, when the boy was found masturbating in the attic. His father removed his wide, worn leather belt from around his bulging belly, laid the child over a sawhorse, and lashed his buttocks until blood ran down his legs while Juana, Paquito's mother, looked on stony-eyed and his sisters tried to mask their delighted gloating.

Yet this same savage father often gave vent to a yearning *solea,* an Andalusian blues of the kind Enrique used to favor, and on rainy evenings I'd hear his high, rough voice cry out:

Madre mía del Socorro,
de la noche a la mañana
me perdí sin saber como.

Lady of Solace,
between night and morning
I lost myself without knowing how.

Perhaps it was that yearning for solace that prompted the carpenter to shuffle barefoot and bloody over the cobblestones in the Lenten festival among a throng of devout supplicants, flagellating his bare back with a bamboo stave. As the months went by I came to realize that the kind of harsh contrasts Paco presented was not a conflict of opposites so much as a tension between complementary elements, the yin and yang of Iberian experience.

Most of all there was the bullfight, with its ritualized confrontation of a powerful wild beast and a lightfooted man armed only with a red cape and a thin sword. If the matador won this encounter gracefully, he was the darling of the crowd. If he bungled the killing, he was cruelly booed from the ring by the unforgiving mob. Several *corridas* I saw in the Granada ring were botched when the matador could not find that small gap in the animal's nape where the sword must slip between the shoulder blades into his heart. While the exhausted beast drooled blood, its black hide wet with sweat and fear, the desperate man rose once again on tiptoe, sighting along his blade. At that point, the howling mob appeared to prefer to see the matador, rather than his noble adversary, die. If a killing was not done with *duende* – grace – it remained raw and unredeemed, an act of pure cruelty. With true *duendismo*, the crowd's collective spirit soared in celebration.

In the bullring brute fact and poetic metaphor were fused. The matador in Lorca's "Lament for Ignacio Sanchez Mejias," fatally gored by a horn in the thigh, hears flutes resounding in his ears, while the bull stands alone with a high heart. "I will not see it!" the poet cries out, but he knows all the same that he has to look.

And I, too, had to look. I had to look at the fact that Leila could never be dismissed from my life. I had to reconsider the cruel way I had damned her as an impostor. The memory of our last meeting left a persistent, dusty aftertaste in my mouth, a dryness in the throat I could not assuage, and I began to realize that I had to confront Leila once again, and decently, before I could be sure if I truly had become my own man. But I knew I wasn't yet quite up to such a truly graceful act.

* * *

In the spring I left Granada to find an isolated corner of Andalusia where I could think things through in peace and quiet. After a few days of travel on local buses and trains I found San Jose, a village on Cabo de Gata, the cape on the extreme southeastern tip of Spain where it juts out into the Mediterranean. If you looked due east you might, with inspired vision, see all the way across the entire width of the Middle Sea to Jerusalem.

San Jose was less a village than a cluster of a dozen or so houses on the edge of a cliff by the sea. It was so primitive that all of its supplies, including water, had to be brought in daily by donkey from a town ten miles inland. The local fishermen worked the small bay below by the ancient means of trawling a net across its mouth, then laboriously dragging the sodden net and its tiny catch onto the beach by hand.

The only cafe in the village was actually a local fisherman's living room. The fisherman's wife, Maria, rented me a cave in the cliff and offered to feed me my meals. The mouth of the cave was closed off with a wall and two doors. The left door led to my dark, cool, whitewashed den, the right one to a donkey's stable. I could smell the stable's warm, straw-filled odor during the day and listen to the beast's raucous braying at all hours of the night.

At first, shut in my cave, reading my books, I felt absolutely safe. The cliff itself seemed to protect me, insulating me from the powerful expanse of sea and sky. I emerged only to climb up the path to Maria's living room to eat, or to walk along the beach at sunset to watch the net being hauled in, to inspect the catch of stingrays and sardines that would be my dinner. The peacefulness of the place was almost palpable, a thick cloak wrapping me in its embrace. At dusk I gazed out from my the mouth of my cave at the colors of a dying sun reflected in the sea; ultramarines, apple greens and cobalts fading to violet then purple then charcoal. In that sunset visiting sardine boats glittered like tin cutouts, their engines tapping out a steady beat. Occasional spring storms drove billowing baroque clouds across the dome of heaven toward some distant thunder while bursts of rain brought forth a host of wild white narcissi crowding the drenched fields, filling the air with mingled scents of lemony sweetness.

The days were serene, but the nights were scary. Leila's ghost came at me through the thick cave walls, a huge phantom perching on my chest, cackling in my face, deriding me for daring to conjure her up. Other times she hovered in the shadows, watching me with anxious, angry eyes. Our spirits struggled chest to chest, and sometimes I feared I would be crushed by her powerful presence. It was a terrifying experience, yet I sensed that Leila's shadow wanted me to wrestle her to the mat, to match her, if I were man enough. Each morning, waking from troubled dreams, I was suffused with a mixture of relief and regret. In my mind Leila was simultaneously a ghost and an "impostor," a threat and a phony. To resolve the confusion I simply had to see her face to face.

But how would I overcome the intense shame I now felt about the rough way I had treated her in Paris?

* * *

On my return to Granada I realized that I had lost the card Leila had given me with her address in Dijon. A telegram or phone call to Max would supply the information, but I was reluctant to involve my father. I hadn't told him that I had seen Leila, though I knew it was possible that she had mentioned our meeting. If she had, he had not said a word to me. Anyway, my business with Leila had nothing to do with Max. Now as always he was on the sidelines, willfully blind, perhaps, and essentially irrelevant.

In one wild, momentary impulse I almost phoned Rory to ask for her advice. After all, she had been there with Leila and me, had witnessed the scene, gauged the emotional temperature. I wanted ask her some painful questions, like: Had I wounded Leila so deeply that she might not be able to forgive me? Was I wrong to reverse my attempt to sever our connection completely? Should I discount my original instinct of self-preservation, my feeling that I should "break clean"? Now everything was muddied with remorse, and I was paralyzed.

In the end my only confidant was the faithful Moro. The dog adopted me, taking to lying outside my door waiting for me to toss him a crust or invite him for a walk. When the days and nights were cold and wet I could hear him shivering and I let him come into the room and curl up near the kerosene heater. There he lay, snoozing, from time to time cracking a bilious eye to check if I was still there, his temporary, miraculous friend and master. I say temporary because I knew, and he seemed to accept, that our connection was passing. From bitter experience, Moro was aware that all human beings were skittish in their affections, could as easily kick as stroke him, switching moods from moment to moment. To my credit, I never pretended that we would be together forever, and he never seemed to resent that fact of life, except for an occasional stoically accusing stare.

"What do you think, amigo?" I asked him. "You've been around, you know how things are. What's your advice?"

Cocking his narrow black head, the dog looked almost wise, and for a moment I half-expected him to answer me. When he didn't, I supplied his response, drawing upon my intuition of what his streetwise answer might be. Move on, *jefe*, he'd surely urge, don't cry over lost bones. The only hope any of us creatures have is to dream of fresh morsels, even if they never happen. Like the man said, life is nasty, brutish and short, and there's no time to waste on regrets.

"But Morito, I love her!"

My outburst startled us both. To make amends, I tossed the dog a cracker, which he gulped down in one greedy swallow.

"Yes, I love her," I repeated. "Leila is the love of my life."

I could never have made such a naked confession to any human being, not even to myself, but Moro was another species. Besides, more than anyone I knew, he had learned the hard way to read the human heart in all its awkward attitudes and confusing contradictions.

"Do I have the balls to tell *her* that, my friend?" I asked him. "Just walk up to Leila and say, man to woman, 'I love you'?"

What a leap that would be! To discard all reservations, strip myself naked, exposed to destruction. But then, she had already laid herself bare. "After you, every man is second best," she'd said, handing me her heart. And I had damned her as an impostor!

"How can she ever forgive me?" I asked the dog.

Moro's boiled, yolk-yellow eyes were fixed on my face. I could see he was concerned, sensing trouble in my tone, and in his experience trouble of any kind usually resulted in a kick in his butt. Yet I hoped he was also worried about me, his ephemeral friend. And there was something in his expression that stiffened my spine, some *picaresco* conjecture linking Moro to tough Iberian literary archetypes like Lazarillo de Tormes, that sly servant to a blind man who abused him cruelly as a matter of principle. "Pain is the price of wisdom," as Enrique liked to say. What happens happens, the dog's grave look implied.

twenty

One cold day in March I found myself at the ticket counter of Iberia Airlines at the Granada airport buying a seat on a plane to Paris. I say "found myself" because that was exactly how it seemed. That morning I had gotten out of bed still dazed by dreams, dressed, packed a shoulder bag, and told my landlord I would be away for a week or so. I also gave him an extra few hundred pesetas to buy bones for Moro, but I suspected he would likely kick the dog's ass and pocket the cash. "*La vida es asi*," I shrugged in answer to the dog's mournful stare, hoping that Moro's talent for survival would see him through, as ever. If we found each other on my return, so much the better. If not, well...

Whether the sleepwalking state in which I traveled northward was spontaneous or self- induced, it served to dull my doubtful mind while I changed planes in Madrid, crossed Paris on the Metro, and took the express train to Dijon. The journey consumed most of an entire day, and by the time I emerged from the station in Dijon it was dark. I asked a passing police officer where I could find the Notre Dame church Leila had mentioned was close to her apartment, and wandered off in that direction. A passing thought, *what the fuck am I doing?* bubbled to the surface of my mind. I missed a step, stumbled, and dropped into a wicker chair outside a small café.

Sipping a *café crème*, I slowly took account of my location. I glanced more attentively at the narrow street, admiring its mixture of medieval timbered frontages and patterned glazed tile roofs above an array of lively small shops selling everything from bread to jewelry. Across the way was a wine boutique and for an instant I panicked, wondering if it was the place where Leila worked. Turning my head, I glimpsed the edge of a grand church façade several blocks distant, and the waiter confirmed that it was indeed the Church of Notre Dame.

She is close—!

The thought shivered me, sending an icy spasm from my nape

to my spine. Suddenly I was once again that eager boy waiting for my mother to come to my bed. She was there before me, regarding me with her smoky green eyes, compelling me with a look of love. Back then, when Leila would regard me that way, all passion offered, all passion expected, her face burned deep into the coils of my brain. Remembering that on a strange street in a strange city, my mind was clouded by a confusion of terror and hope.

She is close…

An electric shock ran through me, a different kind of shiver, thrilling every nerve in my body. She's my touchstone, I said silently. My magical woman. My mother and my lover. Whatever happened, whether I was ultimately created or destroyed, I had no option but to offer myself to Leila.

But what if she had now closed her heart to me? What if my harsh ways had impelled her to shut down tight? Turning my face toward the church, I began to pray to some vague deity, *Lord, let that not be so…*

Several sluggish hours passed. I lingered at the café, ordering a series of coffees I hardly remembered drinking. My conscious mind was blank, I could not think up the simplest strategies for finding Leila, not even looking her number up in the local phone book. Back in Granada I had tried to contact the Dijon directory but was frustrated by my poor French and the unreliable connection. Now I felt I had no option but to hang around in her vicinity and hope that she would find me, as if I were an abandoned infant left in a basket on a street corner. Time dribbled by in a daydream that seemed endless, almost eternal as my mind retreated deep into its own inexpressible obscurities.

"*M'sieu?*"

Surfacing abruptly, I found the waiter hovering over me with worried eyes. "*Vous voulez quelque chose?*"

I assured the man that I was fine and ordered yet another coffee. He suggested I eat something, indicating a pastry shop a few doors distant, and I thanked him for his concern. Though my stomach was still too tense to tolerate food, I felt light as air. The journey into some far region of my head had left me with a surprising hope that I might after all have the resources of spirit and imagination to redeem my bungled actions. For some strange reason I suddenly believed I had the youth and the desire, the energy and the inspiration to reinvent both Leila and myself, and I was impatient to begin.

Stirring from my languor, I wandered down the narrow street toward the church. The Gothic façade was all that Leila had claimed for it – an arcaded stone frontage elaborately carved and gargoyled, topped by noble twin towers. I noticed that some of the porch's stonework had been chipped and damaged, probably during the Revolution, when mobs took out their anti-clerical fury on the architecture. Inside Notre Dame the graceful nave, bounded by galleries, was a soaring womb.

Seated before the altar, I gazed entranced at the glowing stained glass windows in the north transept depicting popular thirteenth-century Burgundian saints. This was only the second time I had been in a church, and this place was very different from the primitive building I had visited in La Mancha. Christianity was capable of magnificence, I realized; a transcendent sublimity belying its long history of horrors. In a small side chapel the image of the Black Virgin, Notre-Dame de Bon-Espoir, stared back at me from out of the depths of her ancient maternal memory. Kneeling at her feet, I mumbled a silent prayer, pleading for Leila's forgiveness, asking to be allowed to find her in the church's shadow.

As I was leaving I picked up a small booklet in English about the church's history. Flipping the pages under a streetlight, I noticed a paragraph about the small sculpture of an owl on one side of the church. "Legend has it that if you rub the owl your wishes will come true. In Medieval times the owl was a symbol for members of the Hebrew race and it was believed that rubbing a Jew's nose brought good luck." The bluntness of the wording startled me for a moment, but I immediately searched for the owl. It was life-size, carved almost casually into the angle of a buttress, its body rubbed smooth by centuries of Christians hoping to conjure some Hebrew sorcery. Since my own magic was badly in need of replenishing, I gave the stony creature a vigorous rub.

Wandering on, I found myself in a street of narrow, half-timbered houses whose ground floors were occupied by shops selling antiques and boutiques featuring mustard and wine. In one store window a charming poster of the Burgundian wine country celebrating St. Vincent, "Patron des Vignerons," depicted the famous vineyards of the Cote D'Or as leaves on a vine. Peering at the display in a wine shop, I was transfixed by an object that looked like a large shiny black and silver metal praying mantis rearing up on its hind legs. It took me a while to figure out that it was an elaborate corkscrew, a device to fit around the neck of a wine bottle. This must be one of the devices for which Leila was a *vendeuse*, one of the mysterious accoutrements she may have made her métier. But I was beyond mockery at that moment. All I wanted from that corkscrew, and from the other objects populating the shop window, was a clue to her whereabouts.

On impulse, I rang the bell beside a carved door next to the shop, hoping she might be living in an apartment above, or that someone might know of her. Before leaving the café I had checked in the local phone book and hadn't found a listing for Leila, and this long shot might be my last chance to find her. After all, how many wine shop employees could there be in Dijon? Too many, a small voice replied as I waited for a response to the seemingly silent bell.

After a long pause I heard faint footsteps behind the door. My heart was racing, expecting a miracle, and I braced myself to greet Leila. What would I say? What would I do? Fall on my knees and beg forgiveness like a bad boy? Embrace her like a lover? Exercise decent restraint, maybe..?

The door opened, but not on Leila. A florid, big-bellied man with silver hair stood there, his expression a perfect fusion of courtesy and suspicion. In a rush I told him in English that I had come from Los Angeles looking for my mother. I don't know why I said Los Angeles, except that I felt fifteen again, a lost pup. Realizing this, a flush of shame suffused my face, and that seemed to soften the stranger's wariness.

"Actually," he said, in fluent, accented English, "I know of this American lady. I believe she lives around the corner, in the Rue Jeannin. If you will pause a moment, I will search my memory for her address." Tilting his head, he closed his eyes in solemn concentration. I waited breathlessly, hanging on his gestures as if he were an oracle about to reveal the secret of a riddle. "Number seventeen," he said at last. "Dix-sept rue Jeannin." His tone was portentous, his words drummed my mind. "Dix-Sept rue Jeannin," I echoed fervently. He pointed down the street. "Around the corner." Thanking the man profusely, I hurried away.

At Number Seventeen I found a brick-fronted house with a wide double door. There was only one bell with no name tag, connected to an intercom, and I rang it impatiently. When a disembodied voice answered, I blurted out Leila's name. The lock clicked and I pushed the door open. I was in a small courtyard. In one corner a circular wooden staircase led up into a dim upper region. I was about to climb the stairs when Leila appeared out of the dark.

The surprise of seeing me transformed her face. At first the shock seemed to age her several decades in an instant. Then, just as suddenly, she flushed like a girl with huge, liquid eyes. "Joel..?" she said hoarsely. "You?"

"Me," I replied, holding out my hands.

Leila stepped backward at first, as if about to be attacked, then she shyly reached out to embrace me. "Joel," she murmured. "It's you." Her tone implied that the "you" she recognized was the son she remembered from better days, not the unpleasant adult who had given her a hard time a while back.

"Yes. Me," I said, acknowledging her meaning.

Releasing my hand, Leila led me upstairs to her apartment. At first it seemed as tiny as a doll's house, just two small dimly lit rooms, a cupboard-sized kitchen and a bathroom. The flock wallpaper with a busy gold fleur-de-lys pattern made the space seem even tighter than it was, and the plush velvet sofas and a multitude of cabinets and side tables laden with objets-d'art crowded the reddish rugs. "My hideaway," Leila said, awaiting my judgment on her nest with a mixture of pride and apprehension.

"Cozy," I offered. Realizing that was faint praise, I added: "Lovely. And so – compact."

"I always wanted an elegant space," she declared with some defiance.

"You deserve it," I said. She regarded me askance, wary of derision, but I reassured her with a smile. "Truly," I continued, adding clumsily: "Elegant woman, elegant space."

Leila offered me a glass of wine, and while she fetched the bottle and glasses I sank into a sofa. The exhaustion of the long, confusing day, that had begun so many hours before and so many miles distant, both physically and mentally, hit me like a wet sack behind the head.

Yet I still had so much to say, so much to explain before I could rest. But as Leila returned with a small tray bearing a decanter and two crystal wine glasses, all I could think to say was, "I rubbed the owl."

Leila blinked, then nodded. "The Jew's nose?"

"Yes."

"In France, being Jewish is very particular."

"Especially for *une sale Juive*?" I teased, recalling her unpleasant childhood memories.

Leila shrugged expressively. While she poured the wine I watched her face. One moment her expression reflected the brittle fake Frenchiness I'd so disliked, the next it was glowing. The contradiction bemused me and I wondered if I had the will to reconcile these aspects, to cherish Leila in all her manifestations. In truth, however, I had no choice. I simply had to lay my heart open to whatever face she chose to show me. I had hurt her horribly with my rough disdain, and it might take the rest of my life to get her to really forgive me – not as a mother forgives a son, but as a woman forgives a lover. I'd have to prove, with every act of devotion, that I deserved her affection. In short, I would have to "seduce" her, as she had previously "seduced" me.

But how to begin? Should I just launch into an abject apology? Or should I ease into it? And would she be amenable? Or even capable of again opening her heart to me? Perhaps the shriveling of her soul I'd thought I perceived in Paris was a valid insight into her condition. Maybe she truly was the woman I had damned as an "impostor." The possibility chilled me.

"Cold?" Leila asked, seeing me shiver. "Would you like a sweater? You look exhausted!"

"Leila—" I began, and choked. There was so much to say, and I seemed to have so few words.

"I know," she said, touching my hand. "I know, Joel. Tomorrow, maybe. For now just let's drink our wine – a rather delicious Montrachet I've been saving for a special occasion – and let it go, okay?"

"Okay," I muttered gratefully as she uncorked the bottle.

She poured two glasses, handed one to me, and raised her own in a toast, after first relishing its bouquet with an appreciative sniff. "To us," she said. I nodded, and we drank. I was thirsty and soon emptied my glass, and on an empty stomach the wine immediately clouded my head, overwhelming me with drowsiness. "Another?" Leila asked, offering the bottle. When I dazedly refused, she produced a red rubber device fitted with a small spout and a plunger. She twisted the thing into the neck of the bottle with a precise, practiced gesture.

"What's that?" I asked.

"A vacuum wine saver."

"What does it do?"

"It seals the bottle and keeps it fresh," she explained. "A few quick strokes of this piston removes all vestiges of air trapped in the bottle, recreating the vacuum seal. When you want to pour next time you simply slide up this collar and the wine comes out of the spout."

"Why not just put the cork back?"

"Reinserting the cork forces oxygen into the bottle, destroying the bouquet, killing the vintage."

"You know your stuff."

Leila gave me a sharp look, then relaxed when she saw I wasn't mocking her. "It's my *métier*," she said proudly.

"You must tell me all about your profession," I mumbled drowsily.

"You can sleep here, if you like," she said tentatively. "That sofa is quite comfortable."

"Thanks." By now my eyelids were so leaden it was a struggle to keep them from closing. Leila eased me down on the sofa, tucked a cushion under my head and removed my shoes. She draped a duvet over me. "I love you, Leila," I murmured as I fell asleep. "Really."

The last word I heard was her whispered, "*Yes.*"

twenty one

THE LOW SUN *of dusk throws deep lines of light through the alcoves of the Hall of the Ambassadors. Twilight darkens the Hall's colored wood ceiling as the sinking sun sets fire to the splendid purple, green, and orange mosaics covering the great room's walls and floors.*

Sultan Muhammad V sits on his throne in the northern alcove. Surrounded by his councilors, the Conqueror is absently listening to a droning poem of praise by court poet Ibn Zamrak. Behind the Master of Granada the steep walls of Qual'at al-Hamra, The Red Citadel, fall away on one side to the river ravine, on the other to the gardens of the Generalife. In the east the snow-capped peaks of the Sierra Nevada are silhouetted against puffy clouds backlit by the dying sun.

As usual, Muhammad is dressed simply. A plain crimson cloak drapes his body from throat to heels to protect him from the cold winds blowing down from the sierras; a matching headscarf frames his cheeks. At his side is Habiba, the only woman in the room, the ruler's most trusted adviser, and my friend.

While the poet intones his interminable paean, the Sultan beckons to me over the heads of his courtiers. The sycophants part like the Red Sea before Moses as I approach the throne. I touch my fingertips to my brow in homage and wait for the great Caliph to speak.

"I have work for you," Muhammad tells me. "I want you to create a new courtyard to the royal palace. A place of perfection, an earthly paradise, with golden domes where the light is pure honey. I want a palace that flows like water, glistens like moonlight, glows like this red sun at dusk. I want it anchored to the earth yet sailing among the stars. I want an architecture that melts into music, that has the rhythm of a song and the melody of the spirit." The great king pierces me with his gaze. "Can you give me this?" he demands.

Seeing that I'm speechless, the Caliph continues. "You may have everything you need to make a masterpiece. You may call upon the best artisans in the civilized world, from the Mudejars of Castile to the Persian craftsmen of Damascus. I want richness without vulgarity, quality without exaggeration, an effortless beauty that soothes the soul and waters the spirit like good wine. If you succeed, you'll be immortal. If you fail, I shall pluck out your eyes and throw your broken body into the ravine. Do you accept these terms, Jew?

"Yes, my Lord," I answer humbly.

"Habiba has faith in you, and I have faith in her. We'll see if both of us are right. If not, you'll be dead and I'll be bankrupt."

I steal a glance at Habiba, who smiles discreetly. I bow to the Sultan and withdraw, my heart hammering with joy and terror at the challenge my king has thrown at me from his throne. Habiba, walking beside me, is silent. "You can make it happen!" she exclaims.

Taking her hand, I kiss her fingers, breathing in the rose fragrance of her soap. She laughs, puts her palm over my face like a blessing, then leads me to a stone bench in a corner of the Court of the Myrtles. Her touch is warm and comforting and the sympathy in her light green eyes makes me feel I'm not alone in my struggle to give shape to this place and this time, to create a precinct of true transcendence. "There's so much to give meaning to here," she says softly. "God and man, earth and sky, the private and the public, grace and grandeur..." She falls silent, and for the thousandth time in our long friendship I wonder why I've never asked this extraordinary woman to be my wife...

"Joel?"

Startled awake, I saw Leila peering down at me. My mind still clouded with visions, I exclaimed, "Habiba?"

Leila cocked her head. "A woman?"

"Dreams."

"Bad?"

"Oh no." Rubbing my eyes, I saw that Leila was dressed for work in her elegant black suit. Her face was masked by make-up. "Leila—" I began, then choked. There was just too much to say, and no easy way to say it.

"I have to go to work," she said. "There's coffee in the percolator and fresh croissants, and butter in the fridge. Here's my business card, and a tourist map. If you want to come see me, you'll find the shop on the Porte Guillaume, that looks like a small Arc de Triomphe, ten minutes walk from here. It's this red spot I've marked. Meet me for lunch, okay?" I nodded, and with a quick motherly kiss on my cheek, Leila left the apartment.

As I assembled breakfast my brain was busy with down-to-earth questions. How had Leila come to be in Dijon? How did she become to be in the wine business? Was a there a man involved? This thought prompted a flash of jealousy, and I had to remind myself of her declaration that all other men were "second best."

The croissants were delicious, especially when loaded with the butter I slathered over each chunk before dunking it in my coffee. It struck me that the breakfast Leila had provided was the kind a mother would give a son, and I wondered if that was meant as a signal that she wanted to make her renewed connection with me essentially maternal. On the one hand I felt it would be comforting to just have Leila be my mother, to let her become the conventional mom she had never really been. On the other hand, I yearned to make love to her, to hold her in my arms, to plunge into the world of her unique sexual magic.

Were the two modes irreconcilable?

When I was an adolescent, having Leila as both lover and mother seemed easily fused. The roles had overlapped, the boundaries were fluid, maternal love and erotic excitement had never really seemed opposed. But now we were both adults, so the old balance was disturbed. I could no longer blindly, gloriously follow the urges of an unformed heart and mind, and Leila could no longer assume to lead me where she wished. Perhaps, too, she had since suffered spasms of remorse at having "seduced" a vulnerable child. I'd seen no signs of this as yet, and I fervently hoped she was free of such folly. What had happened between us when I was young transcended accepted notions of what was "proper" or "correct." To me, the only crime was her desertion, and I'd now forgiven her for that – though I still wanted to know why she had left me so abruptly.

There could only have been two reasons, selfishness or guilt, and I hoped it was the former. If she had run away because she felt she was at fault for having made me her lover, I would be very disappointed. Such a reaction would have been commonplace, and that just wasn't her old style. So her reasons must have been purely selfish, as her one letter to me had plainly stated: *But you see, it was your life or mine, and in the end we're all selfish monsters…* For Leila, selfishness was totally in character, and I reconciled myself to that, so long as she could now be thoroughly selfish about us. Leila was my one true hope of glory, my female guide into the enchanted realm, and I hoped with all my heart that she would go on being faithful to her own genius.

* * *

After breakfast I wandered around Leila's apartment, wanting to reconnect with her by soaking up the atmosphere of her home. The feeling of the place differed from the old family house in Santa Monica; though Leila's style had always been tasteful, the apartment's ambiance was more formal and less relaxed, and rather stuffier. That might be because it was also a lot smaller, I reflected, with less space for her *objets*. Or it could reflect a shift toward a more constricted state of mind.

For one bad moment I feared that Leila had made certain fixed decisions about herself, judgments about the way she ought to be that might well exclude the possibility of ever again making me her lover. Clearly her original escape to Paris, her hope of finding "a magical world," had been disappointed. The first excitement – *I am in Paris! Alone* – had obviously drained away, and she had since become the "shriveled" woman I'd presumptuously judged her to be at our previous meeting. Now it was up to me to reopen her heart.

What did she really think of me now? I wondered. Significantly, I could not find any photo of myself, though I searched everywhere. There wasn't even a picture of me as a child. Leila hadn't wanted such reminders, it seemed, and that was rather discouraging.

The day was crisp and bright when I came out into the busy street. The people on the sidewalks and in the cafes seemed prosperous, apart from a few bedraggled, shivering Africans selling secondhand clothes and cheap watches off mobile racks. An old-time *clochard*, almost a stage tramp in that affluent burg, sang a boisterous, off-key ditty to the amusement of a pair of watching *gendarmes*. Down a side street I glimpsed an open-air market with a flower stall, and I stopped to buy Leila a bouquet of hothouse violets.

Maison Robert, Leila's shop in the Porte Guillaume, had a frontage barely ten feet wide. From the street the dark, narrow interior seemed so stuffed with goods it appeared impenetrable. When I entered, a doorbell tinkled a few bars of "Frère Jacques," and Leila emerged from the shadows. "You brought me violets!" she exclaimed delightedly.

"A lover's bouquet," I declared, with a mock bow.

Leila blushed slightly, just enough to reveal her embarrassment, or pleasure. She put the flowers to her cheek with a shy smile, and I wanted to kiss her. But just then the doorbell sounded and a man entered.

As Leila chattered to the customer in a wonderfully fluent French, I examined the contents of the shop, marveling at the sheer array of objects and devices displayed to serve a dedicated drinker. They included all manner of corkscrews, corkpulls and bottle stoppers; decanters and decanter drying stands; glass-fronted cadenzas and mahogany wine and stemware racks; cowhide wine tote bags and hardwood wine chests; liquor flasks, crystal goblets and antique chalices; gilded and chrome-plated champagne "keys" – pincers designed to ease out corks; wine bottle napkin rings, cognac "pipes" and martini "misters;" fancy silver and pewter *taste-vin*; portable martini sets and trivets for displaying vintage corks; wine holders in the shape of butlers, jolly monks and monocled tipplers – and a host of things I could not identify. The crowded space exuded a smell of rich woods and subtle polish, an aroma of wine casks, an air of obsessive luxury.

What a serious mystery the French have made of the simple act of swallowing booze, I thought. To me, the ceremonial appurtenances crowding the boutique were either eminently civilized or essentially silly, or both together, and as I listened to Leila's practiced patter I wondered once again how she had come to be such a seemingly adept mistress of this arcane arena.

At one o'clock Leila locked the store and we went for lunch to a neighboring bistro specializing in mussels. "I remember how you used to love my *moules*," she said, and I didn't contradict her. As an aperitif Leila ordered cassis, a drink made from a blackberry liqueur mixed with Aligote, a light dry white wine. "A Burgundian delight," she explained proudly. The mussels were delicious, "flown in from Brittany this morning," and in the euphoria of good food and wine I began not to mind Leila's animated Gallic mannerisms.

"What are your plans?" Leila asked as we sipped our coffees. Her tone was tentative, uncertainly maternal, as if she were unsure of her rights or the current character of our relationship.

"To be with you."

"But what about Granada? Your studies?"

"How I use this time in Europe is up to me."

"Do you have enough funds?"

"Sure." Reaching across the table, I took her hand. "Listen to me, Leila," I urged. "At our last meeting – yes, I was hateful. And I did hate you, for leaving me, dropping me like a hot potato or a used Kleenex, or whatever." She tried to pull her fingers free but I held fast. "In the last few years I fooled myself that I'd kicked you loose, stopped loving you, but that just isn't possible. Fact is you're the most important person in the world to me. You're my love, my life. You know?"

Leila stared at me, amazed. It was, perhaps, the first time ever that I had truly astonished her.

"What do you say?" I asked. "Leila?"

"I'm not—" she began, and choked. With great deliberation she drank some water. "It's different, now," she murmured.

"How so?" I demanded disingenuously.

"You're older. I'm older." With a helpless shrug she repeated, "Older."

I gazed long and hard at her face. The more I looked at her, the more the original Leila came clear through the scrim of disillusion.

Releasing her hand, I leaned back in my chair. "You are the woman I love, my magical female, the only one who could ever carry me away, far above the clouds. You are my dream and my hope. My Leila."

"Oh God," she gasped. "What am I to do?"

"Love me. That's all."

"That's all?" she echoed.

She began to weep, and in the flow of tears the false crust masking her true face seemed to crack and melt away. "Oh God, oh God," she murmured helplessly, over and over. Seeing her so naked and unguarded, so ravaged and so ravishing, my heart swelled with sympathy and joy. When we parted I kissed her on the lips, and she smiled.

* * *

That night, after a light supper Leila prepared, she excused herself to shower and wash her hair. I wasn't sure if that was her usual evening habit, or if she was preparing herself for me. Whatever it was, I was content to drink the cognac she provided and wait for her to reappear. I'd declared myself, and now I had to just wait and see what might follow. Though my fate hung in the balance, I had rediscovered my true purpose after years of wandering in the wilderness, and that made me feel very sure and happy.

Leila spent well over an hour in the bathroom, perhaps delaying the moment when we would be face to face. Her dallying reminded me of Rory's reluctance to emerge from the bathroom the first time we made love – the first time I had ever made love to any woman. Was Leila also shaving her calves, believing, as Rory claimed, that "men hated women with hairy legs"? When, finally, Leila reappeared she was wearing a toweling gown and a towel wound around her newly washed hair. "Hair gets so easily soiled in the city," she said, offering an unsolicited apology. She sat beside me on the sofa and I handed her a glass of cognac. "To us," I toasted.

Moving around behind her, I removed the towel and began to rub her hair dry. She shivered, perhaps with pleasure, perhaps with apprehension, or maybe because she was chilly after her bath, and I suggested she move to sit on the floor in front of the gas fire. Leila let her damp hair hang loose, hiding half her face behind a dark veil. She slumped into a self-absorbed posture suggesting surrender and I wondered what was going through her mind.

I tried to jump inside her skull, to see us through her eyes. In Paris she had been confronted by my rude hostility. She must have been shocked and hurt by the hard look on my face; a look not only of resentment but of blunt disdain for the person I felt she had become. Then I had turned up out of the blue in a very different mood, offering apology and love, and she must be agonizing over which of these attitudes represented my true feelings. I couldn't blame her if she suspected that I might now be playing an elaborate game, to set her up, expose her to some terrible attack; get her to lay herself bare, then stick in the knife of my old hurt and hatred.

After all, what did we really know about each other after such a long separation? In the six or so years since I had last seen her I'd grown from a teenager into a young adult, and she had completely changed her way of life. It must have been a struggle for Leila to metamorphose from an idle Santa Monica homemaker and mother into a busy *vendeuse* living alone in a foreign country. I had to admire her spirit, and wonder if there was some part of her that resented my abrupt intrusion into the new existence she had contrived. It was a strange existence, though, I had to say. A narrow one by any measure, considering what I knew of the treasures of her soul.

In many ways we had become strangers, and I had to ask myself if I really had any insight into how Leila might now feel about our old connection. Apart from regret or remorse, what did she think when she looked back to the time when we were lovers? Did it seem utterly remote, a different life in a distant country, not quite real? Maybe she had come to think of that era as a wild aberration, even a period of danger, a moment when she had risked her soul, and mine. Perhaps, when she thought about our shared past, her residual sensation was a shiver, a frisson of amazed escape from a terrible disaster.

And what of now, this moment? Did she think she could trust me? Or was she silently asking me what every woman asks a man when it comes right down to the wire: *Who are you? What are you? What do you want from me?*

There's the famous passage in the Old Testament about the visit of the Queen of Sheba to Jerusalem, to test Solomon with "hard questions." The King was famed as a sage and a wonder worker, and the Ethiopian lady wanted to see if he was all he was cracked up to be. Maybe she suspected that the old monarch, the fabled lover of a thousand women, might turn out to be just another big male bullshit artist. The Bible says that Solomon gave the Queen "all her desire." But, tricky devil that he was, Solomon laid down a floor of mirrors in his palace to peer under skirts – to see if, according to rumor, her legs were covered in a thick fur. Did he really want to discover whether Sheba was half-woman or half-beast? Or was this a sly strategy to undermine the Queen, because he feared that her necromancy would prove true and expose his supposed magical powers as mere chicanery.

"What are you thinking about?" Leila asked, jerking me out of my reverie.

"Us," I answered.

The glow of her body – the female heat, life's molten core – came at me in waves of warmth. Gently, I began to slip the gown from her shoulders. I tried to push it down to her waist but she grabbed my hands and cried, "No!" When I protested she exclaimed,

"My body – it's old. *Ugly!*"

Her expression was excruciating. I yearned to pull her into my arms, but I held off, respecting her anguish. "No, Leila," I said softly. "You're never ugly to me."

Twisting around, she scrutinized my face, searching for its true intention, anxious and afraid. "Really?" she murmured. "But I'm an old woman. Your mother—!"

"That never bothered you before," I countered with a smile. "You were you, and I loved you for it."

"But Joel," she sighed. "Joel…"

I lifted her chin, made her look at me. "Back then we were a pair of innocents, each in our own way," I began. "Me, because I was a kid. You, because you're you. Now we know more, and maybe also less. But we're still essentially us, surely?"

"Are we?" she murmured. "Are we?"

Rising, I reached down for her hand. "Enough chatter. To bed." Pulling Leila to her feet, I led her toward the bedroom. The bed was narrow, I noticed, almost a spinster's cot, covered with a flower-patterned duvet. Helping Leila out of her gown, I eased her under the covers. As I undressed she watched in rapt fascination, relishing every detail of my body, which she had never seen fully grown.

"You're a gorgeous man," she murmured. "*Superbe.*"

I raised the bottom of the duvet and kissed her foot. My tongue slid lightly over her toes and sole, making her wriggle with delight. While she was distracted I slid my fingers up her calf, against the grain of the downy hair, and she released a painful sigh as she surrendered to the wave of warmth carrying her away.

Lifting the covers, I regarded her naked body. It was so fabulous I wanted to weep with joy. Her figure had matured – the small breasts a little softer, the nipples darker, the bulge of her stomach a bit looser – and the overall impression was stunningly female.

"Marvelous," I sighed.

"Truly?" she murmured.

"Truly."

I stared at her face, so open, loving, sexy – intensely alive, her cheeks glowing, green eyes darkened by desire. This is the face I would like to drown in, I thought.

Urging her to turn on her stomach, I slipped a pillow under hips. I bent down to lick her spine, traversing her backbone from nape to coccyx and back again, tracing words like "fuck" and "cunt" and "love" with my tongue tip. She shivered, arched her buttocks, sighed. I ran my wet lips down to the backs of her knees and up her thighs, then down again, to her ankles and the soles of her feet and her toes, then up along her calves, nipping at her skin. Easing her thighs apart, I tugged gently at her labia with my lips and teeth, my nose against her anus, my tongue probing her cunt. I sucked deep until she came, one orgasm following another, tide upon tide of pleasure.

Parting her ass cheeks, I set the tip of my cock in her swollen vulva. As I penetrated her she released a weeping gasp. I held still, every nerve, every muscle, every follicle and fiber tensed to the point of explosion.

"Go deep," she panted as I prolonged the pause. "Please?"

I obliged, pushing in all the way, so deep I felt her cervix. She came at once, howling, and I shoved harder, feeling her vagina grip my prick and squeeze and let go, squeeze-release-squeeze, until I spurted everything I had, blood, bone and flesh, into her body.

twenty two

LEILA WAS UP when I awoke. I heard her moving around in the kitchen and the aroma of fresh coffee floated in the air. Pale sunlight outlined the window and I could hear the muted sound of traffic beyond thick walls. I lay in bed listening to the rhythm of my breath, stretching out the moment. A sense of peace permeated my bones, a feeling that I had come home, that I was in tune with eternity. Flashing images of last night's fucking sent electric jolts through my nerves, but these small excitements only deepened my serenity.

Last night I had made love to Leila not as a boy but as a man, and the pride of it swelled my heart. Back then I had often felt I wasn't her match in passion or courage, but now I'd come close, and that was marvelous. I did not flatter myself that I was her erotic equal; I already knew that no man can ultimately measure up to a woman's sexuality, but I believed I'd given everything I had.

It thrilled me, too, that Leila had not lost her ability to abandon herself to the act of love. The shriveling I had sensed in our earlier meeting had been no more than skin deep; the amazing female energy was still there under the surface, full force. I had a prideful image of myself as Moses striking the desert ground with his staff, summoning up the life-giving spring lying in wait under the dust. Was it vain of me to believe that I was the one and only male who could crack the shell she had built around herself in these past years? Certainly, it seemed she hadn't met any other man, in Paris or Dijon, who had the touch. But that wasn't really surprising, given our fated connection. I was made for her, made *by* her, for just this purpose.

So why had she run away?

That old question rippled the surface of my tranquility. This time, though, I tried to really think it through, not from my side but from hers. In her letter she had insisted she was acting out of selfish motives – insisted too insistently, perhaps. Maybe the real reason wasn't selfishness but an apprehension that, with me, she was committed to a pathway that might well turn out to be a dead end. A way of being that might not lead anywhere, not for conventional reasons of guilt or "psychology," but because I might not grow up to be the man she needed to fulfill her. That would have been a cataclysmic disappointment for her, and it would also have left me with aspirations way beyond my talents – a double tragedy she had perhaps hoped to forestall by fleeing.

That had to be it; none of the other possible explanations were adequate. And if that were so, where did it leave her now? I wanted to know the answer. I leapt out of bed, pulled on my pants and shirt, and hurried into the kitchen.

"Leila?" I cried.

Her back was to me. She was dressed for work, armored for the day, and I didn't know what face I would see when she turned around. When she did, I couldn't quite decipher the ambivalence of her expression. Her cheeks were glowing, her mouth was soft, but her eyes were tinged with apprehension as well as tenderness. "I'm late," she murmured.

Taking hold of her shoulders I shook her gently. "Leila," I repeated. "It's me." She dropped her eyes, and I gently raised her chin. "It's me." She shivered, wordless. "Go to work," I said. "We'll talk later, okay?"

Grabbing her coat, Leila almost ran toward the door, like a child eager to escape parental scrutiny. At the last moment she turned and flashed me a look of mingled love and worry before hurrying away.

I kept away from Leila's shop that day, to give her time to recover her composure. I understood that I would be the very last person she'd want to see right then wandering among the credenzas and wine savers, the *taste-vin* and champagne keys; if I had walked into her shop she wouldn't know where to put herself. After clearing away the breakfast dishes and making the bed, I went out for a breath of air. A few streets away I came upon Notre Dame and paused to admire its façade. In the light of day I could take in the details of the double tier of "blind" arches supported by slender colonnades, a delicate presentation for a Gothic church. Gargoyles poked out their jeering heads between the tiers, mocking the architecture's formal gravity.

Dijon was a charming place, very satisfied with itself, yet slightly repellent in its smugness. It seemed an odd town for someone like Leila to have settled in, and I tried to puzzle out her purpose. Perhaps Paris had proved too tough for her, or maybe just too full of disappointments, a fantasy that had not lived up to her dreams. I had a sense of Paris as a hard town under its surface charm, a milieu that was much more ruthless and unforgiving than Santa Monica. There had been something naïve in Leila's dream anyway, a very Californian flight of fantasy that must have crashed hard on the boulevards of the City of Light, leaving Leila bruised to the bone.

This thought enraged me momentarily, rousing a fierce instinct of protectiveness. "Don't come here to be human!" I muttered out loud, drawing some odd glances from passers-by. Still it was sad that Leila had had to find a hideaway in this pleasant but somewhat stifling place. They don't know who you are here, I said to myself, angrily. But then, I guess you'd also forgotten who you are, Leila, until last night.

Last night... What a time that had been! A watershed in the history of the world, no less.

But what follows?

Circling through the maze of Dijon's streets, I tried to think my way through the implications of our coming together. I knew what I wanted, but Leila's feelings were enigmatic, I feared, and I had to try to understand them. I enjoyed a young man's hopefulness, that sense of endless possibility, but she was a mature woman, scarred by sadness. I yearned whole-heartedly for the enchanted realm that only she could lead me into, but she clearly had reservations that I could only guess at. Perhaps I ought to draw back a little, leave her room for doubt, not be too over-eager. But my desire was to go for the moon, let loose all the dammed-up feelings I'd harbored these past years. For me, the doors of perception were cleansed, and infinity was in plain view.

"If I can do this, I'll be half way to heaven," I declared out loud. But was half way good enough...?

"I must take you back to see the Alhambra again," I told Leila as we were having dinner. "It's an amazing place."

She stared back at me blankly. Her mind seemed far away all through the meal of salmon poached with leeks and capers in white wine that I had shopped for and prepared. When our eyes did meet she seemed dazed, not quite there, and I could make no real contact.

"Leila," I said gently. "Talk to me."

She stiffened defensively. "Ah," she murmured. "This salmon – delicious. Who taught you to cook?"

"I taught myself, living with Max. This is one of your old recipes. And why are you just picking at it?"

"On no, it's delicious." She dabbed her mouth with her napkin. "Yes. Delicious."

"Then eat."

Dutifully, Leila swallowed a forkful of salmon, chewing distractedly, as if eating were a duty. She put her fork down carefully. "I can't do this," she mumbled. "Sorry."

"If you're not hungry—"

Her eyes filled with tears. "I want to, but I can't."

My heart sank as I began to realize what she was saying. The solid floor under my feet seemed to crumble away, leaving me suspended over nothingness. Through dazed eyes I stared at Leila, trying to make sense of her cry – *I want to, but I can't* – fearing its implication. I yearned to shake her, not yet quite believing that she could actually be rejecting something so amazing as *us*. But from the misery clouding her face it seemed she was doing just that. Yet I couldn't be angry. She looked so unhappy my impulse was to hug her, hoping also that the warmth of an embrace might melt her resistance. But the tight way she held herself suggested an unbreakable resolve, so I kept still and said nothing, holding my breath, waiting for her to continue, dreading what she might say.

With great effort she looked me in the eye. "My life is over, but you have all your life ahead of you, Joel. All your life," she repeated emphatically.

Through the fog of my own disappointment, I struggled to understand what she was really saying. Was she afraid of getting hurt by opening her heart to me without reservation? Did she actually think she was "old" or "ugly"? Or did she simply distrust her own instincts, that had once led her to make me her lover? If that was the reason for her reticence, I wanted to reassure her, tell her she was the best thing that had ever happened to me; that she had transformed my life, opened my eyes to possibilities I never could have imagined on my own. Then it struck me that she might think that I was trying to force her to play a part that was unreal, to be falsely "magical," perhaps. A flush of shame heated my cheeks at the thought of it, and I wondered if it was true. If it was, it would be unforgivable. Leila wasn't there just to fulfill my fantasies, I argued silently. At least, I hoped not.

"Leila, all I ever want is for you to be yourself," I said emphatically. "Just that."

"But I'm not myself. Not that `myself,' not any more." She shivered graphically, as if a ghost had passed over her grave. "My life is over, Joel. Over." Taking a deep breath to calm herself, she said, "Everyone has one time of glory, if they're lucky. I had it with you, back then. But glory fails, you can't live there forever. And you never have it twice."

A sudden illumination struck me. "Is that why you ran away?"

"I couldn't bear to let you down. Better a quick cut in full flood that a slow leaking away."

"Is my `glory' over too, then?" I challenged.

Leila looked at me, watching my face, as if she were honestly trying to make up her mind. "What we had back then was *my* glory," she said, choosing her words. "I seduced you into my way, because I needed to, because I was dying on my feet. And you were irresistible. Utterly irresistible. And you were mine."

"Maybe you simply don't trust me," I replied hotly. "Perhaps you think I'll abandon you as you once abandoned me. But I'm ready to give everything I have, hold nothing back, forever."

Leila took my hand. "Your loving, faithful heart – that's your own magical way." She smiled for the first time that evening, a lovely smile, warm and fond. "It's hard to resist you, sweetheart. When all's said and done how can any mother resist a beloved child's cry? And I want to respond as you wish me to, want to with all my heart. But I'm older and wiser than you are. I know that my race is run. You must have the grace to let me be."

Sitting there, at Leila's table, I felt the ceiling slide down and rest its huge weight on my neck. Bitter thoughts roiled my head. What devious intentions were her specious arguments concealing? Yet in all honesty I had to ask myself again if the Leila I wanted was someone I had fantasized, a creation of my own fervid imaginings. But that couldn't be. What I had experienced with her in the past – and last night – was no illusion.

"You're a lovely, loving man, Joel," Leila said gently.

"So. What now?" I asked miserably.

"Now I'd like to be your mother, plain and simple. And you're my son, plain and simple."

"Just like that?"

"Just like that."

I shook my head. "Not possible. Not after – everything."

"That's sad," she murmured. "Then you must forget me. Get over me. Move on."

"That's pretty brutal."

"Just factual. I'm French, remember. Under all the charm and fancy we're a very factual bunch. We always come to terms with reality, even if it's unpleasant, or even degrading. I hope there's a touch of that kind of blunt pragmatism in you." She smiled wryly. "Fact is, I have *un ami de mon age*. Lucien. A pediatrician. He lives in Beaune, about sixty kilometers from here. We see each other most weekends. We're very nice together." Her mouth wobbled. "Not glorious, but very – *raisonnable*."

I gaped at her. "You don't mean—?"

Leila nodded. I wanted to blast her with outraged fury, but my anger was undercut by the look on her face. Her expression was truly excruciating, a raw fusion of self-pity and regret with a brave but unsteady attempt at demonstrating her determination to be *raisonnable*.

In that instant I knew that Leila would never be truly "French," not in the way she pretended to be, anyhow. She would always be in limbo between the Californian dreamer who once seemed to believe that anything was possible, and the all-too-*raisonnable* Frenchwoman. My heart flooded with pity for her, and I wanted to take her into my arms and rock her, whisper sweet lies in her ear, do anything to make her smile. But such an act of false comfort would only prolong the agony, for her and for me.

"I'll leave in the morning," I said quietly.

"In the morning," Leila echoed. "Okay." She gazed at me, eyes lucent with tears.

"I love you, Joel," she murmured. "You will always be my *petite bête d'amour*, the true love of my life."

I shrugged, and we fell into a deep, shared silence.

twenty three

THE JOURNEY BACK to Granada was as vague as when I had traveled the other way. On the plane I tried to conjure up that dreamed-of time when Leila and I were lovers, but no matter how tight I squeezed my eyes I could not return to that fabled place, and I was constantly thrown back into the heartbreaking desert of the dried-out landscape Leila had apparently decided was her true and present home. It wasn't my territory and never would be, and as the plane's wheels hit the tarmac at Granada's airport I was consumed by a desperate need to rediscover my own ground, my own place in the world. I took a cab from the airport directly to the Alhambra, hoping the Red Citadel would refocus my sense of who and where I was.

On the way the cab cut through the Albaicín, close to my neighborhood. At one red light I glanced into the local butcher shop, and what I saw there made me laugh out loud.

In the late afternoon hour the shop was crowded with housewives buying their supper chops and steaks, shouting out their orders at Pepe the butcher lording it on a raised platform behind his scrubbed marble counter. Most of the women shoppers wore matronly black dresses, and each one had a pair of dusty paw marks on her buttocks.

The mark of Moro!

The dog often did his dance in the butchershop, leaping madly into the air behind the crowd to beg for the scraps of fat it amused Pepe to toss over the heads of his noisy customers; the row of buttock paw prints on those black female behinds was a graphic record of Moro's efforts to keep from toppling over. I looked around for him as the taxi moved on, hoping to catch sight of that dogged survivor, but he was nowhere to be seen.

The taxi dropped me at the Gate of Justice. The guards, who knew me well, waved me through. I hurried through the grandiose Renaissance palace built by the Christian emperor Charles the Fifth into the Moorish Court of Myrtles. Slipping through several side doors I made my way into the Lion court and into the Hall of the Two Sisters. The splendid room was empty, and for the first time I felt I could stand still and breathe deep.

The square chamber was roofed by a Dome of Heaven, a classic Islamic filigree of faceted golden honeycomb vaulting, designed to give the illusion that it was turning in rhythm with the sun, moon, and stars. "This dome is the Palanquin of Solomon hung above the glories of its chamber, rotating in its gyre," the Jewish poet Ibn Gabirol wrote. Now, at sunset, an iridescent light illuminated the vivid beehive, lightening my heart. "Here even the dreamer will refresh his desire," reads a line of Ibn Zamrak's verse inscribed on the wall.

Sitting in a corner, my ear attuned to the hiss of the nearby fountain and the rustle of the water channels in the adjacent courtyard, I tried once again to puzzle out Leila's true motives for rejecting our reunion.

Had she simply wanted to kill the connection to the boy who had worshipped her, loved her with all his body and his heart? – using the phrase," just factual," as a knife to cut the enchanted cord. Maybe, in her heart of hearts she wanted my soul to shrivel on its own. Perhaps, unconsciously, it was too hard to accept that I might survive our severance feeling whole and hopeful if she was reduced to the merely *raisonnable*. I could understand that; some defeats are only bearable if your companion goes down with you.

I walked to the narrow lookout opening onto the small courtyard of the Draxa Gardens. Beyond the weathered Roman tile roofs the jagged white peaks of the Sierra Nevada were outlined by the setting sun. The crystal glitter of that distant snow was spread before me, the gold of the Dome of Heaven was at my back. "*This* isn't `factual'!" I exclaimed, "Never!" and began to weep. Deep, sighing sobs exploded in my stomach, forcing their way up through my throat, shaking me from head to toe in a paroxysm of release – a moment of both death and refreshment, an end and a beginning. Afterward, I felt hollowed out. Empty but new, open to anything.

* * *

Moro caught sight of me the moment I entered the Guiterrez's courtyard. Instantly, he leapt up on his hind legs and did a wild jig, circling madly, pink tongue dangling from his jaw. I apologized for not having a bone for him, but his joy at seeing me seemed quite unmercenary, a pure-hearted ecstasy. My room smelled stale and I threw open the shutters to let in the crisp night air. Across the courtyard I could see Paco bending over his worktable and heard the rasp of his saw. The smell of the paella his wife Josefina was preparing in the kitchen drifted toward me and I realized how hungry I was. Dropping my backpack, I shut the door and hurried down the road to the Bar Moderno, a neighborhood restaurant and tavern, with Moro at my heels.

The place was simple, with scratched marble tabletops and rough iron chairs that made a scraping sound when moved over the chipped tile floor. Ignacio, the patron, ran back and forth behind the high bar that ran down one side of the room, its counter loaded with *tapas* laid out in white saucers. In the months I had frequented the place I'd never once seen Ignacio's body below his massive paunch, and I imagined him as a giant hermit crab inhabiting a stolen shell – much like Max in his wheelchair. "*Señor Joel!*" he exclaimed as I entered. "*Mucho tiempo sin verte.*" When I told him I had been in Paris he shook his jowls, expressing a sage distrust. "*Los franceses, nunca se confían.*"

I wolfed down a heaped helping of a wonderfully greasy lamb stew, along with a carafe of rough-edged red rioja, and followed with a crème caramel and a cup of Ignacio's harsh espresso. Ignacio offered me a cigarette and I smoked it slouching back in my chair.

The bar began to fill up with local people taking a break from work to down a glass of *tinto* and munch a tapa or two. One of the specialties of the Bar Moderno's array of snacks was a plate of fried sparrows dipped in honey – tiny, crunchy corpses coated in sweetness. The room's hard surfaces, resonating with loud Andalusian voices, turned the place into a giant birdcage filled with human crows and parrots.

Glancing out into the night I caught a glimpse of Moro cringing by the door. He yearned to enter, to cadge scraps, but he knew that Ignacio would send one of his waiters to kick his butt. "*Aquí vivimos sin bicharracos*" – without vermin – Ignacio liked to declare, excusing my sympathy for the animal as a silly foreigner's quirk.

Stuffed with good food and drink, I drifted into a Moro reverie. To dispute the harsh reality of his canine condition in a context that considered him "vermin," the brave dog had created his own transcendent domain.

Dancing transported Moro from dismissal as a despised *bicharraco* into an imaginary paradise where juicy bones and scraps of fat rained down out of the air – a graceful triumph over brute circumstance. I was filled with admiration for his hard-won victory.

To reward him, I ordered a plate of fried liver and took it to the door. The dog began to hop about as soon as he saw me, and the liver disappeared down his gullet in a trice. Then, suddenly, his yellow eyes glazed over and he fell to the sidewalk with a thump. His legs jerked and saliva dribbled from his jaw, as if he were in a fit. It seemed that the rich food, a radical change from his usual spare diet, had knocked him out. Kneeling down, I stroked his sleek black head, murmuring my apologies. Moro's eyes closed and I feared he might die, killed by kindness. But in the next instant he struggled to his feet and trotted away into the night, an inky shadow soon dissolved in darkness.

That was the last I ever saw of him. Moro simply vanished, and though I asked many locals and hunted through the neighborhood, and even waited outside Pepe's butcher shop for several mornings, I could find no trace of the dog anywhere. "They come and go, these strays," Pepe shrugged. "That is, if they manage to avoid extermination." The Spanish noun he used carried an overtone of annihilation, of being literally wiped off the face of the earth. I took Moro's disappearance as a signal, signifying that it was time for me, too, to move on, go home, return to Los Angeles and get on with my life. I wasn't sure just what that life might be, but it was waiting for me all the same.

* * *

Max rolled toward me with a big smile as I entered the Santa Monica house on my return from Granada. "Joel!" he cried, "Give us a hug!" As I bent over to embrace him in his wheelchair I was surprised by the slightly stale smell his flesh and clothes exuded – an old dog's odor, tangy yet somehow appealing. "I really missed you, son," he said, leading me toward the living room. "Living alone is no fun."

The house looked shabby yet comfortable, a bachelor's pad. Although Max hadn't changed the furniture, the atmosphere of the home was suffused with an air of amiable decay, as if, like its owner, it was cheerfully shambling toward the end of its days. "Ricarda, my housekeeper, left us some lunch," Max said. "Tuna sandwiches, like you like." I didn't recall liking tuna sandwiches, but I munched on one with some relish all the same. We chatted about this and that, and it was clear that Max was well settled into his old groove, "living out his life sentence."

"So, you saw our lady," Max said, coming to the point as soon as it was seemly. "How is she?"

"Old."

Max nodded. "Finally."

"Finally."

A slow smile parted his lips. "I could never quite live up to the old Leila," Max drawled. Flashing me one of his sly, sardonic grins, he added, "But maybe I can live down to the new one?"

I blinked at the quiet cruelty of this remark. Did Max hate her that much? And did he still think I was merely a fellow "Leila survivor"?

His assumptions and his attitudes repelled me, but I knew there was little point in challenging them. Max had made peace with his own bitterness, achieving a sort of perverse serenity that allowed him to dribble the rest of his life away. It wasn't my place to dispute him, even if I could. As he liked to say, everyone has the right to go to hell in his own fashion.

"What are your plans?" he asked, breaking into my thoughts.

"I think I might try and be a teacher," I replied, without too much reflection. "Maybe enroll at UCLA, get a graduate degree in education. I want to talk to Mr. Morales, my old Spanish Lit teacher."

Max nodded. "You'd make a good teacher. You have the humanity. And you could live here, with me. We'll be buddies."

"No." The syllable was so emphatic Max blinked. "This place has too much history," I added, trying to soften the rejection.

"Too much Leila, you mean, eh?"

"And too much `Joelly.' "

"Right." He made a face. "And too much Max, eh?"

"That, too."

We locked eyes, man to man, exchanging understandings. Then, slowly, his assumed assurance crumbled, his face seemed to come apart. It was like watching a bowl crack in slow motion, the fault lines in the glaze opening to expose raw clay. "Honor thy father, Joel," he muttered. "Honor thy father."

"For `going to hell in his own fashion'?" I said tartly.

Lifting his chin, he said with a kind of pride, "For being a really accomplished *cojo*." He laughed. "All parents are toxic, Joel, and you're quite correct in wanting to shake us both loose." I said nothing, and after a moment he continued, in a quiet voice. "The lessons that both Leila and I, in our diverse ways, have to offer may well be of no earthly use to you whatever. They're probably poisonous, truth to tell – *mierda absolutamente pura*, in the famous phrase."

He held out his hand. "I'm trying to be truthful, okay?"

"Okay."

We shook hands solemnly, and in that instant, recognizing his odd kind of achievement, I loved him without reservation. Max liked to say that the true measure of a man lay in the way he dealt with inevitable disappointment, and there was a dignity in the manner in which he had made disillusion his best and only true friend.

Maybe he laid it on a bit thick at times, but that was surely forgivable. It wasn't his fault that he had encountered Leila at a time when he was very young, still whole in body, and openhearted enough to believe in the possibility of transformation. Too late he had discovered that the rule, drink deep or touch not the waters, applied to all categories of knowledge. Max's true meanness had been his desire to diminish Leila, negate her marvelous spirit out of spite, and I didn't want to fall into the same self-murdering trap.

After lunch I excused myself and went for a stroll along Palisades Park. The ghost of Rory seemed to hover, and I wondered where and how she was. Her sad goodbye, *Adiós amor mío*, echoed in my ears. Rory was then, this was now, the end of the beginning.

I leaned on a concrete parapet, staring out to sea. The high sun hammered the ocean's skin into sheets of glistening, faceted bronze, an effect as brilliant in its own way as the glowing honeycombs of the Hall of the Two Sisters. One was made by gods, the other by men, and both were charged with the intimation of a magical dimension beyond the ordinary way of being. I had relished that realm with Leila; and I promised myself that one way or another, I would never stop trying to reach it again, even in transgression, and even if it killed me. In the end my magic might well be inferior to hers, but it would be earned, with another woman, somewhere, sometime. And it would be more genuinely my own. "I am a *lover*," I said out loud – a simple statement of fact.

postscript

IN THE YEARS following my visit to Dijon, I saw Leila infrequently, perhaps three or four times before she died of a cerebral aneurysm, at the young age of 59. Once, when I was touring Europe with my first wife, Rachel, we met for lunch in Paris. Twice Leila came to California on business, to contact vineyards from Santa Barbara to Sonoma County, and sell wine accessories to local merchants up and down the state. At the time I was still married to my second wife, Carol. Needless to say, neither of my wives liked Leila, and she returned the sentiment, so the visits were brief. Anyway, we had little to say to each other; everything that mattered had long since been said and done.

Unlike my own liaisons – all childless – Leila's relationship with her pediatrician lasted until he died. Unlike me, she was free of expectations, so far as I could see; that old marvelous, magical light had long vanished from her eyes and she seemed content to be a thoroughly ordinary woman in the bourgeois French fashion. Unlike me, she never again seemed to long for the delights and dangers of sexual sorcery, which I still seek, and often find, in every woman I come close to.

Yet even now, after writing this story, I still find it almost impossible to keep Leila in focus. Where I was once too deep within her personality, I was later too distanced from the mundane character she became, and so I have never be able to fix upon a point of view that might bring her into sharp relief. To me, Leila can never be just another person; she will always be a phenomenon, loved, adored, hated, despised, disdained, forgiven. In short, a marvelous woman; my mother.

"We swim too deep in the female waters" – Max's old comment; but these oceans are the source of life. Leila's particular wellspring dried up, for her own sad reasons, but all the same she gave me the most valuable of all gifts – the key to the magical domain and its Golden Rule: *a man's deepest delight derives from a woman's pleasure.*

If I ever forget that, I'll be lost.